To Seduce a Stranger

By Susanna Craig

To Tempt an Heiress
To Kiss a Thief

To Seduce a Stranger

Susanna Craig

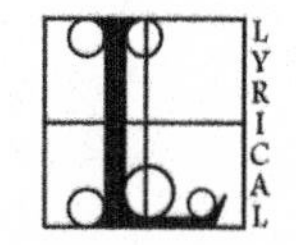

LYRICAL PRESS
Kensington Publishing Corp.
www.kensingtonbooks.com

To the extent that the image or images on the cover of this book depict a person or persons, such person or persons are merely models, and are not intended to portray any character or characters featured in the book.

LYRICAL PRESS BOOKS are published by

Kensington Publishing Corp.
119 West 40th Street
New York, NY 10018

All Kensington titles, imprints, and distributed lines are available at special quantity discounts for bulk purchases for sales promotion, premiums, fund-raising, educational, or institutional use.

Special book excerpts or customized printings can also be created to fit specific needs. For details, write or phone the office of the Kensington Sales Manager: Kensington Publishing Corp., 119 West 40th Street, New York, NY 10018. Attn. Sales Department. Phone: 1-800-221-2647.

First Electronic Edition: April 2017
eISBN-13: 978-1-60183-619-9
eISBN-10: 1-60183-619-8

First Print Edition: April 2017
ISBN-13: 978-1-60183-620-5
ISBN-10: 1-60183-620-1

Printed in the United States of America

To my daughter:
may you never outgrow your love of stories

ACKNOWLEDGMENTS

While writing this book, I have been backed by an amazing group of people: my agent, the marvelous Jill Marsal; all the folks at Kensington who help turn my stories into books and get them to my readers, including Kimberly Richardson, Rebecca Cremonese and her team, and especially Esi Sogah, whom I am blessed to have as my editor; my university colleagues, who have shown enthusiastic personal and professional support for this new venture; Randi Polk, who supplied the lovely French turns of phrase in this book (any errors are my own); Amy, who never lets me panic; and finally, my family, especially my husband, who is my inspiration for everything.

Prologue

Ravenswood Manor, Gloucestershire
June 1775

For some time now, the parlor maid had been neglecting to sweep into the nook between the bow window and the high-backed sofa in her ladyship's receiving room. The wide beam of afternoon sunlight was thick with dust motes that settled softly on the floor, dimming the luster of the damasked furniture and coating the hems of the rose velvet draperies.

The maid's shortcomings suited the boy just fine. In the dusty, narrow crevice, he had built a world he did not wish to have disturbed. An entire battalion of soldiers stood perpetually at the ready, apparently unconcerned at their precarious field position; flanked on two sides by the wall and the sofa's back, they could only advance or retreat, and as they were English soldiers, retreat was never an option.

On this day, however, they faced a new enemy.

Just yesterday, the boy had begged for a ship that he might expand into a navy, although he knew his father thought him too old for such playthings. Hardly had the request been out of his mouth before Father had erupted, insisting that no son of his would become . . . well, he wasn't sure quite *what* his father had said, but it had begun with "arse," a sure insult and one never to be spoken in front of a lady, which was probably why Mama had very nearly swooned when she heard it.

A heated exchange between his parents had surely followed, but the boy had been spared from it by being sent to his lessons. He ought to be there again now, but he had played truant instead and sneaked back to his favorite hideaway as soon as he could manage it. To thwart his father's prohibition, he had pinched his mother's sewing basket from the table as he passed, thinking it would make a fine pirate's ship. Next, he set to work scraping the painted uniforms off three soldiers whose leaden expressions made them the most likely candidates for notorious men of fortune. With a flourish, he drew a wavy line in the dust on the floor to mark out the shore and positioned the ship with its broadside facing his unsuspecting troops.

As the pirate captain knelt to touch off his cannon, the boy heard his mother's light footsteps, followed by a tread he could not immediately identify.

"So kind of you to drop in, Mrs. Henderson," Mama said.

Mrs. Henderson was the vicar's wife, a heavyset woman with a prominent nose and hair the color of a mouse's hide. But she always smelled of gingerbread and was kind to him and the other boys tutored by Mr. Henderson's curate, Cummings.

"Will you take tea?"

"It's very kind of you, I'm sure, but I can't stay, my lady. I only called to see if young Ravenswood was unwell. He wasn't at his Latin lesson today, and Mr. Cummings seemed to think that he wasn't quite himself yesterday."

"Oh, that!" Mama laughed, a shade too brightly. "He was petulant because his father forbade him a new toy." Her words made him bristle. "Boys will be boys, Mrs. Henderson. But I'll see to it he does not miss another lesson."

A long pause. "And you, my lady—are you quite well?" It seemed Mrs. Henderson was not content to let sleeping dogs lie.

"I? Why, yes, of course," replied Mama.

The boy heard the click of the door latch, and before he could wonder who had dared to close a door that Father never allowed anyone to close but him, he heard Mrs. Henderson say, "My lady, I know it's not my place. But that's an ugly-looking bruise."

When Mama had come in last evening to say goodnight, he had seen the bruise at her hairline near her temple, only partially hidden by her lace-edged cap. He could picture her slender hand rising now to shield her face from the other woman's sight. "It's nothing. I—I tripped and—"

"No need to make excuse, my lady. But perhaps a poultice—?"

"Oh, no, no." She brushed the suggestion aside. She did not like anything that drew attention to her supposed clumsiness, he knew. Neither did his father.

He heard Mrs. Henderson's footsteps cross the carpet quickly and when she spoke again, her voice was low. "I know we mightn't have much time to speak freely, my lady. Isn't there anything a body can do to help you? Perhaps if Mr. Henderson spoke with his lordship?"

"Oh, God, no. *Please*, Mrs. Henderson. Say nothing more."

"I *will* speak, my lady. I can't do otherwise. It's abroad in the village what's become of your parlor maid." His mother gave a hiccup of surprise. "You dared to speak on her behalf, I suppose."

Someone stumbled to the sofa and sank down upon it—Mama, by the sound of it; the bulk of Mrs. Henderson soon followed. Their voices were quieter still, but now, only inches from his ear, he could not help but hear them. "I thought perhaps I could persuade him to let her stay on—in the village, of course, not here—at least until the child is born . . ."

"But he wants no evidence of his crime hereabouts?"

The sofa creaked as one of the women shifted. "What would you have me say, Mrs. Henderson? I cannot speak ill of my husband."

"No, of course not." Mrs. Henderson managed to sound at once wry and sympathetic. "Isn't there somewhere you could go?"

"How could I leave my son?"

"Do you fear for his safety, then?"

Mama laughed again, but the sound was suddenly strange to him. "I fear for his *life*, Mrs. Henderson." The boy crouched lower in his hiding spot, careful not to disturb the orderly ranks and files of soldiers at his feet.

"Dear God in Heaven! Do you mean—?"

"I mean that if left to his own devices, my husband will raise his son in his image. So now, while I can, I intervene. His mother's influence may be the only stay against a violent nature."

A violent nature? Did Mama believe he was fated to turn out like Father? People seemed to delight in telling him how he took after the man. In looks, certainly—he was big for his age, and dark where his mother was fair. Mr. Cummings insisted that must be where his quickness came from, too. Neither Latin nor algebra required much effort. *But what if*—the boy glanced down at the soldier still clutched in his hand—*what if that is not all I have inherited?*

"When he's sent to school, however," Mama continued, "I will leave. A visit to my sister's—an extended holiday, we shall say." He had never heard his mother use that tone of voice. It was something more than angry, more than stubborn.

"Oh, my lady." Mrs. Henderson clucked her tongue. "But in the meantime . . . ?"

Mama rose to her feet and crossed to the door, opening it wide. The sudden gust of air through the room swirled the dust on the floor at his feet. A sneeze threatened, tickling deep in his nostrils, but he pinched the bridge of his nose to keep it at bay. "It was kind of you to call, Mrs. Henderson."

The sofa protested once more as the vicar's wife stood, and he heard her shuffle into a curtsy. "I am at your service, your ladyship."

They left, and the boy was alone again in the dusty silence. He rubbed his thumb back and forth over the figure he held, as if it were some sort of talisman. When the other boys had teased little Molly Keating about her freckles, Mr. Cummings had told him it was a gentleman's duty to protect a lady. How he wished he were a pirate captain! What wouldn't he do then to keep his mother safe? He would whisk her away across the seven seas, take her somewhere his father could not harm her again.

Alas, he had no ship, no cannon, not even a cutlass. He shoved angrily, impotently at the sewing basket, which plowed into the soldiers lining the shore, breaking their ranks. She could leave when he did, she had said. But he would not be going away to school for more than two years. Terrible things might happen in that time. If only it were in his power to leave *now*.

He studied the pirate's painted face. Father was fond of saying that every Bristol merchant was a pirate at heart. And they had ships, the boy knew. He had seen them once when Mama had taken him to the harbor on an outing. If there were pirates so near as Bristol, he could run away and join them. He supposed Mama would worry about what had become of him. Mothers did worry, he knew. But she would forgive him if she were able to leave this place.

Away from his mother's gentle guidance, he risked becoming more like his father. But what choice did he have?

His shoulders rounded under the weight of his decision, the boy began to pack up his soldiers. Perhaps his father had been right all along, for he suddenly felt far too old for such playthings. At the least, he would try very hard to be grown-up enough not to long for the day when he could come home.

Chapter 1

Bath, May 1797

Despite a gift for spinning stories and building castles in the clouds, Charlotte Blakemore had never gone so far as to imagine that her late husband would leave her a fortune.

It soon became clear that her stepson had not imagined it either.

Robert, the new Duke of Langerton, stepped forward and twitched the will from the bespectacled solicitor's hands, as if he suspected the man of fabricating. Neither of them actually said anything, however.

The incredulous squeak—"*Vraiment?*"—could have passed only Charlotte's lips.

"Yes, truly," said Langerton, lowering the parchment and fixing her with a hard stare.

It was not as if Langerton had been left nothing. As heir to the dukedom, with all its properties and a considerable income attached, Langerton was now one of the wealthiest men in England. Still, it was quite clear he objected to the fact that his father's substantial private fortune—whatever was not entailed or otherwise bequeathed—was to be divided among him, his sisters, and Charlotte. And not equally, either. Charlotte was to receive half.

Without saying anything more, Langerton returned the will to the solicitor and resumed his seat. A feeble ray of morning sun poked between the dark curtains covering the library window and picked out a few silver threads in his dark hair. Although he was not yet forty, the strain of the past few weeks, beginning with his vocal disapproval of his father's second bride, had aged him.

The remainder of the will's terms—gifts to the servants, sundry personal effects to those who would treasure them—passed by without comment. Charlotte hardly heard them. Sitting stiffly beside her, Langerton no doubt imagined she was calculating the interest on her inheritance. The thoughts flitting through her head were actually closer to a disjointed prayer of thanksgiving, however.

Thank God she would not have to return to her aunt.

Not that her father's sister, Baroness Penhurst, had been cruel, exactly. But no one who knew the woman would call her kind. *Bad enough that James had to sow his wild oats with a Frenchwoman,* Charlotte had overheard her lamenting more than once. *Did he have to saddle me with the baggage?* "The Earl of Belmont's natural daughter," people called her when they were inclined to be polite. Which they rarely were.

"That's far more than you would be entitled to receive by dower rights alone." Langerton's voice broke through her ruminations. The solicitor was stuffing papers into his worn leather case. "You must be pleased."

Charlotte drew herself up. "Nothing about your dear father's death has brought me pleasure, Robert."

His lip curled. Did he really expect her to address her stepson as Your Grace?

"Next you'll claim you were madly in love with him."

George Blakemore, fifth Duke of Langerton, had been gentle and caring, and Charlotte might honestly have answered *yes.* She *had* loved him, in the way one loves a sweet, grandfatherly man—fitting, since she was just four-and-twenty and he had been well past seventy when he had proposed. No one had been more taken aback by his offer than Charlotte, not even her aunt, who had done her best to dissuade her old friend from this act of madness—*kindness*, he had corrected when he and Charlotte were alone.

Lady Penhurst always was a right dragon, George had told her with a laugh. *No need for you to live under her thumb forever, Lottie.*

No one had negotiated marriage settlements on her behalf. Aunt Penhurst had refused to attend the ceremony. Perhaps it was an inauspicious beginning for wedded bliss—but bliss had been beyond Charlotte's expectation. It was enough that the exchange of vows in Bath Abbey just a few days after Easter had ushered in six weeks of the closest thing to peace she had ever known. Six weeks, broken by his heart seizure. Not the first he had suffered. Sadly, however, the last.

"Where will you go?" Robert asked, taking up the position behind the desk once the solicitor had vacated it.

"London." A note of wariness crept into her voice. "Your father's will—"

"Blakemore House is a residence of the Duke of Langerton." As he spoke, he began to rearrange various items—the inkstand, a paperweight, his father's seal—with a possessive hand. "And I do not intend to share it with the fortune-hunting daughter of a French whore."

Long years of practice had taught Charlotte how to disguise what she felt—fear, dismay. Even joy. Although her feet itched to fly from the room, away from her stepson's smirk, she refused to give him the satisfaction. "Fortunately for you, you needn't. Your father specified the house was to be mine."

"You have at best a *lifetime* interest in the property, to be clear," he corrected, crossing his arms behind his back and looking her up and down. "But if I were you, I would not put a great deal of faith in the promises of that particular piece of parchment."

Her hard-won composure deserted her. "You mean to—to—?" As sometimes happened when she was distressed, the English words flew from her head, leaving only French, and that she would not speak before him again.

"Fix my father's mistakes?" Robert supplied in a mocking attempt at helpfulness. "As best I can. There can be very little doubt that he was not thinking clearly when he married you. To say nothing of his state of mind when he rewrote his will."

Her lips parted on a gasp. "How can you be so . . . so *cruel*?"

"To you? Nothing so easy, ma'am," he said, making the last word sound like an insult.

"To your *father*," she corrected. "To the memory of a decent, generous man. You would have him called mad merely to serve your own selfish ends?"

A dismissive flick of one hand. "The damage is already done. Since your hasty marriage, he's known far and wide as a crazy old fool. The words are whispered behind every drawing room door in Mayfair, tossed about like dice in a gaming hell. How you must have plotted and connived to pull off that marriage," he said with a shake of his head, as if reluctantly impressed. "But the world knows it for a farce, Charlotte."

"A farce? How dare you suggest—?"

"I *suggest* nothing. You convinced a doddering old man to sign his name in a parish register. Can you prove he knew what he was about? No," he said, answering his own question. "Because he did not. Then you persuaded him to leave an exorbitant sum to some person he believed to be his wife," he continued. "But given his mental state, your marriage was invalid from the start. Now it's up to me to restore the natural order of things."

The natural order of things. Spiteful dukes and mean-spirited baronesses on top. The Charlottes of the world on the bottom.

"Such a ploy will only humiliate the family and tarnish your father's memory," she said, lifting her chin and striding from the room. No matter Robert's accusations, she *was* a duchess. At the doorway, she paused. "I will pray that time tempers your grief enough to make you see it for the foolishness it is."

He stepped within arm's length and fixed her with a narrow-eyed glare. A chill scuttled down her spine. She might have thought he meant her harm—if she could imagine him dirtying his hands with the effort. Should she call a footman? Or the butler? Would they dare to act against the Duke of Langerton if she did?

In the end, however, he waited only long enough to force her into betraying her own nervousness. She giggled. And when she attempted to stifle the sound, a satisfied smile curved his lips, and he slammed the library door in her face.

Then, and only then, did she allow herself to run—down the corridor, up the stairs, and to her bedchamber.

"Was it as bad as you'd feared, ma'am?" asked her maid, Jane, from the dressing room.

"Worse." Charlotte paced to the window and looked down on the garden. Just two weeks ago she had sat beside her husband on that very bench and admired the spring blooms. Now, they had already begun to fade.

"Never say His Grace left you with nothing?"

"If only he had, Jane, I might be better off. Instead he left me so much that his son grows vindictive. He means to forestall my claim to any inheritance by contesting the will . . . by contesting the validity of my marriage . . ." Without conscious thought, her eyes darted to the perfectly made tester bed in the center of the room.

The sight of it catapulted her back to her wedding night, when her new husband had stood beside her on the threshold to this room, patted her hand, and told her she had no cause to feel apprehensive. *I will not disturb your rest, Lottie dear*, he had told her. And he had not—not that night, nor any other.

She had not exactly been saddened by the discovery he did not intend to share her bed. Certainly nothing her aunt had told her had given her cause to look forward to what happened between husband and wife. And the late duke *had* been an old man, hardly the stuff of any girl's fantasy. Not that she ever permitted herself *those* sorts of fantasies.

Still, she had felt a pang of something—something for which she had no word, either in French or English—when he had brushed her knuckles with dry lips and wished her good night before retiring to his separate chambers. She had always been so very lonely, especially at night, when the house grew still but her mind did not.

She had let herself imagine that, perhaps, married life would be different.

Entering from the dressing room on silent feet, Jane must have caught the direction of Charlotte's gaze for she said only "Oh," in a quiet, knowing way.

Jane knew how things had stood between her mistress and her husband, of course. Such matters could hardly be kept from one's personal servants. How many others suspected the truth? Could Robert somehow use it as evidence against her? The late duke's *mind* had been perfectly sound, but all in her marriage had *not* been as it should have.

"They won't do you as they did poor Lady Cleaves, will they?" Jane asked.

With fingertips suddenly turned to claws, Charlotte gripped the windowsill for support. She had forgotten all about the Cleaves affair, although it had been on everyone's tongue just over a year ago. Lord Cleaves had accused his wife of infidelity and announced his intention of suing for a divorce. Lady Cleaves had countered with a petition for an annulment on the grounds of her husband's impotence, claiming their four-year marriage had never been consummated. Detailed accounts of the proceedings had been published in the papers and laughed over in none-too-hushed tones. Aunt Penhurst, for one, had enjoyed snickering over the stories of Lord Cleaves's failed attempts to demonstrate his capacity in front of the officers of the court. Meanwhile, Lady Cleaves had been forced to undergo physical examination by two midwives to prove she was . . . What had been the legal term bandied about? Ah, yes: virgo intacta. Then, Charlotte had not been quite sure what it meant.

Now, however, she knew all too well.

Heat swept up from Charlotte's chest, crossed her cheeks, and settled in the tips of her ears, leaving her fingers cold.

The world could laugh at her if it chose. She was half French, the daughter of a loose woman. She was used to derision, used to suspicion. She had never cared a jot for the world's good opinion, and she knew she had done nothing to earn its censure.

But she could not bear to think of anyone laughing at a man who had been so very, very kind.

As she stared down into the greenery, her eyes unfocused, a movement on the edge of the garden caught her attention. Someone in dark, nondescript clothes, those of neither a servant nor a gentleman, stood almost hidden by the stone pillar at the corner of the fence. Perfectly positioned to see both the house and the mews. A thief? But it was broad daylight.

"There's a man," she began, turning away from the window and gesturing behind her.

Jane nodded eagerly and came forward. "Now, that's the ticket, ma'am. A man. There must be some chap you took a fancy to, once upon a time. Someone you'd like to . . . That is, you might be a widow, but you're still just a bride at heart, and a bride has a right to look forward to—well, you know what I mean. No one would have to be any the wiser."

Charlotte's jaw had grown slack as understanding dawned, so that it was an effort to muster a sound. "Jane!" She giggled nervously once more—drat it all. Dropping her gaze to the carpet, she said, in what she hoped was a scolding tone, "Surely you aren't suggesting that I—that I indulge in—?"

"*Me?* Why, 'twas you who mentioned a man," said Jane, leaping to her own defense.

"Yes. A man. Standing just outside the garden gate." Charlotte nodded toward the window, still unable to raise her eyes. "I wonder what business he could have there?"

Jane hurried across the room to take a peek, then shook her head. "Not a soul about, ma'am. He must've moved on."

Charlotte looked again, but Crescent Lane was empty, just as Jane had said. She scoured every cranny she could see from the window before pushing away and turning back into the room. What foolishness. Robert's threat had made her jittery, that was all. She had nothing to fear from some poor fellow out for an afternoon stroll. Probably just the kitchen maid's new beau.

"We are going to London, Jane," she announced, straightening her shoulders. Duchesses did not slouch. To say nothing of giggle.

"Ma'am?" Jane spun away from the window and looked her up and down. "Now?"

"Now."

Fortunately, her trunk was ready. She had come to her marriage with only a few dresses, and those had been replaced too soon by a new wardrobe—of somber black crape, rather than the lavish spring gowns her husband had urged her to buy. The old dresses had already been packed away.

Into a valise Jane placed a few necessaries and a black gown almost identical to the one Charlotte was wearing. A second valise was soon filled with a similar set of items for Jane, all that would be needed for a night—or perhaps two, given the rapidly lowering sky—on the road.

To the first bag Charlotte added one final item: a battered volume of French poetry that had belonged to her mother. That connection alone would have been enough to make it precious to her, of course, but of greater practical interest were the banknotes now tucked inside. Interleaving the book's thin pages was everything that remained of the pin money she had been granted on her wedding day. Six weeks ago it had seemed an exorbitant sum. Now, however, if Langerton had his way, it might be all that stood between her and an ignominious return to Aunt Penhurst.

If she would even be willing to take Charlotte back.

When the footman arrived to carry down the trunk, Charlotte placed her bonnet on her head, lowered its lacy black veil over her face, and strode from the house. Jane followed, a valise in each hand.

By the time the driver stopped to change horses at a coaching inn east of Chippenham, the fine morning had indeed turned to rain. The inn yard was a slurry of mud, as travelers either hurried to depart before the weather got worse, or lingered in hopes of improvement. Charlotte and Jane picked their way to the door of the inn and were shown to a private parlor to wait.

From the window, Charlotte watched as people darted among the carriages, their faces hidden beneath umbrellas or the brims of hats, the brighter hues of servants' livery contrasting sharply with dull-colored, sensible travel garments. Everyone eager to get to the place they belonged.

All except Charlotte, who had never really belonged anywhere.

Under the eaves of the stable, one man stood apart, not hurrying to get out of the weather but looking up at the windows of the inn. A man in a dark, nondescript coat. Despite the distance between them and the blur of raindrops against the window, she felt certain it was the same man she had seen outside the garden that morning.

And he was watching her watch him. Her heart battering against her breastbone, she forced her suddenly frozen fingers to release the curtain. It swung back into place, leaving only a square of muslin where the reflection of her face had been.

An awful suspicion began to form in her mind. Had her stepson ordered her watched?

She shivered now as she had not allowed herself to shiver when his cold eyes had skimmed over her in the library. Robert would stop at nothing to piece together a suit that might keep her from inheriting. Whatever information this stranger could gather might easily be twisted into evidence of her bad character, proof that she was not the sort of woman a duke would choose to wed. At least, not if the duke in question were in his right mind.

No. *Impossible.* Robert was not the sort to go about hiring spies. Aunt Penhurst had been right. She must stop letting her imagination run away with her.

But what if it wasn't her imagination?

Her anxious gaze settled on Jane, pouring tea at a table nearer the hearth, clad in one of the better dresses Charlotte had given up for mourning. Jane was so similar in size and shape to Charlotte, the spotted cambric had required almost no alteration.

"I'll be glad to get back to London, Your Grace," Jane said. As Charlotte took the steaming cup she offered, the spoon rattled in the saucer. "Gracious, ma'am! You look as if you've seen a ghost."

"No." Charlotte clamped the silver against the china with her thumb. "Not a ghost." She felt certain her vision had been all too real. "Have you a sweetheart in town, Jane?"

"No, ma'am." The girl reinforced the denial with a vigorous shake of her head, but a blush pinked the apples of her cheeks. "Not to say so."

"Family, then?"

A nod this time. "My sister. Married to a butcher in Clerkenwell."

It is not as if I am sending the girl into the abyss, Charlotte tried to reassure herself. Jane was eager to return home. Charlotte, on the other hand, had no real home to which she could return.

She stood and studied their paired reflection in the mirror above the mantelpiece. Jane was prettier than she, with her plump cheeks and upturned nose. The veil would hide those features, though, and the coif of nearly black hair behind might have been Charlotte's, but for its tendency to curl.

"Jane, I wish you to change dresses with me."

Dark brows shot up her forehead. "Ma'am?"

"I want you to go on to London, alone. We shall switch clothing before we return to the carriage, so anyone who saw us enter may think I am you, and you are I. Before the carriage leaves, I shall slip out and away."

Jane's eyes grew wider still. "Why on earth would you do such a thing, Your Grace?"

"Because I wish—" The answer was easy enough, really. Nothing more nor less than she had always wished. Charlotte had often been lonely. But she had never been left alone. Widowhood, for all its sorrows, had held out the promise of independence to her. Langerton, and whatever mischief he planned, threatened to take even that away. A challenge to the will, scandalous aspersions heaped upon her, a watcher at every window? She would be little better than a fish in a bowl. "I wish some time out of the public eye. To—to grieve. And I hope in that time, the new duke will come to his senses."

"But where will you go?"

"I don't know." *North—a little cottage in the Lake District, perhaps? Or south, back to France?* The possibilities were limited only by the number of banknotes she had stashed away. "But even if I did, I would not tell you." When Jane looked offended, she explained,

"So if anyone asks, you may say honestly that you haven't any idea where I've gone."

Jane shrugged and began to unpin her dress. "If you wish it, ma'am," she said in a tone that quite clearly communicated her suspicion that Charlotte had gone round the bend.

When the innkeeper announced their carriage was ready, two women departed exactly as they had come: one all in black, drawing surreptitious glances of sympathy even as her own expression remained hidden behind her dark veil; and another, a servant, equally invisible to the eyes of the other travelers, carrying two small bags.

Once inside the carriage, Charlotte strained her ears to hear over the patter of rain on its roof, waiting for the sounds of the postilion mounting, the rattle of the whip in its socket. Then she gave Jane's hand a squeeze, picked up her valise, and slipped out the door opposite just as the carriage rumbled into motion, intending to disappear into the anonymous bustle of the inn yard.

At almost the same moment, two other carriages started away, a lone rider arrived, and all was in chaos, but one sweeping glance revealed no sign of the man in the dark clothes. He must have fallen for their deception and followed the coach. Now she needed only to board the next stage, wherever it was bound. Any direction, that is, but the one in which the Duchess of Langerton was believed to be traveling.

With fumbling fingers, she tugged the hood of Jane's cloak more securely into place, then reached into her bag for the book, for her money. Nothing but fabric met her touch. She dug deeper, up to her elbow in the satchel's meager contents, before opening it wider and forcing herself to look, to confront the truth her fingertips had already revealed. No book. No black crape. Just her second and third best dresses and Jane's underthings.

In her haste to escape the coach, she had picked up the wrong valise.

Even as she groped frantically for her reticule, she remembered slipping it around Jane's wrist to complete the costume. She had nothing with which to complete her journey to a new life. No money for coach fare, not even a coin for dinner at the inn.

Growing wetter and colder by the moment, she stumbled blindly back in the direction of shelter. There would still be a way to go on, there *must* be a way, if she took just a moment to think—

She saw the valise fly up and heard the side-seam of her dress rip almost before she felt the hand on her arm jerk her to safety. A mail coach thundered through the place where she had been standing a moment before, spraying her with mud and the driver's curses as it passed.

"Look sharp!" someone shouted from his place at the rear of the coach, and just as quickly as it had come, the danger was past.

"Are you harmed?"

A man's voice, low and close—accompanied by the realization that the wall against which she had been thrown was actually a man's chest, that the pounding in her ears was his heart hammering beneath her cheek.

Although her knees shook with the exertion, she forced herself upright and away from his support, determined not to draw more attention her way. "No," she said.

Or at least, that was what she had meant to say. But the word curved in her throat and left her lips as "*Non*."

In these days of revolution and war, most people seemed to be alarmed, even repelled by her French heritage, but on at least one memorable occasion, it had been an excuse for unwelcome familiarity. Would the strong hand still cupping her elbow drop away or grip her harder?

The stranger did neither. "*Vous êtes française*," he merely said. *You are French*. It was not a question.

Something about his accent disoriented her. He did not speak French like an Englishman—at least, not like an English gentleman, one who had been tutored in the language from childhood, had spent time in Paris on the Grand Tour, and thought himself a fine fellow when he dropped a romantic phrase or two in some unsuspecting girl's ear.

Still less did he sound like a Frenchman, though.

She mustered the strength to take another step backward, to free herself from his touch, to look at him while she formulated a reply.

If she had imagined his voice unsettling, she was totally unprepared for his eyes, which were the soft, welcoming blue of a summer sky, startling in a deeply tanned face. He must have lost his hat during the rescue, for rain dripped from dark curls plastered to his forehead, and ran in rivulets down his cheekbones and along his strong jaw.

His clothes offered no more enlightenment as to his status than had his voice: plain, well-tailored, but not elegant—even aside from being spattered with mud. No one would mistake him for a man of fashion. A merchant, perhaps. That might explain his having a few French words at his disposal. But he was as broad-shouldered and brown as a farmer.

Zut alors! Had she grown as snobbish as Robert? What bearing did the cut of the man's coat have on the fact that he had snatched her from almost certain death beneath the hooves of those horses? Even less did it matter how blue his eyes or how broad his shoulders. Although those shoulders, and the strong arms beneath them, certainly had played their part. And as for his eyes . . .

Even as she watched, a shadow flickered across them, and for the second time that day, she found herself being inspected with a sort of curious frown.

Tugging off one glove, he raised his hand and brushed the pad of his thumb beneath her eye, flicking away a clump of mud. Beneath his surprisingly warm touch, her own skin felt cold. She shivered, then darted her gaze away from his face to discover her dress and Jane's cloak were all but ruined. Although the state of her clothes was the least of her worries, she found herself blinking away tears.

Shock. She drew her shoulders back and lifted her chin. "I must t'ank—*th*ank you for saving my life," she said, marshaling every trick she had learned to make her English sound perfectly . . . well, *English.* And failing miserably.

Nevertheless, he paid her the compliment of replying in the same language. "I was simply in the right place at the right time. May I be of some further assistance, Miss . . . ?"

The hesitation at the end of his question begged for an introduction. "Lottie Blake—" she began, unthinkingly. *Blakemore*, she had been about to say, as if she could afford to go about revealing her real name to anyone who asked.

But it little mattered, because before she could finish, his brows dove downward. "Lottie?" he echoed disapprovingly. "*Charlotte*, surely."

She had never really been fond of the nickname. Her aunt had begun it, disliking how *Charlotte* rolled off a French tongue. Before that, Charlotte could hardly remember having been called anything at all.

It felt doubly strange, then—doubly good?—to hear her given name now, even on the lips of a perfect stranger.

"Yes. Charlotte," she agreed, "Charlotte Blake." It was a comfortable alias, at least as fitting as *Her Grace, the Duchess of Langerton* had ever been. Although the muscles in her legs still quivered, she managed a curtsy. "Very pleased to make your acquaintance, sir."

"The pleasure is mine, Miss Blake." He bowed in return. "Edward Cary, at your service."

Chapter 2

Perhaps if he had not been so foolhardy as to touch her, Edward might have been able to pluck his hat out of the muck and simply walk away. The streak of mud across her pale cheek had been a distraction, but the chill of her skin felt like a call to arms.

"Allow me to take you back to the rest of your traveling party," he said, bending to pick up her valise and a good portion of Wiltshire clay along with it. He had a few choice words for the person or persons who had left a young woman to wander about a bustling inn yard unescorted on a wet, gray afternoon.

"I thank you, Mr. Cary. But that won't be necessary." She reached for her bag, making no move to take his arm. "I am traveling alone."

Alone? His chin jerked upward as if he had been struck by the word, sending more cold rain where it assuredly was not welcome. A few drops found their way beneath the upturned collar of his greatcoat to trickle down his neck and along the valley of his spine.

So much for the celebrated beauties of England in the springtime.

In twenty years, he had forgotten how the damned chill settled into one's bones. Or perhaps, when he had last felt it, his bones had been more forgiving.

Doubtless he ought to prepare himself for frequent repetition of the facile assertion that his time in the West Indies had thinned his blood, although he rather suspected that his blood was the same consistency it had been when he had left England as a boy. Suppressing a curse, he turned toward the inn, still carrying her satchel, stepping deftly around a puddle that promised to be deep.

"Sir," Charlotte Blake called after him, "you have my—"

"Come." Spoken from between teeth clenched against chattering, the word sounded like a growl, even to his ears. "We'll sort it out inside."

After a moment's hesitation, she followed. He could hear her picking her way across the ruts behind him, then felt her hand tugging on the valise. "I do not wish to go inside, Mr. Cary." She had managed somehow to hone her soft French accent to a stern English edge.

But they were already to the inn, and he stepped into the warmth and dryness it promised, pulling her with him when she did not release her satchel. Hoping to secure a private parlor for Miss Blake, somewhere she might freshen up, he was forced by the crowd of stranded travelers to make do with the bustling public room instead. Dark walls were adorned with a series of cheap prints depicting charming country scenes that did not bear comparison with the gloom beyond the room's windows. Fingers of heat beckoned from an enormous stone fireplace, curling just out of his reach. Near it sat two young men who, by their looks, had been traveling in an open gig. Small puddles had formed on the floor around their boots and beneath a third chair, where their coats drooped and dripped. With a jerk of his chin Edward evicted them from their table and installed Charlotte in the seat closest to the fire, facing out into the room.

"How came you to be here alone, Miss Blake?" he asked, taking the chair opposite and setting her bag at his feet.

"I was traveling with my employer," she said. "I am a lady's maid."

"Oh?"

What fueled his skepticism he could not say. Her dowdy clothes, perhaps, which were far from the quality or style in which fashion-conscious lady's maids usually dressed. Or her voice, which even as he contemplated his reaction, shot through him with a throaty, "*Oui.*"

The "lady" she served might be anyone, he told himself, tamping down his suspicion. Miss Blake could hardly be blamed for taking employment with some parsimonious social climber who hoped to bolster her status with a real French maid.

"And you were somehow separated?"

"As we were returning to London from Bath," she explained, "I informed her ladyship I wished to be released from her service. When she resumed her journey a short while ago, she did so without me."

"What?" At his exclamation, several heads in their vicinity turned. No maid in her right mind would have quit under these circumstances, to be turned loose in the rain at some roadside inn. Which meant the situation had likely been reversed. He tried to imagine what might have possessed a lady of rank to dismiss her servant so abruptly, to abandon a young woman at the side of the road. Insolence? Theft? Or worse?

"Have you another situation lined up?" he asked, trying to make the question sound idly curious.

"No." The word seemed to have been jarred loose by a violent tremor that passed through her body—whether cold or shock or anger, he could not be sure.

"Brandy," he barked to the barmaid as she danced past on her way to deliver two more pints to the ousted bucks. When she returned with a single tumbler of amber liquid and set it down before him, he pushed it toward Charlotte. "Drink this."

His offer was met with a sharp shake of her head. "No. Thank you."

"Purely medicinal. It will help with the shivering."

Although it must have cost her tremendous effort, her shoulders and hands and knees stopped shaking. "I assure you, I am f-fine."

"Are you always this stubborn?"

As if to prove the extent of her self-control, she raised perfectly steady hands from her lap and rested them on the edge of the table. "If you must know, Mr. Cary, I haven't any money to pay for it."

No money? That only confirmed his suspicions. Just a moment past, his bones had ached with cold; now, his blood threatened to boil. Someone had meant to condemn a vulnerable young woman to the village poor house. Or the village whorehouse. Stretching out one finger, he scooted the glass closer to her. "My treat."

Her lips twitched and her nostrils flared, but in the end she lifted the glass to her lips and carefully sipped its contents. "*Merci*," she said as she returned it, three-quarters full, to the table. He had expected watery eyes or a choking cough. What he got was a wry sort of smile. "But you ought to know you have been cheated. No Frenchman would honor that beverage with the name of brandy."

A laugh rumbled in his chest. "English palates have been stunted by the war, no doubt," he said. "Nevertheless, it brought some color to your cheeks."

He had meant it as a statement of fact, not a flirtation, but Charlotte's gaze dropped to where her hands still rested on the table. "I should go."

"Go where?"

"I do not know," she said, pushing back as if she would stand. "It does not matter."

"Let me help you. Take you where you wish to go. Or give you coach fare, at least." The offer was past his lips before she could rise and walk away, before he could consider its wisdom.

At last she lifted her eyes to him, large in her still-pale face and such a deep brown he could not see where her pupils ended and her irises began. Separated from her only by the width of a small table, he could almost see his reflection in those dark eyes, but nothing of what she was thinking. She shook her head. "Why should you do such a thing? We are strangers. It would be most improper for me to travel with you or to accept your money."

"I've been away from England for many years. Things have no doubt changed in my absence. But I was taught to believe it at least as improper for a gentleman to leave a lady stranded."

"How can I be sure you *are* a gentleman?" Her lips quirked upward with the question as her gaze skimmed over him, cool but openly assessing.

A very good question indeed. The particular ways in which he had proved his character over the years would mean very little now he was back to England. "You cannot."

His answer produced an unexpected nod of satisfaction. "How long have you been away?"

"Twenty-two years. Most of my life," he explained at the slight widening of her eyes.

"Where?"

Was it his imagination, or did she hesitate over that simple question?

"The West Indies. Where I was employed variously as an errand boy, a shipping clerk, and most recently as the manager of a sugar plantation," he added, before she could ask.

"An overseer, you mean. A driver of slaves." Her English was better than she had led him to believe. She seemed to know the terrible burden those words carried, at least. "Are their lives really as bad as one reads about?"

Debates and discussions about abolition had begun to circulate in English drawing rooms, he knew, but he had imagined them occurring out of the earshot of servants. "I do not know what you have been reading, Miss Blake. But the vast majority live and die in conditions far worse than you, in all likelihood, can imagine." He certainly had not come back to defend slavery and the planters' way of life.

He might have separated himself from the implications of his statement. After all, he had worked for most of those same years to improve the conditions of the slaves under his supervision as best he could. But he had not come back to England to defend himself, either.

A long silence hung between them, filled by the noises of the public room. "Where do you go now?" she asked at last. One of the two men at the next table shot a glance her way and murmured something to his companion, who craned his head around.

All at once, Edward realized it was not her muddy clothes or disheveled hair that kept attracting their notice. Not even, perhaps, her accent. No, their heads had been turned by her large dark eyes, high cheekbones, and full lips.

Hers was a beauty perhaps not currently in fashion in England, and not the sort to which he himself had typically been drawn, but he could hardly deny there was something attractive—in the magnetic, irresistible sense—about Miss Charlotte Blake. Even her dowdy, ill-fitting dress did not disguise it. Had some lord's head been turned by his wife's maid, with or without the maid's encouragement? If so, his lady could not be blamed for seeking to remove the temptation.

But how careless, how callous simply to throw that temptation into another man's path.

"Gloucestershire," he replied to her almost-forgotten question. The answer seemed to satisfy her. He might have said nothing more. Yet recklessly he added details to his story. Details that brushed against the truth. "I have a long-standing arrangement with a gentleman regarding the management of his estates. He will, I hope, be glad to see that I am at last able to assume my responsibilities on his behalf."

"A clerk. A slave driver. Now a steward for a man of property," she said, ticking off each title on her gloved fingertips. "I believe I have my answer, then. You are *not* a gentleman."

Edward chose to laugh. "I fear many will agree with you, Miss Blake."

Convincing them otherwise would be more than enough to be going on with. He needed no additional challenges. Certainly, he should be grateful Charlotte Blake had refused his assistance. Right now, he ought to rise, drop a coin or two, and be on his way.

Before he could move, however, she sucked in her breath and dropped her gaze to the table, murmuring words he could not catch, perhaps in French. He thought for a moment that her reaction was embarrassment, inspired by her sudden awareness of the young men's interest. But they were not seated so as to be visible to her when she looked at him. Or rather, *past* him.

Twisting in his chair, he swept his gaze around the public room. The crowds had thinned once the east-bound stage had come and gone. Here and there, a few travelers lingered. Near the doorway, an older man in a dark coat stood speaking earnestly with the innkeeper, who listened with his arms crossed over his chest before shaking his bewigged head.

When Edward returned his attention to Charlotte, he discovered she had moved her chair away from the fire, shifting closer to him. With her back to the room, she pulled up the hood of her cloak, drawing it securely around her face.

Who or what she had seen remained a mystery to him, but it required no great feat of penetration to understand that behind him lay something she wanted desperately to avoid.

"Mr. Cary," she whispered, her voice muffled, "I find I must accept your offer of assistance, after all."

"Of course. Let me pay your way on the morning stage to London."

An almost imperceptible shake of her head. "I must leave *now*. Just—please, will you take me with you?"

"To Gloucestershire?" Picking up his hat with one hand, he brushed away what he could of the partially dried mud with the other. "What would you have to do there?"

She studied her gloved fingers where they lay curled in her lap. "I am willing to work, Mr. Cary. Perhaps your employer will have need of a servant? I will repay your trouble," she insisted.

"I cannot promise . . . That is, the gentleman who owns the estate is . . ." *Prone to misconduct where serving girls are concerned?* An understatement, surely.

"Not in residence?" she supplied. "I suppose a wealthy gentleman of property would prefer to be in town for the Season." There was a certain wild eagerness in her eye when it met his. "So much the better."

She was afraid. Afraid of being seen. Afraid of being recognized.

Had any part of the story she'd told him been true?

"Please," she urged, glancing from beneath her hood toward the door. "May we go?"

Undoubtedly, spending two-thirds of his life in Antigua had affected him, shaped him. People would make assumptions about the sort of man he had become in such a place, and they might not always be wrong. But he had never been the sort of man who could ignore the plight of a woman in danger. His life experiences had not changed who he *was*.

From birth: Edward Cary, Viscount Ravenswood.

And when his father's hard heart at last calcified to the point at which it no longer beat, he would be the Earl of Beckley.

Whether anyone would accept him as such after all these years was another question entirely.

With a curt nod, he gestured her toward the door. "All right." As she turned away from him, he reached for the almost-full tumbler, downed its contents in a single swallow, and grimaced.

She had told the truth about one thing, at any rate. He'd be damned before he'd dignify that swill with the name of brandy.

When Charlotte saw the horse, she began to have second thoughts about her request for aid. She'd imagined speeding away from the inn in a carriage, curtains drawn, unobserved by passersby. The discovery that he intended her to share his mount was, to say the least, alarming.

"Do you ride, Miss Blake?" he asked as he strapped her satchel to the saddle before swinging up with apparent ease.

Standing just out of reach of his outstretched hand, she shook her head.

"You aren't frightened of horses, are you?"

"No." The reply came quickly. Too quickly. That sort of obvious lie had on occasion earned her a rap across the knuckles or a pinch from Aunt Penhurst. She could hardly hope that Mr. Cary would prove less astute.

At least, however, he did not seem to be as quick-tempered.

"You're perfectly safe," he insisted, his voice warm and his eyes smiling down on her. "Samson here is one of the most—er, placid animals I've ever encountered."

Placid? No judge of horseflesh, she could not be sure whether he was sincere or merely trying to sound reassuring. The distinctions between a sway-backed nag and a high-strung racehorse were entirely lost on her. All of them were enormous and behaved unpredictably, as far as she was concerned. Looking about the muddy yard, she was forced to acknowledge that she had little choice, however. It was either back to the inn, or up.

Had the man questioning the innkeeper been the same man she had seen earlier? And if so, had he spotted her?

He was probably nothing more than a newspaper man, on the hunt for fodder for a gossip column. Well, she did not mean to stay and give him what he wanted. Laying her hand in Edward Cary's, she set her toe on his boot and allowed him to pull her up in front of him.

"All set, Miss Blake?"

Tangling her fingers in the horse's dark mane to hide her nervousness, she held her spine rigid. One of those wretched nervous giggles bubbled in her chest, but she fought it down. Although the ground looked to be an alarming way off, and the toss of the horse's head made her certain they were about to be thrown, she managed to nod in acknowledgment of Mr. Cary's words.

"Try to relax," Edward said, his voice low and calm. "Samson can feel your fear. We won't let you come to any harm. Trust me."

Another awkward laugh almost escaped her. How ridiculous to speak of trusting a perfect stranger.

Although, of course, she *was* trusting him. At least a little.

What choice did she have?

Concentrating on each muscle, she forced her limbs to ease. The task proved far more difficult than the one she had set for herself in the public room: keeping herself from shivering and tossing back the tot of brandy like an old sailor. For one thing, the change in posture made her uncomfortably aware of the breadth of his chest against her back, the band of his strong arm about her waist. When he guided the horse around a treacherous-looking rut, she could feel the flex of his muscled thighs along her hips and legs.

No one had ever held her so close.

Well, that was not entirely true. Someone must have, when she was a child. Surely she had once been nestled against a breast or dandled on a knee, although she had no memory of it. More recently, there had been that Mr. Sutherland, a friend of her cousin Roderick, the young Baron Penhurst. Late one night, Mr. Sutherland had grabbed her on the servants' stairs and tried to steal a kiss . . . and a bit more. She had made short work of his roving hands with the press of a pointed heel to his instep, and had taken secret delight in the fact that he had still been limping when he left the house three days later. When Aunt Penhurst had asked him the cause of the injury, he had looked pointedly at Charlotte before claiming he had tripped, sparing her for once from having to make up some story that her aunt would never have believed.

In any case, if physical contact was not quite unprecedented, it was still unusual enough to leave her feeling a bit breathless and longing to sit up straighter again, if only to fill her lungs properly and shake off the unaccustomed sensations. She would not do it, of course, because she did not want to incur Samson's, or Mr. Cary's, displeasure. Besides, the change of posture had made the motion of the horse almost bearable.

At least, until Mr. Cary urged him to a faster pace.

"O-oh!" The jarring motion of the trotting horse rattled the gasp from her chest.

"Tell me, Miss Charlotte Blake." His voice in her ear was a distraction, as she suspected he had intended. "How does a Frenchwoman come by such an English name?"

"My—" *Husband*, she had been about to say, but she bit the word off just in time. "Er, that is, I—my father was English."

"But you were raised in France?"

"Yes."

Usually, that fragment of her story was sufficient. Anyone who did not know the rest was quick to sketch in the blank spaces, rarely to Charlotte's advantage.

"By your mother?" Mr. Cary prompted.

So he wanted to hear the damning tale right from her lips, did he? Knowing what use gentlemen like Mr. Sutherland had made of such information, she was loath to supply it. Only the late Duke of Langerton had ever been willing to overlook her shameful origins, and look where that had got him.

What would Edward Cary do with the truth?

Based on what he had told her, she suspected there might be more than a few unsavory bits in his own past. Young men did not leave England to work on West Indian sugar plantations if they were secure of a future at home.

Perhaps he was a foundling, as his story suggested. Perhaps they were two of a kind.

But she could not afford to find out.

"My mother died when I was a young child," she answered at last. An infant. In truth, she had no memory of the woman at all. "I was raised in the household of her brother, a wine merchant in Rouen."

"Who taught you English?" he asked after a moment.

"My uncle rented rooms to an English poet and his . . . sister." Even as a child, Charlotte had recognized the lie for what it was. Dorothy, the poet's mistress, had divided her time between copying his work and keeping him from committing some act of self-harm in a fit of artistic despair. "When she had a spare moment, she invited me in to converse. To improve her French, she always insisted, although she spoke it flawlessly."

Those few hours, snatched away from dismal years, had been some of the only bright spots in a childhood that had required her to grow adept at storytelling: tales to entertain her younger cousins to keep them from getting underfoot; small lies to explain the bruises, the tears, the torn dresses inflicted by the older ones; outright fabrication when grim reality simply could not be faced. Over time, the truth had begun to blur around the edges. Sometimes, she was no longer certain which was memory and which invention.

The horse's hooves slipped a little as he shifted onto a more northerly path, but she had forgotten to be frightened of its movements. "When I was not quite sixteen, we began to hear terrible rumors of blood flowing through the streets of Paris. The poet hurried to see for himself, insisting his sister return home. Much to everyone's surprise—including the poet's, I don't doubt—she did. I begged her to take me with her."

"It was not she who left you destitute back there?" There was something encouraging, almost comforting about the edge to his words, as if he hoped one day to have an opportunity to chastise the person responsible for her present predicament. What would he say if he knew she alone was the one to blame?

"Oh, no. Once we arrived in England, she helped me to track down my father's sister, and I went to her. It was she who . . . gave me my start in service."

Not a lie. Not really—although Mr. Cary might beg to differ if he ever had cause to hear the whole story. Despairing of making any kind of match for her brother's "sallow-faced, sickly bastard," Aunt Penhurst had made use of her instead. Household mending, at first. Later, when she had proved she could write a neat hand—in English, no mistakes—she had graduated to a sort of unpaid lady's companion. Not quite a lady's maid.

Not so well treated. Never so well dressed.

And if Aunt Penhurst had not snapped her fingers once too many times in the presence of the Duke of Langerton, Charlotte might be there still. Right at this moment, she was no longer persuaded that the old duke's interest had been entirely beneficial. Certainly, the new duke's did not seem to be.

Would she rather be back in the Penhurst household, then? Or riding through the damp countryside in the embrace—for there could be no other word for it—of a man she did not know, escaping . . . what? Her stepson? A stranger in a dark coat? Society's sneers?

She could have faced any one of those challenges.

But why should she have to?

Power flowed through the muscles in the horse's neck, warming her fingers, and when she stretched slightly forward, Samson responded by moving faster, his new gait smooth and swift. Charlotte welcomed the wind as it rushed past them, rippling her hood, loosening the pins in her hair.

No one knew where she was. No one knew who she was.

She ought to have been frightened.

But for the first time in her life, she felt free.

Chapter 3

In Edward's dreams and nightmares, his last glimpse of his childhood home had been late at night, light pouring from the windows as he sneaked away into the dark forest. In actuality of course, it had been morning, the birds had been singing, and his mother had walked with him almost into the village, where he was to have his Latin lesson with the curate.

He had never made it to the vicarage. Instead, once his mother had planted a goodbye kiss on his cheek—one he, as a would-be young man, had been obliged to protest—he had turned and headed south, meeting up with the mail coach in Marshfield, a village a few miles down the road. So sure had he been of his decision to leave, he had actually managed to fall asleep on the way to Bristol.

Well, he was awake now, although he felt quite certain Charlotte was not. His arm was beginning to ache where she leaned against it—a welcome distraction from the aches he felt in other places. The very last thing he had needed was to ride for hours with a woman's soft arse pressed into his groin.

At first he had imagined it a simple matter of leaving her at the next crossroads with a few coins for the stage, so she might travel wherever she had a mind to go. But her evident tension had soon made him realize she feared being followed by whomever she had fled. So they had carried on despite the drizzle. Surely, given Samson's increasingly plodding steps through the mud, his baggage coach would overtake them eventually, and she might travel inside, in reasonable propriety and comfort. By late in the day, however, it had become apparent to him that they were not to be so fortunate. His last hope had been the inn they passed just as the rain broke and darkness began to fall. They could rest for the night, finish their travels by daylight. But innkeepers asked questions for which he hadn't any good answers. What *was* his relation to the young woman with whom he was traveling in such an unconventional fashion? So they went on, under the moonlight, completing the final stage of a journey he had delayed too long already.

Still, when he caught his first glimpse of Ravenswood Manor, he drew up the reins, bringing Samson's ambling gait to a halt.

Just ahead, buttery stone gleamed among the trees, painted white by the light of a rising moon. But there were no candles in the windows as there had been in his dream, no smoke rising even from the kitchen chimney, no sign of human habitation at all. Only the shadow of an owl, a dark gash across the pale façade, as it swooped silently in search of some unsuspecting prey.

"Miss Blake," he said, tightening his grip on the reins even as he shifted his left arm to rouse her. "We're here."

She did not start as he had expected. Perhaps she had not really been dozing, although when she spoke, her voice was husky as if with sleep. "*Nous sommes où?*"

"Ravenswood Manor," he said. "Principle seat of the Earl of Beckley."

"An earl?" The title brought her to full alertness. He knew he was not imagining the alarm in her voice. She had reason to be wary of the aristocracy, certainly, given her treatment at its hands, but surely the lady she had served would not waste her time with further retaliation. Was it the woman's husband she feared, then? From whom was she trying to hide?

"It does not look as if he is in residence."

"No." Brambles had been allowed to crisscross the path, and the front gardens were in shambles. When he dismounted, no one answered his shout toward the stable block, and as his eyes passed over the front of the house, he saw a broken window high above. Total neglect. And not of recent date. "It does not look as if *anyone* is in residence."

He looped the horse's reins around a piece of crumbling statuary, some lesser Greek god missing one ear and his nose, then reached up to lift Charlotte down. As he trotted up the steps—two at a time, despite their depth—and pounded his fist against the front door, he could feel her hesitating, lingering beside the horse, as if she expected to have to make an escape.

Defeated by silence in answer to his knock, he was about to turn and join her when he caught a sound from inside the house. Shuffling footsteps across a stone floor, followed by the scraping sound of the bolt being drawn. The heavy paneled door swung inward, and in the darkness of the cavernous entry hall stood a man of indeterminate age, clutching a tallow candle, heedless of its oily drips.

"Here at last, are ye?"

It was not the greeting he had expected. "Where is Jewkes?" Edward demanded, resurrecting the butler's name from some corner of his memory.

"Don't know nobody by that name," the man said. Jewkes was almost certainly gone, of course. Everything would have changed in twenty years. But the former butler's replacement looked—and smelled—more like a shepherd. "Who're you?" The man raised the candle higher, looking sharply into Edward's face.

Edward nearly choked on his reply. "Cary," he said at last. Would the name reveal enough? Too much? But only the dimmest light of familiarity flickered in the man's gaze. "Is the family abed?"

"Dunno."

"Are they here, man?"

"Naw," he said, and spat. "His lordship went t' Lon'on years ago. Ain't none from t' family lived here since." With that, he turned and walked back into the house, and as he did not slam the door behind him, Edward followed, forgetting for a moment that he was not alone.

The pattering sound of Charlotte's feet trying to catch up caught him by surprise. "But you seemed to be expecting us?" she asked.

The man paused but did not turn as he replied. "'Spected them trunks b'longed to somebody." Resuming his shuffle, he led them past broken furniture moldering in disarray and priceless portraits rotting beneath swags of cobweb. Bile stung the back of Edward's throat.

"So, my things have arrived?" he asked, forcing a note of calm into his voice.

A laugh wheezed from the man's lips, almost extinguishing the candle. "Aye. All of 'em."

Eventually, they came to what had once been the servants' quarters, and the man opened the door to the butler's room, where a sagging rope bed and a rag-covered chair passed for coziness. In a spacious manor full of once-elegant furnishings, what would have possessed a vagrant to take up residence in this meager chamber? But the pile of empty bottles discarded in one corner answered Edward's unspoken question. Proximity to the wine cellar had been the lure of this particular room.

"You are the, ah—the, er—?"

Charlotte's soft voice was a raft of tranquility in the noisy sea of chaos rushing through Edward's brain, and he grasped for it like a drowning man. "Caretaker?" he supplied, uncertain whether she fumbled for an English word she did not know, or merely a word, any word, to describe the man's role in the rubble of what had once been Edward's family home.

"I guess you can call me that, if you like. I'm what's left. Samuel Garrick, by name. Used to be second stable boy. When there was horses." Nonchalantly, he took his pipe from his waistcoat and lit it with his candle, producing a cloud of even more noxious smoke, if such a thing were possible. "You fixin' t' stay, Mr. Cary?"

Words simply would not come. How in God's name had his father let this happen? When Edward had run away, he had told himself he was saving his mother's life. But he had always let himself believe he could return to Ravenswood one day.

This time, Charlotte came to his aid. "Mr. Cary has just returned from the West Indies. The earl is expecting him to serve as steward of this property."

Garrick shrugged. "Don' know nothin' 'bout that." His dark eyes glimmered with interest as they looked Charlotte up and down. "An' who're you?" Even disheveled and travel-weary and surrounded by squalor, she was striking, and Edward supposed the man could be forgiven his inquisitiveness.

But the answer to his question was not an easy one.

Although Edward could never have imagined what he would find when he got here, he had allowed his anxiety over returning to Ravenswood to cloud his judgment where Charlotte Blake was concerned. People who ran roadside inns were not the only ones who asked inconvenient questions. Of course a young woman traveling alone with a man would excite speculation. He had meant merely to help a mistreated lady's maid. Instead he might have ruined her.

What plausible explanation for their peculiar arrangement could he offer? If she did not look quite so exotic, he supposed she might pass for his sister . . .

"I," Charlotte began, unperturbed, tugging loose the fingers of one glove, "am Miss—"

The candlelight struck gold on her fourth finger and sent forth a dazzling gleam. A gold band. *A wedding ring.* Too much to hope that it had not caught Garrick's eye.

"Mrs. Cary," Edward spoke over her. "My wife."

Even as the word passed his lips, he feared it was the sort of promise on which a man might eventually be expected to make good. Except that she was already married. *Good God.*

With what sort of woman had he saddled himself when he made that rash offer of assistance? A lady's maid? Perhaps. He half suspected, given her own account, that she was some English adventurer's by-blow. For all he knew, a French spy to boot. Any and all of whom were the last sort of woman he needed or wanted.

Pale-faced and wide-eyed in response to Edward's claim, Charlotte sank onto the chair behind her, then leapt up again when the pile of rags on its seat screeched and hissed.

"Mind the cat." Garrick puffed lazily on his pipe, while the affronted feline stared unblinkingly at Charlotte for a long moment before beginning to lick its sleek black fur back into place. "So you was in the West Indies too?"

"Er—ah." Edward began to fumble for an explanation, but Charlotte stepped smoothly into the gap, gathering her gloves in the palm of one hand and drawing back her shoulders like a damned duchess.

"No, Mr. Garrick," she said. "I was companion to a widow, the widow who owned the property Mr. Cary managed in . . ."

For reasons he could never have explained, even to himself, Edward softly inserted, "Antigua."

She bristled. "Of course I know that. Didn't I write out the direction often enough? I was in charge of her correspondence," she explained to Garrick. "One day, on a whim, I added a line of my own to the bottom of one of her missives to Mr. Cary. Some question about the weather, wasn't it, my dear?"

Edward started. He had almost forgotten he was meant to be an actor in this little play. He should stop her.

Instead, he nodded. "Er, yes. I believe it was."

"My"—she began, and then shook her head with a sly little smile cast in Edward's direction—"*our* employer rarely looked at the letters herself, you see, Mr. Garrick. Mr. Cary and I began to correspond. When he returned to England, he paid a call on my mistress, and—"

"And that, as they say, was that," Edward spoke over her, sensing that Garrick's interest in the tale thankfully had begun to flag. "Happily ever after and whatnot," he finished lamely.

Since Samson's hooves had first stepped onto Ravenswood land, Edward's head had been pounding. The state of the house had added nausea to his symptoms of panic. Now his palms were slick with sweat. What sort of person spun lies so effortlessly?

One who'd had a great deal of practice.

Garrick dragged smoke into his lungs and nodded. "Bit of a relief, that."

"I beg your pardon?"

"I was afeared you might say t'other one was yer missus."

"What other one?" Charlotte asked, every inch the suspicious bride.

Around his pipe stem, Garrick gave Edward a toothless, knowing smile. "The fancy baggage what come with yer trunks and things."

"Fancy . . . baggage? I don't know what you—"

A terrible thought struck him. *No.* He had meant to leave every part of that life behind. She wouldn't have. Couldn't have.

But apparently, she had.

Edward made himself ask, "Where is she?"

"Right here, Mr. Edward."

Mari Harper spoke from the doorway, her voice clear, her posture erect. Clad in a respectable blue gown of some plain stuff, she would have appeared unremarkable but for the brightly colored turban wound about her head. That, and the color of her skin of course, such a dark brown it almost disappeared into the blackness of the empty corridor behind.

"Mari!" Frustration sharpened his voice. "What in God's name—?"

"You rode in the baggage cart all the way from London?" Charlotte cut across him, stepping to Mari's side and putting an arm through hers to coax the other woman into the room.

No one could have guessed that Mari's appearance—her very existence—must have come as quite a surprise to Charlotte. "I am almost glad I did not know," she was saying, as if the two were old friends. "I would have been worried sick about you on these muddy roads. You are unharmed by the journey? It was an uncomfortable one, I've no doubt . . ."

"I am well." Mari inclined her head in that regal way of hers. "Mrs. Cary."

Torn between a sigh of relief and a cry of frustration, Edward could not trust himself to speak. So Mari had overheard Charlotte's ridiculous story, had she? Of all the times for her to decide to play along. He had come back to England to reclaim his life. He had no intention of stepping into someone else's trumped-up version of it.

"Now, see here," he began when he had recovered enough composure to speak. The two women drew closer together, a wall of defiance. Garrick plucked his pipe from his lips so that nothing interfered with his broad grin as he looked from Edward to them and back again.

"Mrs. Corrvan suggested I come," Mari explained. "She thought you might have need of assistance."

"How . . . thoughtful of her. I shall have to find a way to express my gratitude." He was half tempted to get back on the road this very night, just for the pleasure of giving her a piece of his mind.

"Mrs. Corrvan always was the soul of generosity," Charlotte confirmed. "And as you can plainly see, we can use all the help we can get. Everything here seems to be in a dreadful state."

Mari acknowledged the truth of Charlotte's words with a dip of her turbaned head, although her eyes never left his face.

He opened his mouth and then shut it again, hard enough that his teeth met with an audible click. "Fine," he said without parting them again. Everything *was* in a dreadful state. And clearly nothing would be resolved tonight. "Is the Rookery livable?" he asked, turning toward Garrick. Charlotte believed he had come here to claim the post of steward and had told Garrick as much. Edward might as well make use of the misunderstanding and claim the steward's cottage for one restless night, before setting out again at first light.

"Depends." Garrick resumed chewing on his pipe stem. "How partic'lar are you?"

"Has it a roof?"

"Mostly. But yer lady ain't likely to stand for it," he added in a confidential undertone.

"Mrs. Cary can be made reasonably comfortable in the housekeeper's quarters with me for the time being," Mari offered.

"Right," Edward said, not daring to look at Charlotte. "Then I'm for the Rookery, and it's back to the stables for you, Garrick. You've horses to tend once more."

He expected an argument, from any or all of them. But when he raised his eyes, Charlotte and Mari were already receding from view, and Garrick was shrugging into a ragged coat. "It'll be good t' have summat to do," Garrick confessed as he paused to relight his pipe before extinguishing the wretched candle's smoking flame.

"There's certainly work to be done," Edward agreed, brushing past corridor walls covered with chipped plaster and peeling paper as he made his way outside, where the rain had begun to fall once more. He hitched the collar of his greatcoat higher.

"Aye. Allus has been. But without a lord, or at least a steward about, there's been no reason—and no way—t' do it. T'weren't easy watching the ol' place fall t' ruin. I'm right glad you've come, sir."

It was not quite the homecoming greeting he had imagined, of course, although he had thought himself prepared for the worst. But his churning emotions made him suspect that in some corner of his mind, he had been secretly nursing a fantasy in which his loving mother welcomed him back with open arms. The sort of story that could only be spun by someone with a gift for invention.

Someone like Charlotte Blake.

Mrs. Cary.

What in God's name had possessed him to say it? What had he been thinking?

The truth was, he had *not* been thinking. The furniture of his mind was in a state not unlike that of the rooms they had passed, dusty and tumbled and shattered. What thoughts he had been able to muster had been solely focused on a quick return to London and the inevitable confrontation with his father, who was now almost an old man. How good it would feel to at last have the upper hand—the advantage in size, in strength. The ability to stand up for himself and others, which he had craved as a child.

In the stables, they met the coachman Edward had hired to haul his baggage as he stepped from one of the stalls. "Ah, Mr. Dobbs. I'm glad to find you here." His words were muffled by the rain. "You'll be returning to London in the morning, I suppose? As it turns out, there's a matter of business requiring my urgent attention—and I understand you don't have an aversion to passengers."

The man swallowed a guilty smile and shook his head. "You'd be welcome to it, Mr. Cary. But I'm afeared we'll have a delay."

"The weather?"

"We-e-ell, in a manner o' speakin'. My off horse, Prince, has a swole fetlock, you see. All that mud." A slow shake of his head. "If we head out again tomorrow, he's like to be hurt worse. These horses is my livelihood. Can't risk it, sir."

"No, of course not," Edward said, mustering a note of false calm. "It won't be a long delay, I hope?"

Dobbs shrugged but did not look hopeful. "Jus' have to wait and see, sir. If that rain keeps up, might be stuck here a few days yet."

A few days?

A steadying breath drew cool, damp night air into his lungs, heavy with the peaty scent of new growth waiting to burst forth. Spring. A time for rebirth.

He considered Garrick's words about the work to be done on the estate. As satisfying as it would be to meet his father with angry words, it might be more beneficial to stay, just a day or two. He could familiarize himself with the lay of the land, assess the damage that had been done, and arm himself with a plan of action to right the wrongs that could still be righted.

A sense of powerlessness had led him to abandon Ravenswood once. He would never abandon it again.

But was it wise to stay here now . . . with his *wife*?

Another deep breath, and this time, he swore he could almost smell the scent of Charlotte's hair, as if it still teased his nostrils. Could almost feel the curve of her waist, as if his arm were still wrapped tightly around it.

He shook off the sensation.

He would not allow himself to be tempted into a dalliance with a beautiful stranger. God knew what might come of it. *Mrs. Cary?* No. That could never be. Marriage—with any woman—was out of the question, even if it meant the Beckley title would die with him.

From the looks of things, it was already as good as dead.

It was only a few steps to the housekeeper's rooms, but far enough for Charlotte to realize that the woman accompanying her, although young and otherwise apparently healthy, had a dreadful limp. As Mari dragged one foot along the stone floor, Charlotte wondered how she had ever managed to surprise them all with her silent appearance in the doorway of Mr. Garrick's dank cell. Regardless of her physical limitation, however, she carried herself like a queen.

Who was this woman whom Edward addressed so familiarly? A servant? A *slave*? Or had Garrick's guess been right? Was she something else to him entirely?

Mentally, Charlotte scolded herself. She had been on the receiving end of assumptions often enough to know how they could wound. And in any case, their relationship was no concern of hers.

She expected to find the housekeeper's room as derelict as the rest of the house, with dust coating every surface and cobwebs festooning every corner. But a candle gleamed from a still-tarnished candelabra, revealing a freshly swept floor, a clean table, and a small, roll-armed sofa with a blanket masking its no doubt tattered upholstery. Through a partly open door on the far side of the sitting room, Charlotte glimpsed another chamber and a bed freshly made with linens that must have been brought in the luggage with which the woman had traveled. How long ago Mari had arrived, Charlotte did not know, but she had certainly kept herself busy in the interim.

As soon as they were through the door, Mari released her arm and turned to face her, sweeping her gaze over Charlotte's muddy gown and tangled hair. She did not speak. Aunt Penhurst was the sort of woman who loved the sound of her own voice, and over the years, Charlotte had grown used to the hum of constant criticism.

She had forgotten how much disapproval could be communicated through silence.

"I am Charlotte," she said after another awkward moment, then extended her hand in greeting. "Charlotte Blake." For of course, whatever her relationship to Edward, the woman must know Charlotte was not Mrs. Cary.

Mrs. Cary. Why had he said it?

Hardly had the question crossed her mind, when the candle's flickering light caught her wedding ring and gave her the answer. It was only an old-fashioned posy ring, a narrow gold band engraved with a pattern of vines and the motto *amore digna*: worthy of love—words that had been meant for some other bride, of course, three hundred or so years ago when the ring was made. Nonetheless, its simplicity had gladdened Charlotte's heart far more than any lavish bauble could have done.

Mr. Cary must have spotted it and sought to explain its existence to Garrick, and anyone else who noticed. An impulse born of misguided chivalry, she supposed—an attempt to preserve her reputation. But why had she not contradicted his ridiculous assertion? Worse, what had possessed her to embellish upon it, as if they had some history together? Her aunt had often warned her that her stories—her *lies*—would lead her into trouble.

But no. She thought of the decay and disarray that lay beyond the walls of this room, recollected Langerton and his spy looming somewhere in the distance. *I am in trouble already.*

"Mari Harper," the woman said evenly in an accent at least as pure as Charlotte's.

Although Mari did not take Charlotte's outstretched hand, she did unbend enough to sit down on one of the rather rickety-looking chairs flanking the table, and she did not protest when Charlotte joined her. The black cat, which had followed them down the corridor, wound its way around Mari's legs with a plaintive *mer-re-row* that echoed eerily in the half-empty room.

Eager to fill the silence that followed, Charlotte tried to explain her presence. "I was stranded at an inn near Chippenham due to a—misunderstanding. Mr. Cary came to my aid. When he described where he was headed, I confess the remoteness of the situation appealed to me." Certainly that aspect of Ravenswood Manor did not disappoint. No one would think to look for her here, in the middle of nowhere. "I had hoped to secure some employment in the neighborhood, although now that I see how things stand . . ." She allowed her voice to trail off. Despite Mari's obvious disapproval of her presence, Charlotte was going to have to make the best of things here.

With . . . her husband.

"You must have come from the West Indies," she said after an awkward moment had passed. "With Mr. Cary."

A guess. A good one, she decided when Mari nodded.

"I suppose Mr. Cary often spoke of returning to England."

"No, ma'am. Never. Not until she did."

"She? Mrs. Corrvan, you mean?"

Another nod. No further information seemed to be forthcoming, however. The questions crowding Charlotte's mind were far too indelicate to be asked, and she suspected she would get no answers even if she could find a way to frame them. Feeling suddenly choked, she loosened the tie of her cloak, then brushed absently at the mud on her dress until she realized dried flakes of it were scattering onto the freshly swept floor.

"This Mrs. Corrvan," she ventured at last, darting her gaze to Mari with apology in her eyes, "she owns the property in Antigua where... where...?" *Where Edward was an overseer? Where you were enslaved? Where you and Edward—?*

"She does."

"I do not suppose she is an elderly widow, by any chance?"

"No." Something wry, not quite humor, lit Mari's eyes. "She is young. And very beautiful."

"Ah." Charlotte lowered her gaze as embarrassment flooded through her, although she could not say why. Something about Edward's expression when Mari had mentioned Mrs. Corrvan's name. Furious and tender all at once. And she suspected he would prefer that no one, especially not a stranger, had caught a glimpse of it.

Well, that seemed to be the only glimpse of his past she was likely to get. Whatever Mari knew, she showed no inclination to reveal anything more of his life. Or her own.

Another lengthy and uncomfortable silence was broken by a thump at the door, which swung open of its own volition, the latch long since having rusted to uselessness. Garrick stood there with a basket in one hand and Charlotte's satchel in the other. He appeared to have knocked with his foot.

"Mr. Cary thought you'd be wantin' your things, ma'am," he said to Charlotte, setting the bag on the floor before carrying the basket to the empty table. "There's bread here," he explained. "And a jug o' water. But don't try to light a fire 'til I can sweep the chimley in the mornin'. Like t' burn the house down for a pot o' tea."

Mari only nodded. "Thank you, Mr. Garrick," Charlotte said, rising. "I don't know where we'd find tea leaves, in any case."

When he had gone, she opened the basket and found half a loaf—torn, not cut—and a stoneware jug, along with two mealy apples that must have been left over from last autumn's harvest. Dividing the store of food, she laid each portion on two clean handkerchiefs she took from Jane's valise. "Given the state of the rest of the house, I can only imagine how this room looked when you arrived, Miss Harper," she said, handing one handkerchief to Mari. "Thank you for your willingness to share it with me."

Caught in the act of drinking, Mari sputtered a little, then passed the jug across. Lifting the heavy vessel, Charlotte drank deeply, gratefully, even as she greedily wished there might also be enough for a wash. She caught Mari watching her when she was done. "You are welcome," Mari said at last. "Mrs. Cary."

"Call me Charlotte," she replied as she took a cautious seat on the blanket-covered sofa, testing whether it would hold her up for the night, or whether she might better make her bed on the floor. "I believe we can reserve 'Mrs. Cary' for the moments when Garrick is about," she explained, curving her lips into a weak smile.

Beneath Mari's assessing stare, she almost flinched. "Mr. Edward deserves a good woman," Mari said at last. Then she pierced the flesh of an apple with even, white teeth and began to chew, leaving Charlotte with the distinct impression that the words had been meant less as welcome than as warning.

Chapter 4

Awakened by repeated taps of a soft paw against her face, Charlotte sat up with a start, causing both the sofa and the cat to mewl in protest. In the gray half-light, the furnishings of the housekeeper's sitting room were little more than indistinct shapes. The sun had only just crested the horizon, and the birds were still serenading it with their songs of welcome. Early as it was, however, she sensed as soon as she rose that she was alone. The door to the inner chamber stood open and the bed within had been neatly made by its silently departed occupant.

The cat stopped pacing along the back of the sofa long enough to sharpen its claws against the tattered upholstery, then stretched. Charlotte stretched, too, and scratched the restless tom behind the ears before pinning up her braids and putting on a clean dress. When she left the room, she took the muddy one with her, intending to brush it off outside. The cat followed.

"Do you have a name?" she asked the cat as she walked into the morning air. Weeds choked what had once been a fine kitchen garden. No livestock grazed in the fields beyond. "I suppose you must have a name," she said, glancing down at the cat as she began work on the dress. Surely Garrick called him something. "But no cat I've ever met has been willing to share it. May I call you Noir, then?"

The black cat paused in the act of cleaning between his hind toes to look steadily at her. Yellow-green eyes blinked once before he went back to his task. Charlotte took the gesture for assent.

When the dress had been improved as much as she could manage, she laid it over a nearby bush to freshen in the spring air. Hopefully Mari could supply needle and thread to repair the seam under one arm that had ripped when Mr. Cary had jerked her to safety.

The sun was fully up now, and she could hear Garrick in the stables nattering to the horses. But no sign of Mari. Or Edward. With a hum of curiosity, she set off down what might once have been a path. At least, snapped twigs and bent grass suggested someone had recently passed that way.

Not a quarter mile from the manor she saw a smaller house, made of the same golden-brown stone, its steeply pitched roof and mullioned windows a copy of the manor in miniature. She guessed it must be the Rookery. A few more steps brought her close enough to hear voices, although the speakers remained out of sight at the back of the house. Noir ventured closer, creeping through the undergrowth in search of some unsuspecting rodent.

"I don't understand why you followed me here," she heard Edward say.

Mari's voice answered him with a question. "To Ravenswood?"

"To England."

"How arrogant you are. Did you not tell me I was free?" The woman's lack of deference rooted Charlotte to the spot as she awaited at the very least a reprimand. Aunt Penhurst would have dismissed a servant who spoke so.

Instead, Edward's reply offered reassurance. "You *are* free."

"And did you not pay me wages for my work these last months?"

"Yes, of course. But—"

"Those wages were sufficient to buy passage on a ship. I was *free* to do so. It does not mean that I followed you."

"Fine," Edward conceded irritably. "Have it as you will. But you still have not answered my question. Why leave? When I put Regis in charge, he confessed to me his hope that you and he might—"

"Marry? No, I think not. I never fancied him." Without conscious thought, Charlotte crept closer, drawn to the story unfolding just out of sight. "In any case, would the whites of Antigua recognize such a union?" Mari demanded. "Could you promise me that my babies would not be snatched from me and put in chains?"

"You have a copy of your deed of manumission."

"A piece of paper can be burned, Mr. Edward. But in England, there are no slaves—"

"Miss Hol—*Mrs. Corrvan* taught you that, I suppose?" Something like impatience edged his voice as he corrected himself. The woman of whom he spoke must have been recently married, for the name did not come easily to his lips.

"She did."

"So what will you do here?"

"Work, I suppose," she answered after a slight hesitation. "Won't someone have me as a cook, or a housekeeper?"

"Is that what you want to do?"

A pause. "I don't know. But it's something to have a choice."

"It is. And while you are weighing your options, you might better have stayed with Miss—*Mrs.* Corrvan. She has two households to manage. To say nothing of how she's wearing herself to a shadow working to raise support for abolition," he added in a mutter. "She needs assistance."

"And you do not? Mrs. Corrvan is leaving for Yorkshire within the week. But she felt certain I might be of some use here—"

"Mrs. Corrvan may go to the devil." He spoke across Mari, and the harsh rejoinder nearly forced a gasp from Charlotte's lips. "She's meddling in things she doesn't understand. Look around." One arm swept outward, a slash of white against the overgrown greenery at the back of the house. "If I'm to succeed at Ravenswood, I'll have to find a way to bring this place back from the brink of destruction. All my concern must be for the farms, and the tenants upon them—if any remain." A moment of silence followed, as if he required a moment to collect himself. "Bad as the state of the manor may be," he added more quietly, "its care is far from a priority. A housekeeper is far from a necessity."

"What of Mrs. Cary?" was Mari's next question.

"Mrs.—? Good God. You needn't pretend—"

"It was you, I believe, who began the game of make-believe," Mari observed. A smug smile tugged at the corner of Charlotte's mouth. "Who is she?"

"I—I don't really know," he admitted. "She appeared to be in some danger, so I—"

"Stepped in to save her. Oh, Mr. Edward. When will you learn you can't save everyone?"

Her gentle question was rewarded with a bitter sound that hardly deserved the name of laughter. "I have known *that* since I was nine years old, Mari. If only I had learned the lesson just a little sooner, everything might have turned out differently."

Nine years old. That must have been when he had gone, or been sent, to the West Indies. What a harsh awakening for a child. But if Mari was right—and Charlotte's own experience confirmed it—Edward still felt a responsibility to take care of others.

"What's done is done," Mari told him. "Now, what do you mean to do with her?"

"If she's an opportunist, she'll soon see there's nothing for her here and be on her way."

Charlotte could not help but bristle at that description of her. *An opportunist,* indeed. Just what sort of opportunity was she meant to be seeking from a man whose clothing and mode of travel and current situation revealed his lack of fortune as surely as hers had? Did he imagine himself possessed of charms that would entice a woman to attach herself to him, regardless of every appearance against him?

Her indignation almost caused her to miss Mari's quiet reply.

"If she leaves, or you send her off, how long before everyone in the neighborhood has heard some rumor about your wife who ran away? Or whom you abandoned?"

"Village gossip."

His easy dismissal did not sway Mari. "Gossip that could ruin you. It will cost you the trust of the people you hope to help."

"You may be right," he agreed after a moment. His voice sank with the reluctant admission, forcing Charlotte to creep closer along the wall, that she might hear the rest of what he said. "And there's always the possibility her fears are genuine. She may have good reason for fleeing to this remote spot."

"Perhaps," Mari conceded. "But how will you decide which is the truth?"

"I don't know." A pause. "What do you suggest?"

Yesterday's rain had left the gentle slope at the side of the house slick with mud—a fact that Charlotte had been willing to ignore until her feet began to slip. It might have been the way the shade had thinned the grass in this particular spot. It might have been the way she was leaning forward trying to overhear her fate. Whatever the cause, as she put more weight onto her left foot, it slid from beneath her. She threw out her hands, swallowed a shriek as both the rough stone wall and the untamed shrubbery eluded her grasp, then skidded and stumbled the rest of the way down the hill, the speed of her descent aided by a thick coating of fallen leaves that must have been rotting there since last autumn.

She landed on her derriere at Edward's feet.

Noir, who had once more been rubbing against Mari's ankles, hissed and arched his back, his tail erect and fluffed to three times its usual size. Mari's eyes went wide and her lips parted in surprise, though no further sound escaped them.

Only on Edward's face did shock war with some other emotion. She strongly suspected him of fighting a smile.

His brown hair lay in tousled waves, not quite so dark now that it was dry. But in the morning light his eyes shone bluer yet, if such a thing were possible. They were fixed squarely on her face as he bent over her, and to her undying shame she giggled like a schoolgirl.

"Good morning," he said drily, stretching out one hand to help her up. "Mrs. Cary."

"I am *not* an opportunist."

Edward looked up from the chipped washbasin, mildly surprised by the outburst. Once on her feet, Charlotte had waited quietly while he persuaded Mari to return to the manor. She had accompanied him wordlessly into the Rookery, even watched without comment while he turned a battered chair upright and made certain it was sound before inviting her to sit down.

But what had seemed like cooperative silence had actually been stewing, it would seem.

"Nor are you a lady's maid," he countered as he handed her a square of damp linen. She was once more coated head-to-toe with mud, and her coil of braided hair had escaped its pins and was slowly unraveling, giving her the appearance of a down-at-the-heels Medusa.

"No," she agreed after she had wiped the dirt from her hands. "I was really more of a lady's companion."

"Mm, yes. So you said last night." Not trusting any of the other furniture in the room with his own weight, he leaned one arm against the dusty mantel. "To an elderly widow with property in Antigua."

Her gaze darted guiltily to the floor. "The lady by whom I was employed *is* a widow, although the family's holdings do not extend to the West Indies, so far as I know. And I did handle her correspondence for a time. Every word."

"Including letters to the gentleman with whom you eloped, I suppose?" He nodded toward the ring on her hand.

That question sent her eyes to the grimy window, as if she hoped to spy a suitable answer somewhere beyond it. "One or two," she whispered, her voice as far away as her gaze.

Would Charlotte Blake—or whoever she was—never cease to surprise him? He had expected a hot denial, some other explanation for the gold band she wore. "You *are* married, then?"

"I was." A pause, then she turned and fixed those fathomless dark eyes on his face. "He died."

Truth. Or such an excellent performance of it that he could never hope to know the difference. It sounded as if an ill-founded and ill-fated marriage had led to her employer's disapproval and dismissal, leaving Charlotte stranded in more ways than one.

And though it ought not, the revelation came as something of a relief. Society gave widows some latitude in their behavior. He had not ruined the reputation of an innocent young woman with his clumsy attempt to help. So long as he did nothing more foolish than he had already done, he would not have to offer her the questionable protection of his name to make up for his mistakes.

"Is there nowhere you can go?" Even if her marriage had caused a rift, surely her aunt or her late husband's family could be made to see reason and do their duty by her.

She weighed the question before replying. "Even if there were, what does it matter if I lack the means to travel?"

"I offered you coach fare," he pointed out.

"You seem eager to be rid of everyone. Even Miss Harper."

"I believe she would be better off in London." He did not need the added responsibility of ensuring her safety. Or Charlotte's.

"With Mrs. Corrvan."

Must her name be on everyone's *lips?* Refusing to speak it himself, he simply said, "Mari is, among other things, an excellent cook. Any household would be lucky to employ her."

Charlotte stood and surveyed the room. The cottage was in an obvious state of disrepair, although nothing like the manor house. For one thing, it hadn't as far to fall. Garrick had spoken honestly about the roof, however. Numerous leaks had left the upstairs bedrooms with rotting floors and mildewed walls. Uninhabitable. Edward had spent last night in this very room, in front of the empty fireplace, hoping the ceiling stayed put.

"Why not this one, then?" she asked.

"I beg your pardon?"

"Or were you depending upon your wife's skills in the kitchen, Mr. Cary?"

"My—? Oh." He dropped his gaze to the floor. "I should never have said—"

"No," she agreed. "You should not. One rescue was quite enough." Then she continued in a slightly softer voice that pulled his eyes upward again. "Nor should I have encouraged it. But what's done is done, and now we must decide what the next step will be. Is Miss Harper right? Will rumors have flown so fast?"

"Well, Garrick believes we are married," he admitted reluctantly. "I certainly wouldn't put it past him to have spent last night at the Rose and Raven, regaling the locals with tales of our arrival."

"So, if I leave now, it could cause a minor scandal."

If she stayed, it would surely cause a major one.

"No," he said sharply. "We cannot possibly—"

"Just what do you imagine I am proposing, Mr. Cary?" Despite her bedraggled state, she managed to convey a good deal of hauteur.

"I'm not quite sure." He lifted one brow. "Mrs. Cary."

"Although I appreciate your generous offer of assistance, I would prefer not to return to society at present. The quiet here suits me. If you allow me to stay, in exchange, I will . . ."

Everything seemed to hang suspended in her pause. But what exactly was he hoping she might offer?

"Why, perhaps I can make this place livable," she suggested, glancing around once more. "I am not afraid of hard work. I could scrub and straighten—earn my keep, so to speak."

His breath, his heartbeat, the spinning of the earth on its axis—all jerked back into their normal rhythms. "It will not be necessary for you to play the parts of both the steward's wife and a scullery maid."

It would be absolute madness to let her stay, on any terms. Only he could not shake the feeling that there was something behind her she wanted—no, *needed*—to escape.

He understood the impulse, even as he knew her attempt was likely doomed to failure.

One simply did not outrun the past.

"You may remain at Ravenswood if you wish," he agreed at last, drumming one fingertip against the mantelpiece. "But not in the Rookery." Having her that close would be an invitation to trouble. Thank God he would be heading to London in a few days' time.

"Very well," she said, sounding relieved, whether at his willingness to allow her to stay, or his plan for keeping himself as far from her as the estate's business would allow, he could not say. Perhaps a bit of both. "Shall I invent some excuse for our, ah, separation?" The faintest blush pinked her cheeks as she spoke the last word.

Trouble indeed.

"I should think the hole in the roof would be sufficient explanation for your residing elsewhere. If it comes up, say I am working to make the place livable again."

Raising wary eyes toward the ceiling, she nodded. "*Certainement.*"

He was beginning to notice patterns in her behavior. She lapsed into French when she was tired or distracted. She giggled when she was nervous or afraid.

And he did not want to know even that much about her.

When she turned to leave he could see debris from her fall still clinging to her. "Wait, Miss Bl—Mrs. Cary," he said, stepping forward. *No, I cannot call her that.* "Charlotte." She paused. "Your dress," he explained. "May I—?" A glance over her shoulder revealed the problem, and she tipped her head in assent.

Setting one palm on her shoulder, he swept the other quickly and firmly down her back to brush away the worst of the dirt and dead leaves. Dissatisfied with the result of his effort, however, he allowed himself a second pass, slower this time, over the same soft curves that had been pressed tight against him as they rode.

Had yesterday's misadventure taught him nothing?

Once more, she held herself rigid beneath his touch. "As to names," she said when he had done, "I believe 'Mrs. Cary' will be sufficient when an address in public is absolutely necessary. Living separately, we shall have little occasion for private conversation, thus no need for intimacies."

Wise words. Too bad they had come too late. He lifted his hand from her shoulder.

As she moved away from him, however, he stayed her once more.

"I think you will agree we have arrived at what is at best a short-term solution. When you are ready to leave, how shall we explain your absence then?"

As the question left his lips, it brought with it an unexpected pang. Ravenswood had always been a lonely place. Her inevitable departure would not make it less so.

"We shall just have to, to—what is the expression? Something about uh, a river—?"

"We shall cross that bridge when we come to it?"

Her shoulders lifted in a Gallic shrug. "If you say so. These things, they have a way of working out," she said reassuringly. "I am really quite good at thinking on my feet."

"So I gathered."

Before she could step away, he reached up to pluck a stray twig from her dark, glossy hair, revealing an angry-looking scratch that disappeared beneath the collar of her dress. When a newly freed lock swept across it, she flinched.

"You should have Mari take a look at that scrape."

"Oh? Has Miss Harper healing skills, as well as culinary ones?" she asked, not looking back at him.

"She has many gifts," he replied. "Including the gift of being able to read people."

"Are you trying to alarm me, Mr. Cary?" Charlotte raised her hand to cover the nape of her neck.

"Not at all. I was merely observing that Mari has always been an astute judge of character. Why should that alarm you?" He snapped the twig between his fingers. "Unless, of course, you have something to hide."

Expecting his words to produce one of those nervous, tittering laughs, he was disappointed to hear her more characteristic giggle turn into something rather more wry-sounding. "If I do, Mr. Cary," she said, pausing on the threshold to study him with her dark eyes, "I would venture to guess I am not the only one."

Then she was gone.

Catching himself staring at the spot where she had been standing, he spun on one foot and left through the back of the house so as not to meet her again. As he strode in the direction of the home farm, he twisted the broken twig absently around his finger.

How had she known?

He had been hiding something for so long, the secret sometimes felt more real than the lie he had been living. For more than twenty years, no one—not even the ever-astute Mari—had doubted he was what he seemed to be: an orphan who had managed through extraordinary luck not only to survive but to become a self-made man.

Coming home meant claiming his true identity. Or at least, he had expected it would.

He had seen almost immediately that there were advantages to continuing the charade of steward a bit longer, however. For one thing, his questions about the estate were more likely to receive honest answers if people believed they were speaking to one of their own.

For another, it provided a modicum of protection from those who might hope to profit from the return of the prodigal son. Charlotte Blake might insist she was not on the make, but he did not know her well enough to trust her. A feigned marriage to plain Edward Cary seemed to suit her just fine, but if she knew he was in fact the son of an earl, she would likely alter her expectations.

Given those uncertainties, he was determined to reveal as little as possible about himself to anyone.

But what if, somehow, Charlotte had already begun to suspect the truth?

Chapter 5

Based on Garrick's description, Edward had pictured Matthew Markham as a man well past his youth, a farmer with a long-standing connection to this land, someone who would remember the old days and be able to help Edward understand what had led to the present condition of Ravenswood. So when he met a tanned, sandy-haired man, a few years younger than he, crossing the field with a sturdy stride, he hesitated.

"Mr. Markham?"

A slight narrowing of dark eyes. "Who's asking?"

"I'm Edward Cary," he said, stepping forward. "The new steward."

"Cary, eh?" Markham echoed. "Some relation to the family, then."

"Distant," Edward lied. Or perhaps it wasn't really a lie. Twenty-two years and four thousand miles had certainly strained the connection. "Your father is Lord Beckley's tenant?"

"He was. He died three years ago."

"My condolences." He paused, considering. "If he's been gone for three years, then you must be the man Garrick told me I'd find. Matthew Markham."

Markham studied Edward for a long moment before giving a single jerk of his chin. "Aye."

While Edward considered what to ask next, the other man turned slightly out of the path he'd been on and kept walking. Edward followed. "You are alone? No brothers?"

His steps did not falter. "Nay."

"How do you manage?"

"I work hard, Mr. Cary," he said, stopping again and sizing Edward up. "And I'd appreciate it if someone would convey as much to his lordship."

"You've been bearing an unfair burden, Markham. For how long?"

"My pa was Lord Beckley's tenant for almost forty years. I worked beside him from a lad. Old Feasby, your predecessor, made over the lease in my name, though it wasn't strictly legal, I suppose, as I wasn't yet of age. Now, I work mostly alone. Hire in a lad or two from the village during harvest, when I can."

Edward scanned the landscape as they passed. To eyes accustomed to sugarcane and the lush greens of the tropics, the alternating strips of field and fallow, both still mostly brown and awaiting the new growth of spring, looked desolate. "How much land have you under cultivation?"

"Not enough."

"What of the rest of Lord Beckley's tenants?"

"There's too few of us, and that's certain. Some died. Others were driven off when they couldn't make the rent. And of course, most of them left when everyone else did."

"When was that?"

"Twenty years ago or so."

"Oh?" Edward tried to mask his curiosity, though his heart knocked in his chest. "What happened then?"

"Outbreak of smallpox. Lady Beckley died of it."

In the damp, heavy soil, Edward stumbled and narrowly kept himself from falling. Long ago, he had forced himself to acknowledge that his running away had probably not been enough to save his mother. But a part of him had always held out hope.

Though they were little more than confirmation of what he had long suspected, Markham's words ripped that fragment of hope right from his chest, leaving something worse than a wound.

Emptiness.

His mother was gone.

"They say his lordship wrecked the house and swore never to return," Markham continued. "'Course, that's just rumor. I never saw the inside of Ravenswood Manor, and I don't know that my pa did either. The servants scurried away like rats from a burning barn, and when folks in the village got word, those who could, left. Naught but a handful of souls there now."

"And the steward—Feasby, was it?" The name was unfamiliar to Edward. "What of him?"

"Not much to keep him here after that. He spent his time on some other property he managed. Up in Derbyshire, as I heard it. Don't think he much cared about this one. He always came quarterly to collect the rents, though. Last quarter day, he didn't bother to do even that."

It was all too much at once. His mother's death, his father's indifference. "To whom did you pay your rent, then?" he asked numbly.

Only after Markham had looked askance at the question did Edward consider he ought to have known the answer if he were who he claimed to be. "An office in London. Leadenhall Street. But I suppose that's about to change?"

"Of course," Edward said, masking his uncertainty with firmness. The last thing he needed was to be the cause of this man's eviction if his rent failed to arrive at the appointed place on the appointed date. But Lady Day was almost a month off. By then, he would have confronted his father and would have matters well in hand here.

As they walked, midmorning sun beat down on their shoulders, but Edward still felt a nip in the air—or perhaps that was just more evidence of his thin blood. He would have called it a late spring, but what did he know anymore? "Between you and me and Garrick, and perhaps some of those lads from the village," he ventured, "is there time to put more land under cultivation yet this season?"

Markham stopped short. "With what, sir? Have you money to pay for seeds, equipment, labor?"

"I have some resources at my disposal, yes," Edward reassured him. Unlike Charlotte, he was far from penniless.

"It's late. Any other year, too late," he said, with another doubtful glance at Edward. A real English steward would know as much. "But it's been a cold, wet spring. Folks who moved too quick lost their seed. We might do to put a bit of wheat or barley in the ground yet."

They were standing now beside the farmer's house, a small neat building, clapboard rather than stone, but in need of whitewashing. Like everything, it was a stark reminder of the work that had gone undone. Markham made no move to invite him in. "Are you a married man, Mr. Markham?"

The other man gave a humorless laugh. "Haven't got much to offer a wife, sir. It's no time to marry, unless you're a rich man—or a man lucky enough to find himself a rich woman. In any case, there's no vicar at the church anymore to do the deed. The living was sold years ago, and I don't believe I've ever seen the man who holds it. His curate is meant to fill the gap, but he's spread mighty thin."

"It would seem you all are." Edward held out a hand for a conciliatory shake. "I hope you'll believe I intend to improve things."

Markham looked down at the outstretched hand, up at Edward, then reluctantly took Edward's hand. "I'll settle for your not making them worse."

It was hardly a vote of confidence, but Edward was in no position to reject it.

"And what of you, sir?" Markham asked after he had released Edward's grip. "Is there a Mrs. Cary?"

Before he could catch himself, he began to shake his head, then tried at the last minute to make it seem as if he had merely been trying to ward off a fly. "Yes. There is. My wife and I are . . . recently wed. She came to Gloucestershire with me, but the Rookery is in such poor repair that I have installed her in the manor. With his lordship's permission, of course."

The farmer managed to look at once skeptical and indifferent. "You sure about puttin' in another crop? Seems like a newly married man wouldn't want to be leavin' his wife's side at sunrise to dig in the dirt."

With an effort, Edward dispelled the unwelcome image of Charlotte Blake, warm and drowsy, in his bed. "As I said, Mr. Markham, I'm here to work."

"Well, Mari," said Charlotte with a smile, having changed into what had once been her very best sprigged muslin, "this is the last clean dress I have to my name. What manner of trouble do you suppose I can get into now?"

Mari lifted the muddy dress from her hands. "Are you English?"

Charlotte recalled what Edward had said about the woman's perceptiveness. Had she fled from one spy straight to another? Well, she would just have to be careful not to change her story. No more inventing. "My father was. I was raised in France, however."

Whether Mari found the answer satisfactory or not, Charlotte was unable to determine. The woman turned and left the room without speaking. Charlotte followed her into the kitchen, where it looked for all the world as if the servants must have fled in the middle of preparing dinner—many years ago. The food itself had long since disappeared, molded into dust or eaten by something, but a kettle still hung over the hearth and pots and pans lay scattered over tables.

Mari nodded toward a scraggly broom. "You begin to set things to rights in here. I'm off to the well, and I'll make sure Garrick's cleared the chimney, too. We'll hope this"—she tapped the side of a rusty cistern near the sink—"will hold water."

Charlotte was used to taking orders. "All right," she agreed and set to work. The tasks themselves—sweeping, stacking, straightening—were largely mindless, but they raised any number of questions. What could have happened here to allow things to deteriorate to such a state? The earl was in London, Garrick had said, and had been for years. While there was nothing unusual about a nobleman residing in Town, especially at certain seasons, she could not imagine why he would have left his estate entirely untended. No servants left behind to care for the place, every sign that the family's departure had been hurried and unplanned.

And Edward—was this what he had expected to find? She had not seen his face when they arrived, was not privy to his first reaction. His overheard words to Mari, however, suggested that things were worse than he had been led to believe. If there were no tenants, no farmers, then the estate had no income. On what did this Lord Beckley live? He must be very rich, or very foolish, if he could afford to let Ravenswood go to rack and ruin. If she were Edward, she might be tempted to refuse a post offered by such a reckless man.

But the edge in Edward's voice conveyed quite clearly that this was more than a post to him. What was his connection to this place, so far from the world he had left?

Two things succeeded in tamping down her inquisitiveness: her hands, sore from sweeping and polishing and scrubbing; and hunger. Once Garrick's approval had been secured, Mari built a fire and set water to boil. Soon, Charlotte's muddy dresses were soaking in a tub in one corner, most of the dishes had been washed, and the kitchen was beginning to look like a place where food could be prepared. If there was any food to be had.

Just as her stomach gave a particularly demanding growl, Garrick entered with a sack of something slung over his shoulder and thumped it down on the table. "You ready for these things now, missus?"

"Ready enough," answered Mari.

To Charlotte's amazement, Garrick and Dobbs, the driver of Edward's baggage coach, brought in sacks of flour and potatoes, dried peas, a haunch of beef, and other supplies. "Mr. Cary must have suspected how things were here," she said as she watched.

Mari made a derisive sound. "Men think of meals, not what goes into making them. Mrs. Corrvan bade me take these things and help him set up his household. But the kitchen in that little cottage? Bah! I say if he's going to eat, he must come here to do it."

He didn't, though. At least not then. Mari prepared a hearty beef pie with astonishing speed, and Charlotte ate with the first real hunger she had experienced in a long time. Though that would have been sauce enough for whatever food was placed before her, she could not deny that Edward had been honest about Mari's abilities. What Charlotte had always considered a plain, dull, English dish had been spiced and seasoned into something almost unrecognizable.

"This is delicious," she said around a mouthful.

Mari accepted the garbled compliment with a nod. "Thank you, Mrs. Cary."

She might have spared the trouble of tacking on that deceptive address, however, as Garrick and Dobbs were eating too noisily to hear her.

"I wonder," asked Charlotte, more hesitantly, "if you would be willing to look at this scratch on my neck? Mr. Cary said you have a healing touch."

"Did he, now?" Mari rose and inspected the injury without further comment, then fetched a wet cloth and laid it across the back of Charlotte's neck. She could not contain the yelp that rose to her lips as the hot water came in contact with the wound. But after a moment, the sting began to ease. Leaving the cloth in place, Mari next retrieved a small wooden box and opened it to reveal neat rows of folded papers and small corked vials. She traced one fingertip over them, settled on a little tub, and withdrew it. "How's that?" she asked as she applied some sweet-smelling unguent to the abraded skin.

Remarkably, the pain faded. "Better. Thank you."

"Hands," Mari demanded, holding out her own, palm upward. Obediently, Charlotte laid her hands across the other woman's, feeling—almost envying—their calluses. Charlotte's skin was red and rough. "Just as I suspected. You're a lady."

Charlotte knew a compliment when she heard one. This was no compliment. "No," she demurred with a glance toward the men. "I'm not. It *has* been some time since I did this sort of work, but I assure you I'm more than capable."

Mari's only answer was to apply another hot cloth to the tender skin of her palms, followed by the soothing balm.

As he shoved his plate away, Garrick gave a hearty belch and patted his stomach. "That'll do. Best get back to sharpening that ol' plow."

"Where's Mr. Cary?" Charlotte ventured to ask as Mari returned the ointment to the box.

"I saw him strike out for the home farm about midmorning. Musta found Markham, I'd say."

"Markham?"

" 'is lordship's chief tenant—almos' 'is only tenant."

"*Only?* But who takes care of all this land?"

"Most of it lies fallow, missus. Guessin' it's yer man's job to change that."

"But . . . Why, that's—"

"That's exactly the sort of work at which Mr. Cary excels," Mari interjected smoothly, shooing Garrick and Dobbs out of the kitchen. Charlotte could have sworn she heard the woman mutter something about *achieving the impossible* under her breath. "And Mr. Garrick?" she called after them. "When you've got that plow ready, turn over the kitchen garden first."

"Have we seeds?" Charlotte asked.

The corners of Mari's mouth lifted. "Not yet. But there will be a way to get some. I think I'll take a little walk," she said, cutting a wedge of the pie, laying it on a plate, and covering it with a cloth.

Bound for the Rookery, Charlotte supposed. "Let me go for you," she offered, although part of her argued that she could surely put her time to better use than having another circuitous conversation with Edward Cary. "It cannot be easy for you to walk so far." All expression seemed to slide from Mari's face. "I only meant—your leg." She stumbled over an explanation. "Is it a recent injury?"

"No."

The single word fell like a slap to the face, setting Charlotte back on her heels and leaving her cheeks flaming. Without sparing her so much as a glance, Mari left with the food in a basket carried over her arm, the only sound the scrape of her lame foot across the floor.

Was there anyone at Ravenswood who didn't have a secret to keep?

Chapter 6

Alone in the house for the first time since their midnight arrival, Charlotte left the kitchen and servants' wing to explore. Perhaps because she suspected Edward would not approve if he knew she was snooping through his employer's home, the grate of the heavy oak door against flagstone sent a thrill of trepidation down her spine.

Retracing the path along which Garrick had led them last night, she entered a long gallery, seeing clearly for the first time what darkness had then hidden. Filthy windows overlooked an empty terrace and dense woodland beyond. On the opposite wall hung a row of mirrors, a few cracked, all mottled with age, reflecting the hazy view. To her right, another door opened onto a dark-paneled dining room, awaiting service of the meal whose remains they had found in the kitchen. Someone, or something—then, or in the years since—had toppled a few chairs, and delicate china and crystal lay in shards on the flagstone, crunching beneath her feet as her hems traced feathery patterns in the dust on the floor.

Back in the gallery, her footsteps echoed in the emptiness. At the midpoint, she crossed the back of the wide central hall and glanced up the staircase, which rose to upper floors cloaked in obscurity. *Later*, she promised herself.

At the far end of the gallery, a second curved door stood ajar, and she slipped into the dimly lit room beyond. The gasp that rose to her lips seemed loud in the high-ceilinged room. Here, too, everything was in disarray. Formerly elegant furniture had been overturned, scattered, and broken. A musty miasma of old paper and books, the odors of a decaying library, settled into her lungs and made her cough. Sun-rotted draperies partially covered a tall bank of windows that once must have offered a spectacular view of the formal gardens, now overgrown and gone to seed. Beyond this receiving room and slightly offset from it, clearly added at some later date, an empty ballroom awaited dancers who seemed unlikely to grace Ravenswood ever again.

Perhaps every creaky old house exuded a bit of mystery, but it was impossible for Charlotte not to wonder what had happened here. What sort of nobleman decided on a whim to quit his estate and, apparently, never return? Even though she had no particular attachment to the place, she felt a certain grief at its abandonment. How could someone simply leave this once lovely old place to rot? Did he imagine a home was easy to come by?

She knew better.

As she wandered around the room, her fingertips left a trail in the thick dust on tables and the curved backs of chairs. From time to time, she paused to set a chair on its feet—until she disturbed a family of mice who had made their nest in the straw and stuffing of one, and they squeaked and scattered to safety. Lifting her skirts almost to her knees so that none of the pests would be tempted to take refuge beneath them, she looked about frantically for Noir. No wonder his fur was so sleek and thick. He hardly had to lift a paw to find a meal in this old wreck of a house. But the cat was nowhere to be seen.

Perhaps Noir and the mice had the right idea. She, too, was tempted to scamper away. What business had she meddling with someone else's house, feigning a marriage with a perfect stranger? She had—whatever Langerton claimed to the contrary—her own house to manage and a real marriage to defend. She had only to ask Edward for enough money to get her to London, and she could . . .

Could what? Ah, that was the rub. Run afoul of the man who had been hired to spy on her? Challenge her stepson and be publicly humiliated? Beg her aunt for assistance and be turned down flat? She had desired only the power to make her own choices. A return to London would likely strip away what little power marriage to the late duke had earned her.

Better to lie low in rural obscurity. Perhaps her disappearance would disrupt Robert's plan. And Ravenswood was an ideal place to disappear. Isolated, abandoned. No one here to raise eyebrows or ask questions. Except Mari, whose interest clearly lay in protecting Edward, not exposing Charlotte.

She understood that impulse. He was strong, steady—certainly worthy of a woman's devotion. Everything he did demonstrated his determination to take care of others. In his hands, she would be . . .

His hands. Awareness chased along her skin where he had brushed off her dress.

Holding herself rigid, she managed to stave off the memory. Those sorts of impulses were the unfortunate complement to an unruly imagination. No one here knew anything about that side of her, the nature she had inherited. She would just have to make sure to do nothing to reveal her secrets, nothing to turn the perspicacious Mari against her, and all would be well.

Suddenly restless, she resumed her examination of the room. *A good top-to-bottom cleaning would certainly improve its condition*, she thought as she glanced around, although there was damage that cleaning could not fix. Some of the furniture looked to be beyond repair, too, and the only solution for the rotted draperies would be to pull them down.

When she tugged one of the velvet panels, it ripped away easily in her hand, collapsing at her feet and cloaking her in a cloud of dust, from which she emerged blinking, coughing, and filthy. Her third—and last—clean dress was clean no longer. Well, there was nothing for it now but to keep on. It had never been in her nature to sit idle, and contrary to Mari's taunt, she was no lady. She jerked down the next panel and the next and the next, until dust billowed through the room like fog, motes turned to prisms by the last rays of the setting sun.

Smoothing a dirty palm over her hair, she gave a satisfied nod. Already, the place looked better.

"What in God's name are you doing?"

Edward's voice came from somewhere over her shoulder, but the dust in the air obscured him from view. As she had feared, he did not sound happy to have found her there. Forced to wait until the dust settled to face him, she gnawed on her lip, stifling a nervous laugh.

Charlotte's dark eyes glittered in the fading light of the room, but every other inch of her looked as if she had lost a battle with a tin of wig powder. Even her eyelashes were pale. As she worried her plump lower lip with her upper teeth, clearly trying to look serious, even contrite, some of that ghostly layer was scraped away to reveal pink flesh. The bitter taste of the dust—it filled his mouth, too—made her sputter.

Despite the grim mixture of horror and despair churning in his gut, the faintest smile rose to his own lips. "If this is your idea of assistance," he said, not stepping toward her, not offering to brush her off again, "I believe I should reconsider your offer."

When she had suggested repaying his help by cleaning house, he had been somewhat skeptical of her intentions, to say nothing of her abilities. He had not considered the possibility she might actually make things worse.

Maybe she and I are two of a kind, he thought, recalling Markham's words.

In his childhood, the place where they now stood had been known as the Great Room, all things to all people. How many times had he been shooed from this room so his father could talk without interruption to men of local importance; played endless scales on the pianoforte as his mother watched over his shoulder; peered unseen around the doorframe while brightly clad couples whirled and bowed across the dance floor?

But the room's days of greatness were long past. Edward's mother was believed to have died of the smallpox, Markham had told him, and gossip suggested his father's grief had been given vent on his surroundings: *They say his lordship wrecked the house and swore never to return.* Edward suspected at least parts of that rumor were unfounded. His father was unlikely to have succumbed to grief.

Had disease taken his mother? Or had the wrath that had been released in this room also been turned onto her? If it had, she would have had no more chance of surviving it than the now-shattered instrument upon which she had once played with such grace, or the landscape in oils above the fireplace, which hung in ribbons as if some ravening beast had raked sharp claws across it. Either way, he would likely never know the truth.

"Are you all right, sir?"

He jerked his attention to the figure by the windows. The light of the setting sun streaming in from behind combined with the dust in the air to sketch a hazy glow around her. "Why do you ask?"

"You look pale, and I thought perhaps . . ."

He laughed, then, because to allow himself to do otherwise might reveal much more than Charlotte ever needed to know. "Pale? You should see yourself," he said, at last holding out one hand to help her over the mountain of moldering velvet at her feet. "But you still haven't answered my question. What are you about?"

"I intend to give this room a proper cleaning," she said, brushing dust from her shoulders and shaking out her skirts.

"By yourself?"

Her chin jutted forward. "If I must. I have lived in many places, with varying degrees of comfort, but never in filth, and I do not intend to start now."

"Are you not comfortably accommodated in the kitchen wing?" She nodded stiffly, obviously reluctant to agree with him. "Then stay there. Don't wander about making a mess of things that aren't yours to touch." An edge crept into his voice as he gestured toward the draperies.

"The mess, sir, was made already," she said, ignoring his hand and stepping past him.

"And I cannot think your employer would wish to find—"

"I've reason to believe Lord Beckley knows the condition of the estate and chooses, for reasons you and I may never fathom, to . . . leave things as they are. We must accede to his wishes."

"Why then did you bother to meet with Mr. Markham?" she challenged. "Why would he hire a steward at all if he meant to allow everything to continue in ruin?"

"He did not—" Edward began, cutting himself off before he could blurt out the truth. "My position is to manage the farms. Not this house."

One day, Ravenswood would be profitable again, capable of supporting the surrounding community, as it had been when he had left it. Already, his plans were blossoming following his conversation with Markham. New seed, new tools, oxen if he could find them. If they managed to get a crop in, afterward he would go to work improving the tenants' cottages, which would better their lives and attract new tenants as well. Once the farm was up and running—and he had met with his father, of course—then he could turn his attention to the manor.

"I can manage the house, if you will let me," she said.

It would certainly keep her busy, out of his way. Nevertheless, he shook his head. He did not want her poking around these rooms, although he could not exactly say why. Perhaps because it felt too much like inviting another person to sift through his own memories.

"But I must do something," she insisted.

"Why?"

She shot him a nervous glance. Clearly she imagined herself in his debt. Did she think that if he declined her offer of help with the house, he meant to demand some other form of repayment?

"Let be," he insisted, ushering her impatiently toward the door.

"Please," she said as he closed the door behind them. "Leave it open. Like so." She held up both hands in front of her, palms facing, about six inches apart. "There are mice, and I hoped Noir might, er, dispose of them."

"Noir?" Edward arched one brow, but he left the door ajar as she had requested.

"The black cat that hangs about. I took the liberty of naming it. I 'ope zat is all right?" She was tired. Her French accent peeped out like the hem of a petticoat, all the more tantalizing when it refused to be concealed any longer.

He shrugged and turned toward the back of the house. If the cat belonged to anyone, it must be Garrick's, for there was no one else to claim it. And he could not imagine the former second stable hand thought of it as a pet.

"Have you eaten? There should be more of Mari's excellent beef pie left. If Mr. Garrick has not got to it already."

His stomach rumbled out an answer. Realizing the necessity of sparing Samson after yesterday's ride, he had spent the day walking the upper farms. Upon his return to the Rookery, he had meant to find something to stave off the pangs of hunger, but he had lost himself in figures instead—times were hard, and everything was dear. Truth be told, he was surprised to find he still had an appetite after that, but his bodily needs demanded to be satisfied, even though his head ached and grief lay like a stone in his chest, pressing his heart beneath its weight.

When they reached the door to the kitchen, he pushed it open and stepped back for Charlotte to enter ahead of him, a part of him reluctant, despite his hunger, to see yet another ruined room overflowing with childhood memories.

But here all was neat, a fire crackling on the hearth, every pot and plate where it ought to be. He might have guessed that Mari would have set the place to rights already. She had always taken a certain pride in a well-run kitchen.

He was not, however, prepared for the realization such a discovery brought with it: It was worse, somehow, to find himself in a place that looked much as it had twenty-five or so years ago, when he had been in the habit of sneaking out of the nursery, past his sleeping nurse, in search of some forbidden treat.

Mari was nowhere to be seen. Charlotte washed her hands, then put the kettle on the hob. After scrubbing his own hands and face, he took the chair at the head of the servants' table—the butler's place—and allowed his eyes to follow her, merely for the pleasure of looking at something that brought back no uncomfortable rush of memory. Or at least, no memory older than a day.

Having cleaned herself up as best she could, she now moved efficiently to prepare him some sort of supper. As he watched her work, he could almost believe she had spent time in service, or at least in a household where she had not been spared her share of domestic duties. Had she waited on her husband—if indeed there had ever been such a man—in just this way?

Charlotte set a plate before him, poured two steaming cups of tea, and then took the seat nearest him, at the end of one of the long benches lining either side of the table.

"Sugar, Mr. Cary?" she asked, lifting the tongs.

He shook his head. "No, thank you."

"I should think you could not bear to do without it," she said with obvious surprise. "I understood it to be common as air where you have been."

"It is." He would never be able to look at sugar the same way he once had, knowing what he knew now about how it was made. And by whom. Every snowy crystal seemed to him steeped in blood. "But its sweetness leaves an aftertaste I would rather do without."

"Oh." She seemed, somehow, to follow the direction of his thoughts. "Some years ago, the abolitionists began a campaign to boycott sugar. We were encouraged to use honey instead. My aunt only laughed and said she thought it would be rather hard on the poor bees."

As she spoke, she fiddled with the handle of her cup, though he could not help but notice she did not drink from it. She had no doubt been about to sweeten it, and his sanctimonious little speech had stopped her. Wordlessly, he took the tongs from her grasp and dropped two lumps of sugar into her cup. "Perhaps it would be," he acknowledged. "Who can say?"

She couldn't be expected to understand the reality of life on a West Indian sugar plantation. He was not even certain he would want her to—in his experience, innocence was a virtue too little cherished. Why inflict on others his knowledge of a horror that their meager sacrifices would do little to abate?

Still, she did not drink.

"Will you not join me?" he asked, noticing for the first time that she had brought only one plate of food.

"The tea will suffice."

He hesitated a moment longer, but in the end, his hunger prevailed, and as usual, Mari's cooking did not disappoint. In what he feared was a most unmannerly display, he had soon cleaned the plate. "How did Mari—?"

"Mrs. Corrvan sent some household supplies with her."

"Ah."

He still could not accustom himself to thinking of Mrs. Corrvan as anything but Tempest—though he should not be thinking of her at all. But this time, at least, the sharp pang he associated with hearing her married name had been dulled by hot tea and good food—and perhaps just a bit by the soft accents of the one who spoke it.

"Was your conversation with Mr. Markham enlightening? How do things stand on the farms?"

"From what I've seen, almost as bad as in the house, I'm afraid," he said, sipping his tea. "Just a handful of downtrodden tenants. It's going to take a great deal of work to make this place function as it ought."

"And money," she added frankly. "Has your employer given you some sort of advance, or at least a line of credit, so that you may undertake improvements here?"

He tipped his chin in a sort of nod. "In a manner of speaking."

Tilting her head to the side, she studied his expression. His indirection had not gone unnoticed. "I have heard stories of those who returned from the West Indies wealthy men. But surely you cannot mean to use your own money to correct the mistakes—the negligence—of this—this—"

"Lord Beckley," he supplied evenly, before she could insert some far less proper noun in its place. "I have an inheritance, from a man I came to know in Antigua. Thomas Holderin. My . . . mentor." It was the best word Edward knew to describe the role the man had played in his life, although he found it wholly inadequate. He might have been tempted to call him a second father, if that label had not already been tainted by his first.

Certainly Edward had never expected to have to use Thomas Holderin's generous bequest to shore up his own family's estate, to right the wrongs his father had committed. Last year, he had given the better part of it to a ship's captain, bribing him to take Tempest—Holderin's daughter—away from the dangers of the island. But just a few days ago, in London, that small fortune had been returned to him, Captain Corrvan seeming to feel he had got a better prize out of the voyage.

"And you mean to invest that inheritance here?" Charlotte asked. His explanation had done nothing to budge the skeptical look on her face.

"I have every reason to believe that any investment of mine will be returned with interest."

Charlotte pulled the empty plate across the table and swept her forefinger across the scattering of crumbs. "I hope Lord Beckley knows how fortunate he is to have you in his employ. I understand very little about the management of property, but I do know that honest, hardworking men are in regrettably short supply," she said.

He did not even know this woman's name, yet somehow she seemed to know him, or claimed to. It was flattery, he reminded himself. Even flirtation. She hoped to ingratiate herself so that he would not turn her away.

In what was either a calculated display, or a totally un-self-conscious act—and damn him if he could tell the difference—she slid her crumb-speckled finger between her lips and licked it clean, then rose to carry the empty plate to the drain board.

"Was Mr. Blake a scoundrel, then?" he asked.

At his question, her gait hitched, but she did not turn. "My husband was . . . naïve. No—that is too strong. He did not always see people for what they truly were."

"And what did he see when he looked at you, Charlotte?"

"That, I could not say." The lift of her shoulders was almost imperceptible in the dimly lit kitchen. "I think, perhaps, he did not see me at all."

The chair scraped across the stone floor as Edward rose, and in the stillness that followed, his boot heels rang as he crossed to stand behind her. At this distance, nothing escaped his eye, not even the way her knuckles whitened where they gripped the plate.

I *see you.*

The words begged to be spoken, but he would not part his lips and set them free. Were they even true?

Along the back of her neck, a streak of grime marked the place where she must have rubbed her hand in a moment of uncertainty, or to ease an ache. Dust still coated her hair. Surely, the gentlemanly thing to do would be to offer to fetch her water for a bath.

But even the thought of making that offer brought with it a host of other, far less gentlemanly, ideas. If he were not careful, he was going to find himself seduced by a perfect stranger. Or seducing one.

"We can never really know another person," he said instead. His breath stirred a loose tendril of hair that brushed her cheek. "At best, we can hope to know ourselves."

And he knew himself well enough to realize he should leave before he did something he would regret. "Good night, Charlotte," he said, stepping away from her and toward the door.

In the dusky shadows of the yard, he met Dobbs.

"Ah, Mr. Cary, sir," the driver said, hurrying toward him. "I was jus' comin' to find you. Miss Mari gave me some sort o' potion for Prince's fetlock, and it looks good as new. Can you be ready t' go first thing?"

Some would have called Dobbs's announcement providential. The perfect excuse for Edward to absent himself from temptation and focus on more pressing business.

Of course, his tenants would not see it in that light. For one thing, he had promised Markham his assistance in putting in more crops.

Behind him, a square of light fell across the ground, a candle shining in the window of the butler's room. Charlotte's room.

Whatever the truth of her story, he had no doubt she was hiding from something.

Gloucestershire was, on the whole, not a bad place to hide from trouble. The undulating landscape and thick forests had provided him an occasional refuge when he was a boy. So, of course, had the old house, medieval at its core but with hundreds of years of haphazard additions that had left nooks and crannies, rooms within rooms, known only to a few.

He thought with no particular pleasure of setting out on the journey to London. Maybe he was still hiding in Gloucestershire, at Ravenswood.

And maybe a part of him was glad not to be hiding alone.

"I'm obliged to you, Dobbs," he said with a tip of his head as he turned toward the Rookery. "But my plans have changed. I'm staying here."

Chapter 7

When Charlotte awoke the next morning, the aroma of frying bacon lured her from her bed. Did dreams have scents? Surely, not even Mari could manage to conjure such a breakfast out of thin air.

Just as she entered the kitchen, Garrick stepped through the doorway opposite, carrying two buckets brimful from the well. "Good mornin', Mrs. Cary," he said, although his eyes never left Mari, who was bending over a skillet near the fire.

Before she could reply, Edward rose from the table. "You'll have half the village here for breakfast if you're not careful, Mari," he teased. Yesterday's strain had eased. With a nod of greeting for Charlotte, he moved to take the buckets from Garrick's hands and carried them to the cistern to fill it. Relieved of his burden, Garrick sat and took up his fork in preparation.

"Well, I only invited Mr. Markham, seeing as he was the one who supplied us with the eggs," Mari tossed back, never taking her eyes off her task.

That piece of information produced a sharp clang of tin against copper, as if Edward had almost dropped the bucket. "You saw Markham? When?"

"Yesterday afternoon. Where there's a farm, there's seed for a garden. And chickens," she added, at last turning away from the fire with a steaming skillet of coddled eggs. "And, once upon a time, a pig."

"Markham spared you all that?" Garrick asked in open amazement, shoveling food from the pan onto his plate before Mari had even set it down.

"My cooking always could work wonders." A smile twinkled in her brown eyes.

Charlotte hid her surprise by busying herself with the coffeepot.

So, the hearty slice of pie had not been destined for the Rookery after all. "Where is Mr. Dobbs this morning?" she asked.

"Went back t' London at first light," Garrick answered around a mouthful.

"Oh!" Mari turned to Edward. "I thought you meant to go—?"

"Two dozen eggs, a flitch of bacon. I suppose Markham gave you the coffee, too?" Edward spoke across her, avoiding the question.

"No. That was among the supplies Mrs. Corrvan sent."

"Mrs. Corrvan?" This time, at least, he did not stumble over her name. But Charlotte could see by the sudden tightness in his shoulders how he disliked having to speak it.

"That's right," Mari confirmed, an edge of defiance in her voice as she turned her attention to dishing up the bacon.

"Ah, yes. Now I remember. Mrs. Cary told me of it yesterday."

Feeling Edward's eyes on her, Charlotte poured four cups of the hot, dark liquid and put one at each place, wondering whether he would prove willing to drink it now, given its origins.

But by the time he joined the other three at the table, he seemed to have put his feelings about Mrs. Corrvan behind him. Again, however, he eschewed the sugar bowl; when it came around to Charlotte, she guiltily dropped a lump into her cup, feeling only slightly better when she saw Mari take two.

"Garrick," Mari asked, passing him the bacon, "is there a hen house here worth the name?"

He waved one hand in the direction of the window and the dilapidated wooden structure beyond it. "Aye, after a fashion."

"Once you've plowed the kitchen garden, see that it's repaired," Mari ordered. The man harrumphed noisily, but at last gave a reluctant nod.

"With any luck," explained Mari, "I'll persuade Mr. Markham to part with a few chicks next time."

"I doubt that." With his fork dangling from the fingers of one hand, Edward looked nothing short of mischievous. "You're out of ammunition. I finished the beef pie last night."

"There'll be something else he'll need, don't you worry," was Mari's tart reply. Their banter this morning was more amiable than the day before, but still nothing like mere master and servant. "Haven't I always found ways to take care of my kitchen?"

"That you have, Mari. That you have. So," he said, pushing back his empty plate, "that's your day sorted, and Garrick's as well, it would seem." Garrick mumbled something around a mouthful of food but made no clear objection. "What of you, madam wife?"

The address made her jump, and her cup rattled in its saucer. "I—I thought I might . . . work a bit on straightening up the house. The family rooms."

Mari paused, a forkful of yellow egg suspended in the air as she looked from Charlotte to Edward. "The family rooms?"

Rising, Charlotte began to collect the dishes from the table. "If Mr. Cary does not object."

Edward stood, too, fixing her with blue eyes that still laughed, though some of the openness had left them. "Would it matter if I did?"

A wheeze of laughter came from behind Garrick's cup. "You ain't been married long, sir, if you're askin' such a blame fool question as that. A woman's like a horse. Can't give either one a free rein and 'spect not to get runned away with. Gotta keep the bit firm and the crop handy, if you catch my meanin'."

The analogy was hardly surprising coming from a stable hand, but Charlotte sensed it nevertheless did not sit well with Edward, whose summery gaze seemed to darken as it shifted to the other man. "I do not believe in whipping horses," he said flatly. "Or women. Or servants—fortunately for you, Garrick."

Undaunted by the thinly veiled threat, Garrick slid one grimy nail into the gap between two teeth and sucked on whatever he had dug loose. "Jus' slaves, then?"

Charlotte hardly knew what came over her. She only sensed that these two men were about to come to blows in Mari's newly spotless kitchen, and instinct told her that if Garrick went down, it would ultimately be Edward who would struggle to rise again. Mari had been right—he could not afford to earn the censure of the people he meant to help.

Stepping between them, she laid a hand on Edward's forearm, feeling the flex of muscle as his fingers curled into a fist. "And what of you, my dear?" she asked, looking up at him, willing his eyes on her. They were intimacies she had never intended to invite, but she could think of no better way to distract him. "How do you mean to spend the day?"

She knew she had succeeded before he spoke. There was surprise in his eyes, but something like gratitude as well, and the coiled spring beneath her hand began to unwind. "I'm bound first for the village to see about ordering some supplies," he said. With his free hand he patted hers where it lay on his arm. Long fingers. Neatly trimmed nails. A gentleman's hands, despite their sun-browned color. "Is there anything you require?"

"Turpentine," she said in her most businesslike tone. "Beeswax. Lye soap." Many years spent in the company of servants had given her knowledge not only of the necessary items but also how to use them.

Squeezing gently, he lifted her hand from his sleeve and turned it palm upward, tracing his thumb carefully around the evidence of yesterday's blisters. The gentle touch, skin to skin, felt more intimate than being held against his body. "You needn't do this, Charlotte," he insisted, his head bowed. For a fleeting moment, she thought he meant to kiss her hand.

She stepped backward, sliding her fingers from his grasp, but not before she felt her pulse quicken and knew he must have felt it, too. Curse her wild imagination! Hadn't she cautioned herself just yesterday about such familiarities?

Oui. Right after the stroke of his warm palm had sent a bolt of lightning through her body, once, twice, forcing her to fight a tremor of longing that he might do it a third time, for good measure.

Desire—so unwelcome—felt like a betrayal.

"Someone should," she said sharply, conscious that both Garrick and Mari were watching. How much had Charlotte just revealed?

She expected Edward to argue with her, but he nodded. "I'll have the things sent. I'm for Markham's farm, after that. He and I hope to put in another field of barley. Don't wait dinner, Mari." And he was gone.

Garrick followed a few paces behind, a triumphant if tuneless whistle on his lips, leaving the two women alone in the kitchen. Determined to behave as if nothing had happened—for nothing *had* happened, except perhaps in her mind—Charlotte bustled about collecting the rest of the dirty dishes.

Mari's eyes had followed the men out the door, some unreadable expression in their depths. She had not taken another bite of her breakfast since Garrick had uttered that terrible word.

Slaves.

Putting aside a stack of plates, Charlotte hesitantly resumed her place at the table and took a sip of her coffee, though it had grown cold. She thought of Garrick's charge, Edward's claim. She thought of Edward's hands, their obvious strength, despite the shocking gentleness of their touch. *We can never really know another person*, he had warned her. But she needed, suddenly, to know what else those hands had done.

"Was he a good master, Mari?"

The words jarred the woman back to the present, and she leveled a sharp glance at Charlotte. "He was never *my* master, ma'am."

"Not your—?"

"Miss Holderin—Mrs. Corrvan, I should say now—managed the domestic servants, of course. Her father saw to the plantation itself," she said. "He was a gentle soul."

Charlotte sent her a skeptical glance. "I was under the impression these so-called 'benevolent planters' were only to be found on the pages of fiction."

Mari conceded the point with a nod. "You would find very few in the world of facts. But then, Mr. Holderin was not a planter. Harper's Hill belonged to his late wife's father. Because we were not his, it was not in his power to set us free. But he did the best by us he could—including grooming Mr. Edward to take his place when he died. In all the years I've known Mr. Edward, he's never raised more than his voice to anyone—and that was mostly to Miss Holderin, truth be told."

Charlotte pushed her shoulders down, trying to make herself relax. There was reassurance in Mari's response. Still, she sensed that something remained unsaid. Perhaps something in Edward's past he would rather not reveal . . . ? But how ridiculous, given her present situation, for her to expect to learn it.

As if Mari intuited her curiosity, she said, "You asked about my limp."

Charlotte nodded uncertainly, taken aback by the sudden change in subject.

"It is an old injury. Acquired when I was a child—in Africa," she began, not meeting Charlotte's eye. "One night, men from a neighboring tribe raided my village. They captured as many as they could find, and claimed us as prisoners of war to be sold as slaves. I clung to my mother and she to me for as long as we could. Until she was killed. One of the men caught me by the ankle and dragged me away from her body. It felt like being torn in two. Something went *pop* inside me, and I fainted dead away." The breath left Charlotte's lungs in a rush, leaving her light-headed. But she did not make a sound. "When I came to, I was chained together with those who remained and marched to the coast. Days upon days. My hip grew worse and worse. When I was at last taken aboard a ship, the surgeon tried to put my leg right again, but by then, it was too late. I have not walked properly since."

"I am sorry," Charlotte whispered, and she was, although she knew that mere words could mean very little, could do very little to heal that injury or any other. "What a painful memory . . . But what made you decide to tell me now?"

"Because I was not ready to tell you before," Mari said simply, and a little sharply. "I have never told anyone that story. But I have been thinking about you . . . and Mr. Edward. You seem worried about the sort of man he might be, having spent so much time in such a terrible place."

Charlotte could not even bring herself to nod.

"I could tell you many stories to reassure you," said Mari. "But know this: He saw me, the day I arrived in the West Indies. Just a boy himself, a few years older than I. He turned to the man with him—Mr. Holderin, although I did not know it then—and said something with such earnestness. I knew no English. But I could guess he was urging my purchase."

Feeling the handle of her cup slip in her suddenly damp palms, Charlotte lowered it carefully to the table. How bewildering for anyone, but especially a child, to experience such a thing. A human being, bought and sold like an animal in the marketplace. "Why?" she whispered. "Why would he enslave you?"

"I was already a slave. Nothing he did or did not do would have changed that. But he knew . . . A girl, with this limp?" She shook her head. "I would not have survived a year on any other plantation in the West Indies. As I came to learn much later, Mr. Holderin had saved Mr. Edward's life. And by begging Mr. Holderin to buy me and take me to Harper's Hill, Mr. Edward saved mine. He was not a good master, ma'am. He was, and is, a good man."

Who deserves a good woman, Charlotte thought, recalling what Mari had said that first night. So why had he saddled himself, even temporarily, with her?

"Thank you for telling me this," she said. "But . . ." Doubt still lingered at the edges of her mind. "Do you never catch a glimpse of something in him, something . . . hard, sometimes?"

Mari nodded. "Oh, yes." She lifted her fork and prodded at the cold eggs on her plate. "I think it's fear."

Fear? Of what could a man like Edward be afraid?

Apparently regretting that she had been so forthcoming, Mari rose suddenly and walked away without speaking. Before Charlotte had recovered from her surprise at the abrupt end to their conversation, Mari returned with a checked apron in a pinafore style, substantial enough that the entire front of Charlotte's gown would be covered when she put it on. "Seems a pity to ruin another dress," she said, holding it out.

"*Merci*," Charlotte replied, hardly conscious of her words.

Mari began to clear their dishes. Plates and silver clattered in the sink as she moved automatically through the familiar tasks of the kitchen, the work she had been doing almost all her life. Charlotte could hear Edward asking her, *Is that what you want to do?* And what had been Mari's reply? *It's something to have a choice.*

"Thank you for an excellent breakfast, Mari. We are very fortunate you chose to come here, or else we might all starve."

"Garrick wasn't wasting away when we arrived," she pointed out as she scraped the uneaten eggs into a bowl and set it at her feet. Noir appeared as if from nowhere and began to eat. "You would have managed. Somehow."

"Perhaps," Charlotte said, although privately, she had her doubts. Tying on the apron, she stepped to Mari's side and began to dry the dishes as Mari washed. "I wonder . . . When you set out for England, is this what you thought you'd be doing here?"

Mari's hands dropped into the water, scattering bubbles and splattering Charlotte. "I never—"

"Don't say you did not have a dream," Charlotte spoke over her. "Everyone does." Heaven knew, she had dreamed of something else every time she had been forced to listen to one of Aunt Penhurst's tirades. If she had not, she might be listening to them still.

"I had been promised my freedom." She shrugged. "It felt . . . dangerous, somehow, to look beyond that. Like tempting fate."

Charlotte could not help but notice that Mari had not really denied having another dream, although she was reluctant to reveal it, even now. Or perhaps she was still figuring out what she wanted.

Fair enough. If Mari had asked Charlotte the same question, the honest answer would have been no. Or, more accurately, *non*. It would be wrong to compare their past struggles, for nothing could compare to what Mari had endured. But when all was said and done, they were both women, caught in a world not of their making, trying to determine the road they would take.

How strange for their paths to cross at Ravenswood.

"Will you let me know when the cleaning supplies arrive from the village?" Charlotte asked, folding the linen towel and laying it aside.

"And where will I find you, Mrs. Cary?"

Mrs. Cary. Not a slip of the tongue, of course. Quite deliberate. Mockery, then? But, no. Not that either, although she could not put her finger on what it was.

"I intend to take a look around upstairs, first," Charlotte said.

"Are you searching for something in particular?"

"No, of course not."

Mari shot her a look, and guilt pricked Charlotte's conscience. But how could she seek an answer if she wasn't yet sure of the question?

Little Norbury—not strictly speaking a part of the Ravenswood estate, although of course it depended on the estate's prosperity for its own—had always been a small village. The stage did not pass through, so there were few visitors, no inn, little to interest a stranger. A church, a pub, and a couple of shops, all of which drew their business from the tenants on the neighboring farms.

No surprise then to find the village in a condition nearly as dire as the manor's.

On the edge of town sat the vicarage—empty, as Markham had warned him it would be. Beside it stood the church, too stark and ancient an edifice to have been much bothered, at least externally, by a few years' neglect. As he walked past, his eyes scanned the churchyard, its moss-covered stones shaded from the early morning light. With a quickening of breath, he entered, passing through a rusted wrought-iron gate whose hinges protested mightily against his touch.

Near the back of the graveyard stood a few taller monuments, divided from the others by another low fence. His feet carried him over the uneven ground, through the narrow spaces between markers that had been skewed and tilted by shifting earth and the passage of time, until he reached that separate space. The family plot.

Cary. The name seemed to press on him from every side. Men. Women. Children—their parents' hope, extinguished like the flame of a candle. The eleventh Earl of Beckley, his grandfather, whom he knew only from the stern-faced portrait in the gallery. Even a pampered spaniel, whose presence there no one had ever been able to explain. Had some clergyman really allowed a dog to be buried in consecrated ground?

At last his eyes rested on the stone he had not realized he had come there to see.

LAETITIA HOWELL CARY
COUNTESS OF BECKLEY
BELOVED WIFE AND MOTHER
DEPARTED THIS EARTH
JULY 18, 1775

"Beloved wife."

In the silence of the cemetery, the sound of his own voice startled him. How had his father mustered the nerve to give such an order to the stone carver? Of course, it might have been the vicar's suggestion, old Mr. Henderson's final attempt to prick his father's conscience. Or perhaps it had merely been the carver's fancy.

The date struck him next. His mother had survived little more than a month after he had gone. Time enough, he supposed, for the smallpox to have struck its devastating blow. What must she have endured in those days between his departure and her death? The realization forced him to shift his gaze.

If there had been an outbreak of smallpox at Ravenswood, would not the churchyard be filled with stones bearing a similar date? Was it possible the disease really had been a rumor fabricated to explain his mother's death? The panic would have been real enough, emptying the village, leaving none behind to ask difficult questions. And if his mother had not died of disease, then . . .

When his hands began to tremble like those of a palsied old man, he turned away, fearing he might either weep noisily or vomit if he stood there a moment longer. It would have been easier to have found his own gravestone in the churchyard. After all, the boy who had left Little Norbury had in truth died long ago. The man who had returned bore him only a superficial resemblance.

By the time he reentered the lane, he had brought himself under control. While there was much here to dismay any onlooker, nothing ought to surprise him now. In the village, he found the general merchant's windows shuttered. The only door standing open was that of the pub. So it was to that venerable establishment Edward turned in search of information.

Almost to the threshold of the Rose and Raven, he could hear someone within, humming a ditty. When he stepped through the door, he saw a thin, fair-haired young woman bending over a bucket, scrubbing tables and floors with the same dirty water. The driving rhythm of her song kept her rag moving at a brisk clip.

"Excuse me," Edward said at last, when she showed no sign of looking up from her task.

She gave a little shriek of surprise at the sound of his voice. "Lor' bless us, what a fright you gave me!" The rag fell into the bucket, splashing her skirts with gray water.

"I beg your pardon, miss. I was wondering if you could tell me where I might find Mr. Toomey?"

"Toomey?" With the crook of her arm, she brushed damp hair from her brow.

"Does Mr. Toomey still own the shop next door?" he asked.

"Ah, you must be Mr. Cary."

"I am." He had not considered how much his question revealed about his familiarity with the place.

"Garrick said you had some tie to the fam'ly," she said, confirming his suspicion that the man had been gossiping about Edward's arrival. Stepping forward, the girl dipped in a clumsy curtsy. "Pleased t' meet you, sir." She wiped her hands on her apron. "I'm Peg."

"You mean Margaret," he corrected automatically. *Peg . . . Lottie . . .* Why must all these young women ruin perfectly lovely names in favor of coarse familiarity?

"Beg pardon, sir?"

"Your given name must be Margaret. Peg is only a shortened version of it, a nickname."

As he explained, she regarded him curiously, her head tipped to one side. "Is it, now?" The girl considered for a moment longer, then shrugged and took up her rag again. "Well, ain't nobody ever called me aught but Peg. Margaret sounds a bit high an' mighty, now, don' you think? People would say I was givin' meself airs if I took t' callin' meself Margaret." Each syllable of the name received an equal share of weight, like a word pronounced in a foreign tongue.

"You may well be right." He tipped his head, partly in acknowledgment, partly to hide his expression of annoyance, mostly with himself. Why did he care what name the girl used? After all, he had once been glad enough to answer to Neddy, when spoken in his mother's soft voice. The fond name had been their little secret; his father would never have allowed him to be called anything but Ravenswood, of course, and frequently had behaved as if a little boy were made of the same stuff as a stone manor house.

So comfortable had the nickname felt, in fact, that when he had left home and found a ship to carry him far away, he had even told the captain his name was Neddy.

Hearing "Neddy" in the captain's drunken, wheedling tone had stripped the name of its appeal. On the rare occasions when the man had been sober, the more ominous "Ned" had proved no better. Worse had been the orders to which his name had been appended. And worst of all, the punishments that had inevitably followed, when he had refused to do the man's terrible bidding.

Without question, Edward's dislike of nicknames could be traced to the day he boarded the *Pearl*.

He cleared his throat. "About the merchant . . . ?"

"Oh, aye. Mr. Toomey's out. Took his wife somewhere near Kingscote t' stay with her mother," the girl explained. "For her lyin'-in. Ain't no midwife hereabouts."

Lying-in? The Toomeys had been far past the age when more children could be expected twenty years ago. *How could—?* It took only a moment for him to realize that the Mr. Toomey in question must be the son of the man Edward remembered. A child who had been in leading strings then was now a man with a family of his own.

Yet another soul who could not be expected to remember, to say nothing of identify, the lost heir of Ravenswood.

"'Spect him back tonight or next day, latest. Summat I can do for you?"

Edward shook his head, stifling his frustration at the delay. He needed to order seeds and other materials if they were to get this crop in, but he could hardly begrudge Toomey his absence under the circumstances. What possible difference could another day or two make in the grand scheme of things?

"Nothing urgent," he said, touching the brim of his hat as he turned to go. Then he remembered his promise to Charlotte. "When Mr. Toomey returns, could you ask him to send some cleaning supplies to the manor, and have the bill directed to me?" he asked over his shoulder.

Another quick bob signaled her agreement. "I hear it's a frightful old mess," she added, slowing his footsteps. "Haunted, they do say."

From somewhere, Edward mustered a smile. "I wouldn't doubt it."

After all, almost everyone he remembered from his childhood there was now a ghost.

Himself included.

Chapter 8

Charlotte stopped on the landing and peered both ways down the dark corridor, wishing she had thought to bring a candle, although it was midday. Every door was closed. The creak of a floorboard made her heart leap into her throat, although only her own footstep could have made the sound. What was there to fear? Just empty rooms in an old, empty house.

Turning and walking to her left, she laid her hand on the knob of the first door to which she came. It yielded readily to her touch, revealing a sitting room with a large bow window flanked by faded velvet drapery. A place where the lady of the house had likely received callers, or gone over menus with the housekeeper. The feminine furnishings were modern beneath their layers of dust—a high-backed sofa, two chairs, a small escritoire. A bright room, despite the grime on the windows.

Which made the blood spattered across the walls quite impossible to miss.

Streaks and smears, rusty-brown with age but unmistakable, created a feathery pattern that looked for all the world like a macabre substitute for wallpaper. On a small oval table, the remains of a delicate glass lamp lay overturned, its crystal pendants smashed against the marble tabletop. A shattered and blood-stained mirror hung above the hearth, looking as if something had been thrown against it with violence.

Downstairs the rooms had been upended, but here it looked as if murder had been done.

What a ridiculous thought. Just her fertile imagination, that was all. Of course there was some rational explanation for the room's condition.

In one corner, the decaying remains of the curtains stirred lazily. Squaring her shoulders, Charlotte smoothed her palms down her borrowed apron, steeling herself to investigate. As she crossed the dusty carpet, her foot settled on a small sharp object that pressed through the bottom of her shoe, into her tender sole, pushing a little yelp of pain past her lips.

Her fingertips sought and found a small metal object. A tiny figure of a man, formed in lead, its painted clothing long since worn away. A toy soldier, of the sort with which boys waged great wars in miniature. What on earth was it doing here? But of course there must have been children here once. Generations of them. It had not always been an old mausoleum of a house.

The curtains rustled again. Absently, she dropped the toy soldier into her apron pocket and stepped closer, reaching out to brush the rotten fabric aside. The soft spring breeze passed into the room through a jagged opening, a broken window pane.

Further exploration found what was left of the culprit behind the sofa: a bird, and not a small one, either. Perhaps one of the ravens for which the place was named. Its feathers had long since disintegrated, leaving only its hollow-boned skeleton.

"Oh, *le pauvre*!"

The sound of her own voice made her jump. What was it about this little room that sent a chill scuttling down her spine even on this sunny day? No grisly crime had been committed here. Just a bird, misdirected by its own reflection, trapped and struggling to escape, beating its head against the glass as it searched for liberty that seemed everywhere promised, always denied.

Intending to pick up the carcass and dispose of it, she bent closer. But her hands would not obey. What was wrong with her? She had never before been squeamish—had never had the luxury.

Colors spun before her eyes and her breath fluttered shallowly in her chest. She, too, had been lured into a bright and shining world—*As my duchess, my dear Lottie, you'll be free to do as you wish*—mistaking it for something better than the one she left behind. Once Robert's intentions had become clear, however, she had been as desperate as this bird to fly from what had turned out to be nothing more than a splendid-looking trap.

For now, she had found a place to rest, to recover her senses. But that didn't mean she had found a way out—or that she would survive her attempt to escape.

Hurrying down the stairs, she soon found herself in the long gallery, and in another moment, she emerged into the sunshine, lifting her face to its warmth, feeling the spring air caress her cheeks. Gradually, her breathing returned to normal.

The cat nudged her ankle and wound his way between her feet, almost causing her to stumble. "Did you want something, Noir?" she asked, bending to stroke him. As if in answer to her question, he started off in the direction of the Rookery. With a frowning glance at her dust-streaked apron and dirty hands, she reluctantly followed; surely Edward was elsewhere at this time of day.

In the end, it did not matter if he was or not, for the cat bypassed the rear of the steward's house to continue along an even less-traveled path, and she went after him, braving the grasping thorns and wayward branches. Once or twice, she thought he had led her astray only to abandon her, but then he would stop and wait, or meow, or appear out of nowhere, curling around her ankles. Curious behavior for a cat.

At last a clearing broke before them, and she spied a little stone hermitage with a thatched roof—a folly, intended only as a picturesque object. Upon closer inspection, however, she realized it was inhabited. Smoke rose from the chimney. From within came the sound of someone singing an unfamiliar, strangely mournful song about a bird. Charlotte shivered. Noir abandoned her and slipped past the rustic oak-plank door. The woman broke off her song and greeted him.

Wary of intruding, Charlotte hesitated at the edge of the trees until Noir reappeared, bringing the woman with him, apparently determined that she and Charlotte should meet. With bent shoulders, the old woman moved carefully, like one afflicted with rheumatism. A dark dress hung loosely on her frail figure; it might once have been fine, but now, many years out of fashion, the garment gave her an almost otherworldly appearance, as if she had been frozen in time.

"Who's there?" When she turned her face toward the woods, Charlotte realized with a rush of compassion that the old woman was blind in one eye.

Charlotte stepped into the clearing and moved closer. "I'm sorry for disturbing you," she said, trying her best to mask her accent. "I . . ."

When had simple introductions become so complicated? Every name at her disposal felt like a lie. Except the one she settled upon, improper though it might be. "I'm Charlotte. The cat—*your* cat, I suppose—led me here, but I did not imagine . . ."

"Pleased to meet you, Charlotte," the woman said, in a voice that was not at all frail, despite her appearance. From this distance, Charlotte could see that the woman was not as old as she had first assumed, despite the streak of white in her hair. Her careful movements came from another cause. Her features were blurred, misshapen by scars, and any sign of youthfulness had been erased by whatever long-ago injury, illness, or accident had caused them. With her good eye, she looked Charlotte up and down, but she did not curtsy or hold out her hand—perhaps either gesture was simply too painful. "People call me Tessie."

The woman's equally unconventional introduction made Charlotte feel as if she was hiding something, too, but at least that was common ground on which they might stand. At a wave of Tessie's arm, Charlotte entered the rustic cottage.

Once inside, the woman sat down heavily, fatigued by the effort of greeting her guest. Noir leapt into her lap and curled into a ball, evidently a familiar and welcome visitor. Although a second chair sat facing the first, Charlotte did not take it, uncertain whether she had been invited to do so.

"I was just out for a walk when I stumbled upon your . . ." A glance at the cottage's rough interior confirmed her suspicion that the building had never been intended for human habitation. But Tessie had managed to make it her own with a few furnishings, neatly kept.

While working on the garden, Garrick had explained to her and Mari that almost everyone who had had the means to leave Ravenswood and Little Norbury had done so many years ago, when an outbreak of smallpox, or at least the rumor of one, had swept through the village. Perhaps Tessie really had been afflicted with the disease and had sought out the empty folly as a place to hide, to recover, to die. Perhaps she simply had nowhere else to go.

"Does anyone know you're here?"

"Some do." One corner of Tessie's mouth lifted in a crooked smile; scars rendered the other side of her face immobile. "Some don't."

"Oh."

What lay outside Ravenswood Manor seemed no less mysterious than what lay within it.

"It is pleasant to have company, though," Tessie said, stroking Noir's glossy fur with one claw-like hand. "The cat is a fine listener, but our conversations are always rather one-sided."

Charlotte only smiled. To allow her lips to part, to laugh, would have been to release one of those nervous giggles that tormented her at moments like this. Not that she had ever experienced a moment quite like this.

"You are new to Little Norbury?"

"Yes." Charlotte nodded. "I—my husband is the newly appointed steward at Ravenswood Manor."

Tessie's knobby fingers paused in midair. "Is Lord Beckley returned to Ravenswood, then?"

Charlotte did not think she could be imagining the note of anxiety in the woman's voice. Did she fear being discovered in this little cottage and turned away from her makeshift home? "Oh, no," she said. "He is in London. I have heard nothing about him coming here."

"Still . . ." Tessie murmured, clearly not reassured.

"You have nothing to fear, ma'am. My husband's concern is entirely for the farms." That, at least, was the truth.

Those words seemed to offer some comfort. "You will not tell him I am here?"

The question felt oddly like a test. How many secrets could Charlotte keep? "Not if you do not wish it." She could see no harm in allowing a frail, lonely woman one little corner of a great estate.

If only Langerton could be persuaded to do as much for her.

"Shall I—shall I come and visit another day?" she offered impulsively. At the very least, she might find a way to share some of Mari's fine cooking.

"Please do," Tessie replied with a gracious dip of her head. There was something so unexpectedly proper in her bearing that Charlotte dipped a curtsy as she took her leave; her own elevated rank seemed a thing from another world entirely. Apparently feeling his duty had already been done, Noir showed no signs of departing with her. He did not even lift his head from Tessie's lap.

Back outside, Charlotte blinked against the brightness of the afternoon sun. The little cottage—a hut, really, although she could not bring herself to call it that—was a place out of time: cool and dark and entirely apart from this warm spring day. It was just the sort of hideaway she had once envisioned for herself.

Somewhere she would not be recognized. Somewhere she could be alone.

But when she considered Tessie's situation, the idea of being alone lost some of its appeal.

Startled by a flash of movement in the trees ahead, Charlotte realized her feet had already carried her almost to the Rookery. Not wishing to be caught spying once more, this time she stepped boldly toward the house, expecting to see Mari or perhaps Garrick employed on some errand.

Edward, who had been bent over the pump handle, straightened as she approached, but not because he saw or heard her. Water still trickled from the pump onto the stones beneath. Stripped to the waist, he scrubbed his hands over his face to wash up, to cool off, or both. A thin, silvery-white scar snaked over the top of one shoulder. His arms and chest were tanned and layered with muscle—as she had known they would be, based on the strength and agility he had displayed in rescuing her.

But knowing a thing, and seeing it, were quite different. She could not seem to keep her eyes from traveling along those curves of muscle dusted with dark hair, down the flat plane of his abdomen, to the place where the hair formed a thicker line that disappeared beneath the band of his breeches.

It was not as if she had no familiarity with male anatomy. She had diapered her uncle's children, and she had once come unexpectedly upon her cousin Roderick in his smallclothes.

But she could not remember ever before feeling curious about what a grown man would look like in the all-together, how it would feel to run her fingers down his chest, along his . . .

Recalling suddenly that she was meant to be a worldly-wise widow, she dragged her gaze back to his face.

As if trying to persuade himself that she was not really standing before him, he shook droplets of water from his hair and blinked his eyes, then snatched his shirt from where it had been hanging and jerked it over his head with a grunt of surprise. The fine linen clung to his damp skin, and quickly grew transparent, revealing whorls of hair and the small brown peaks of his nipples.

He seemed too stunned by her unexpected appearance to speak. Not waiting for him to recover, Charlotte gave a very proper nod of greeting and began to hurry on her way, back to the relative security and familiarity of Ravenswood. She didn't know how many more shocks to the system she could stand.

"Miss—*Charlotte*. Wait. I—"

"Please don't," she spoke over him without turning back to face him, fearing he would offer either an apology or a scold. She wanted neither. "I am sorry for intruding."

"You didn't intrude."

The obvious falsehood lured her back from the edge of the woods. It was almost as if he did not want her to leave.

"I was hoping for a chance to thank you. For this morning," he added in hurried explanation.

Charlotte knitted her brows together. "This morning?"

"You . . . stepped in. Between me and Garrick. Not that it was necessary. I—I meant what I said. I wouldn't have struck him."

From the look in his eyes, she could see he was trying to reassure himself. Recollecting what Mari had told her, she said simply, "I know. It was Mr. Garrick's temper I doubted. I merely wanted to give him a moment to . . . reflect."

Her response seemed to catch him off guard. One of his sun-browned hands brushed along his damp sleeve, precisely where she had laid her fingertips earlier, as if chasing away the ghost of her touch. "Ah. I see. I—I thought perhaps . . ."

"You and Mr. Markham have been hard at work today, I suppose?" she asked, hoping to direct the conversation onto less muddy ground.

"No. When I left the house this morning, I first walked into town, as I planned. On my way back, I decided to inspect the lower farms instead."

"And what did you find?"

For answer, he gave a slow shake of his head. "Nothing cheering. I helped one of the tenants, a man named Weston, free a ram that had got himself stuck in a stile. That's how I came to be—" His eyes darted down and away, a sort of apology for his state of undress. For the first time, she noticed his dirt-streaked buff breeches and scuffed boots. "Weston's too old to manage that farm on his own. The sheep pens were sties, and the ewes haven't been sheared yet this spring.

But I . . ." As the words faded, he shook his head again. "That is, I'm not sure how to . . ."

For some reason, the defeated dip of his shoulders reminded her of how she had felt when she had first arrived in England, surrounded by jabbering voices that spoke a language she had imagined she knew. In private, she had wept while puzzling over whatever strange sounds she had managed to catch. But in public, she had always claimed confidently that she understood what she had been told. Aunt Penhurst had never caught her in that lie.

Sometimes, a lie told often enough became truth.

Charlotte squared her gaze. "I do not recall you ever making mention of sheep in your letters, Mr. Cary."

"My . . . letters?"

"The ones you wrote to me from Antigua, of course. Surely you have not forgotten?"

His eyes sketched across her face, a mixture of incredulity, amusement, and something very like relief in their clear blue depths. "How could I forget, Mrs. Cary?" he said with a small smile. "No, the climate of the West Indies is not favorable to the production of wool."

"In time, you will learn what is required here," she insisted, more quietly. His momentary indecision could not erase his usual air of assurance. "Until then, put Garrick to the shearing."

When he tilted his head and gave an almost devilish grin, sunlight caught his damp hair, a tumble of waves she longed to smooth, its darkness only accentuating the brightness of his eyes. Aunt Penhurst had been firmly of the opinion that only gentlemen could be called handsome. Edward Cary gave the lie to her words.

But perhaps part of his appeal was that he was not, properly speaking, a gentleman—a distinction of dubious merit, in Charlotte's experience. After all, her father, wherever he was, was a gentleman—an earl, like the owner of this derelict estate—and he had abandoned both her and her mother. Then there had been Mr. Sutherland and his grasping, groping hands. And of course Robert, now Duke of Langerton.

The only *gentleman* who had ever lifted a finger to help her had been her late husband. And for that his peers had been ready to cull him from their ranks, if Robert's stories were to be believed.

No, she would rather not think of Edward as a gentleman. Just as she was obviously no lady. Ladies did not have to keep their gazes from wandering down the deep vee of a man's open-necked shirt.

As if aware of her distraction, he crossed his arms over his chest, blocking her view. "By the way, I ordered those cleaning supplies you wanted." She nodded somewhat hesitantly, caught off guard by the reminder of her last-minute request. "They should be delivered tomorrow or the next day."

Hadn't he insisted he did not want her to meddle with the house? What had changed his mind?

She bowed her head and forced her knees to dip in a parting curtsy. "Very good. I shall set right to work."

"You needn't do this, Charlotte," he said again.

For a moment, she could not muster a reply. "Anyone may see that the condition of Ravenswood pains you, Mr. Cary. I am happy to do what I can to help."

It wasn't precisely true. Frankly, she was no longer eager to explore the rest of the house. Would she find more rooms in the condition of that sitting room?

But even as she turned away, she knew she would do it. For however long she chose to stay at Ravenswood, she would need to find something here with which to occupy herself.

Something other than Edward Cary.

"G' mornin', missus."

When Charlotte opened the door, a girl with lank, dark blond hair stood expectantly on the kitchen step, carrying a basket. "I'm Peg. Mr. Cary ordered these things yesterday. For the house." Each piece of information was punctuated with a pause, as if the speaker hoped to prod Charlotte's wayward memory. Only the last detail offered the necessary illumination, however.

"Ah, yes. The cleaning supplies." Charlotte reached for the basket, but the girl, Peg, seemed determined to carry it inside herself. Her head swiveled to and fro, trying to take in every detail of her surroundings. She was no doubt expected to report back to those who had sent her on this mission.

The girl set her basket on the servants' dining table and turned a full circle. "Lor' bless us, missus." Under Mari's direction, every surface gleamed, and Charlotte could guess by the girl's awestruck expression that the space must dwarf the kitchen in any other dwelling in Little Norbury.

"Thank you for bringing these things, Miss—?"

"Jus' Peg, if you please. Though your Mr. Cary would have that it's properly *Margaret*." A skeptical laugh shook her narrow shoulders. "I ain't got no other name. Folks call me Eakins, since it was the Widow Eakins what took me in. But I ain't hers, neither. Ain't nobody's, an' that's a fact."

"An orphan, are you?" The revelation put Charlotte in charity with the girl.

Peg shrugged. "If'n you mean t' ask if me ma and pa are dead, can't say. Someone left me at the poor house, and Widow Eakins needed a helpin' hand at the Rose and Raven, so she took me up."

"The Rose and Raven—that's the pub, isn't it? What do you do there?"

"Clean, mostly. Wait tables, on occasion. An' take care o' the pigs."

"Oh." Were the pigs actual swine or particularly disagreeable customers?

To hide her confusion, she turned her attention to Peg's basket, which contained a round tin of beeswax and a glass bottle filled with turpentine, wrapped in a checked cloth to prevent them from knocking against one another in transit. Well, it would do to start. Absently, Charlotte set the two containers aside and began to fold the worn square of fabric.

A shadow fell across it as Peg backed up until she struck the edge of the table, jarring the items she had brought and nearly knocking them onto the floor. Charlotte looked up to see Mari entering through the kitchen door with a sandy-haired man she did not recognize. He carried his hat before him, filled to the brim with peeping chicks.

"Why, Mari. I didn't hear you come in. Is this—?"

"Matthew Markham, ma'am. At your service." His bow of greeting was slight and awkward, so as not to tumble the contents of his hat onto the floor.

"The pleasure is m—" Charlotte began.

But Peg gasped over her. "Lor' bless us! It's true!" Her gray eyes searched Mari's face with open incredulity. "There really *are* black folks. I've seen pictures of 'em on those plaques," she added in an explanatory whisper to Charlotte, as if she imagined Mari could not understand her words, "the ones again' slavery—with the fellow all bundled up in chains. Mr. Toomey has one behind th' till. But I never—"

"Peg Eakins." Mr. Markham's voice was firm, though he did not raise it. "Mind yourself."

"No need to speak harshly to the girl, Mr. Markham. Her surprise is understandable." Mari half smiled and lifted the upturned hat from his hands, then added in a quiet voice, "You would not like to have witnessed my reaction the first time I saw a white face."

Her speech effectively cut short Matthew Markham's scold. "What are you doing here, Peg?" he asked, more gently.

"Mr. Toomey asked me to deliver some things Mr. Cary wanted."

"Ah. So Toomey's back. I'll tell Cary when I see him. He'll be glad to hear it."

While Mari filled a chipped saucer with water for the chicks to drink, Charlotte began lifting the yellow balls of fluff into a larger basket that could serve as a makeshift coop. "Thank you for the cleaning supplies, Peg," she said when she was done, turning as she wiped her palms on her apron. The girl bobbed a curtsy and slipped out the door, one cautious, curious eye still on Mari.

When she had gone, Mari sighed. "I never thought my coming here would cause Mr. Edward trouble."

"What do you mean?"

"You saw how the girl looked at me. She is afraid, both of what she does not know, and what she imagines she does. The people here have already made assumptions about the kind of man Mr. Edward must be, based on where he has been. The presence of an African woman, a former slave, only adds fuel to the flames."

Charlotte thought of Garrick's accusations, even her own uncertainty about the nature of the relationship between Mari and Edward. "You may be right." With a nod of conviction, she went to the door. "Peg! Come back here, if you please." After a moment, the girl sidled into the house. "We've a great deal of work to do. Could you be persuaded to come back tomorrow with more cleaning supplies and help us put them to use?" Charlotte asked her. "If Mrs. Eakins can spare you, of course."

Peg gave another wide-eyed stare, then a sharp nod. "She sometimes gives me leave t' do aught for Tessie. Don' guess but this'd be the same."

"Tessie?"

Both Charlotte and Mr. Markham spoke the name, with differing degrees of surprise.

"Aye," said Peg, casting a bewildered look at each of them in turn.

"Who's Tessie?" asked Mari.

"An odd old woman who took up residence long ago in a cottage on the edge of the estate," said Markham. "A trespasser. I've been meaning to speak with Mr. Cary about her."

"I already have," Charlotte lied. She could not bear to think of the poor woman turned out of her makeshift little home. "He said she wasn't doing any harm." Markham looked skeptical but said nothing more. "But who is she?"

It was Peg's turn to chime in. "Ain' nobody knows for sure. Widow Eakins says Tessie jus' showed up one day, 'bout the time everybody else were leavin'. 'Cause of the smallpox," she added by way of explanation.

So for twenty years, the woman had simply existed on the fringe of Little Norbury, no questions asked? Charlotte knew enough about village gossip to guess that wasn't the whole truth. "Hasn't she any family?"

Peg shrugged. "So far as I ever heard, don' nobody even know her name."

"What's 'Tessie,' then?"

"A sort of . . . joke, I suppose you'd call it," Markham explained, looking sheepish. "I was only a child then, so I don't remember it, but my pa told me that when she first came, the people who tried to help her thought she put on airs, despite having almost nothing to her name. Said she acted more high and mighty than the Countess of Beckley herself, God rest her soul. So for a time, people called her Countess, and eventually . . ."

"It was shortened to Tessie." Charlotte could not help but think of Edward's refusal to tolerate nicknames. Most people, she supposed, thought of them as signs of affection. But as she well knew, and Edward seemed to understand, they could also be marks of disrespect, weapons in a cruel war to keep people in their places.

"Beggin' your pardon, ma'am, but I have to get back. Widow Eakins'll be wonderin' what's become o' me." With a quick curtsy, Peg slipped past Markham and out the door again.

Retrieving his hat from Mari's outstretched hand, Markham studied its condition before opting not to return it to his head. "I'll say good day as well, Mrs. Cary. Miss Harper," he said, with a bow for each of them.

"Thank you for the hatchlings, Mr. Markham," Mari said.

"It's nothing."

Charlotte suspected it might have been the first untruth that had ever passed the farmer's lips, given the color that sprang into his cheeks when he spoke. A dozen chicks, which would grow into laying hens and cockerels to be eaten, were no small gift, even in the best of times. And these were hardly the best of times.

Once he had closed the door behind him, Mari turned toward Charlotte. "Why did you ask the girl to come back?"

"Widow Eakins would appear to be none too generous. The girl looked as if she could use a few pennies in her pocket," she said, realizing belatedly that if she intended to pay the girl for her work, she would have to beg the money of Edward first. "Or at least a few meals in her belly."

"But the gossip—! She'll be only too glad to tell every soul that enters the Rose and Raven about me, the state of this house, anything that pops into her head."

"I know." Charlotte bent over the chicks, touching each soft, sunny head. When she at last straightened, she met Mari's eye. "I'm counting on it. If the villagers hear that Mr. Cary is bent on improving this place, it will only be to his credit, no matter the source of the information. Peg Eakins can help us persuade the people of Little Norbury that he is a steady and thoughtful man from whom they have nothing to fear."

Mari considered the explanation, then nodded. "You may be right," she agreed, somewhat reluctantly, as she began to busy herself with preparations for dinner. After a moment, she added, "I'll help, too. With the cleaning, I mean."

Charlotte, who had begun to set the table, nearly dropped a plate when she heard the unexpected offer of assistance. "Why, thank you, Mari."

The woman gave a curt nod. "With those soft hands of yours, you'll need all the help you can get."

Chapter 9

"I'm surprised you refused Mrs. Weston's offer of dinner," Markham said, as they trudged across the open field. "You earned it."

The sun was no longer directly overhead, but there was no denying that this was the first genuinely warm day since Edward had returned. Some might even have called it hot. Sweat trickled along the valley of his spine, and he stopped to shrug out of his coat, then swung it easily over one shoulder. Markham had long since shed his.

"I might have done." He was certainly hungry enough. Mari had closed the kitchen three days ago to devote herself to helping with the grand cleaning project. He missed her cooking, and her company, more than he would have thought possible. He would not allow himself to wonder whether he missed Charlotte's company, too. "But it didn't seem to me that the Westons had much to spare."

Markham gave a slow nod. "They don't, and that's a fact." The two men walked a dozen paces before another word was spoken. "They'll do better now, once they sell that wool. The lambs looked healthy enough."

"Indeed," Edward agreed, and Markham laughed, no doubt thinking of the spindly legged, black-faced creature that had butted Edward behind the knees, catching him unawares and knocking him onto the barn floor.

When the empty fields that stretched between Ravenswood Manor and Markham's farm came into view, Markham paused. "Do you suppose Garrick'll be back with that load of seed before nightfall?"

Much to Edward's surprise, Mr. Toomey had walked all the way to the Westons' farm to inform him that the seed had arrived in Marshfield. The eight-mile journey to Marshfield was more than Toomey himself could manage, not wanting to leave his shop unattended for another day. Garrick—tufts of wool stuck to his sweat-damp skin—had offered to go after it before Edward could ask.

"He could be," Edward answered. "But he won't." Garrick had more than earned his pint today, and Marshfield, by his dim recollection, had at least three pubs.

Markham stretched and resumed walking. "Good."

In the shadow of Ravenswood Manor, between the kitchen and the separate paths that led to the Rookery and Markham's farm, they stopped and prepared to part ways. Markham glanced over Edward's shoulder at the house, but said nothing.

How were they getting on inside? Curiosity prickled at Edward, an affliction almost worse than the scratchy fibers of wool that had found their way beneath his clothes.

"Let's step into the kitchen and get something to eat," he suggested.

"But Miss Mari said . . ."

Markham's voice trailed off when Edward swung open the door. He did not intend to be denied access to his own house.

As luck would have it—or not—Mari was at the fireplace heating water, and Edward prepared himself for a scold. But Markham's presence seemed to temper her response.

"I knew you wouldn't last out the week," she said, hands on her hips. Her normally pristine dress was streaked with dust, and her turban was askew. The day's warmth, combined with the fire, made the kitchen shimmer with heat.

"Have you eaten?" Edward asked.

"If you think, Mr. Edward, that I'm going to drop everything to prepare your—"

"I'm not asking you to prepare anything, Mari. It's a beautiful day. Come outside and eat with us." While he spoke, he began gathering a few things into a basket: bread, cheese, wine. Following his lead, Markham stacked plates in a clean cloth and tied it securely around them.

He could see the protest building behind Mari's eyes, like steam in a kettle. But before it could boil over, he heard Markham ask, "Will you join us, Mrs. Cary?"

Charlotte stood in the doorway to the corridor, looking from one to the other. When she got to Edward, her gaze dipped away. "I don't think—"

"Please."

Edward hardly knew whether the word had actually slipped from his lips. But her eyes lifted to his, nonetheless. "If you insist," she said, the reluctance in her voice belied by the way her fingers fumbled eagerly at the knot in her apron strings.

He was past wondering whether he would ever see her looking more like a lady than a maid. Correction: He was past caring. She was dusty, yes, although this time, the apron had borne the brunt of it. Her hair was, as always, slipping from its pins. But the hard work had brought a flush to her cheeks and a sparkle to her eyes. No one with eyes could fail to see her beauty.

"I know just the place," he said, gesturing toward the door with the laden basket. Markham led the way, the bundle of plates in one hand and four tumblers hooked on the fingers of the other. With a sigh—as if the safety of the kitchenware could be secured no other way—Mari followed him.

Charlotte came last, and when she slipped past Edward, she whispered, "*Merci beaucoup*."

He chose to imagine she was thanking him for more than holding the door.

Once outside, he took the lead, heading toward the back of the house, striding across the empty terrace and into the wooded area behind. What had once been a fashionable "wilderness" was now genuinely wild, its carefully manicured paths having long since been reclaimed by the undergrowth. On its far side stood a dilapidated summer house overlooking a largish pond.

In his childhood, it had been one of his favorite haunts. "I, er, stumbled upon this when I was exploring the other day," he told the others to explain his familiarity with the secluded spot. In the shade of a lazy willow, he motioned for Markham to put down his burden. On the square of linen that had contained the plates, he laid the food from the basket. "An open-air feast."

The men spread their coats on the ground to make places for the ladies, then made themselves comfortable beside them on the soft, long grass. Hard work had given them all hearty appetites, and for many minutes, little could be heard above the sounds of eating and drinking. Afterward, Markham told the story of how Edward had been vanquished by a three-week-old lamb, making Mari laugh—a rare sight, in Edward's experience. Charlotte tried and failed to hide her smile behind her half-empty glass.

When he caught her at it, she nestled the base of the glass securely between two folds in the blanket and said, "I was once knocked into the Serpentine by a swan."

"It's a sort of a lake, in London," Markham explained to Mari, so that she might join in the merriment. "In one of those parks where nobs can fancy themselves in the country."

Esoteric knowledge for a West Country farmer. Edward wondered how he had come by it.

As he chuckled with the rest, Edward studied Charlotte's self-deprecating smile. Then her dark eyes lost some of their twinkle, and she suddenly strangled her quiet laughter with her hand, cupping it over her mouth.

Why had she told the story if the memory pained her so?

"I hope that experience hasn't given you a lasting fear of the water," he said, rising. "Come. That pond has been beckoning for the last half hour."

Warily, she accepted his outstretched hand and came to her feet. "Surely you do not mean to swim?"

"I'd like nothing better. But I'll content myself with wading. Join us?" he asked the others.

Mari shook her head almost primly. Markham stretched out lazily in the grass beside her. "Too much trouble."

"Suit yourselves." Edward shed his boots and stockings and tried not to watch while Charlotte did the same.

But it was impossible not to catch a glimpse of her pale feet and delicate ankles as she raised her skirts to mid-calf and stepped gingerly into the pebbly shallows. "Oooh. It's cold!"

Undaunted, Edward walked farther out, until the water lapped at the knee-bands of his breeches. "It's wonderful," he corrected. "Come deeper."

"I couldn't possibly. My dress will get soaked," she protested. But she took two wobbly steps in his direction, all the same.

He glanced toward the shore to see if the others were watching. But Mari was turned toward Markham, speaking animatedly, while the man nodded as he listened, eyes only for her.

Turning back to Charlotte, he asked, "Was it true, the story about the swan?"

Her skirts slipped from her hands and splashed into the water. Silvery minnows darted through the clear water, seeking cover.

"No," she confessed. "Not exactly."

"Then why did you tell it?"

"I . . ." Her shoulders crept higher but did not fall, a sort of half shrug turned into a cower. "I do not know if I can explain."

"Try." The monosyllable was sharper than he had intended.

"When Mr. Markham told the story about the lamb, it made me remember . . ." She twisted back and forth, dragging her skirts across the surface of the pond. "Did you ever hear a story so often in your childhood that you believed it must have really happened?"

"I suppose." Perhaps, when he had been very small. Certainly not the age Charlotte said she had been when she came to England.

"Sometimes, I begin a story, thinking it really happened. And then I recall the truth."

It was a shocking confession. An inability to differentiate fact from fiction was the first step toward the madhouse. Or prison. "What really happened?" he asked.

"Nothing so . . . amusing, I'm afraid."

He stepped toward her, close enough that her hems swirling through the water swept across his bare feet. "Were you often required to be amusing?" The thought was somehow chilling, like Scheherazade forced to spin her thousand-and-one tales to keep her head.

"Sometimes."

"By your husband?"

"Oh, no. In—in France, I used to tell stories to entertain my younger cousins, to keep them from pestering their father. I tried to do as much when I first came to England, but my aunt said she would not tolerate such childish nonsense."

He thought he knew the type. Of greater interest, however, was the unlooked-for revelation about her family. "So you have English cousins as well?"

"Just one. And it was he who was responsible for that tumble into the Serpentine." Her gaze drifted away as she remembered. "His mama insisted that he accompany me on some errand—oh, yes. I recall. To fetch her new hat from the shop. On the way home, he ran off, into Hyde Park. I had no choice but to follow. He jumped at me from behind a bush, snatched the hat from my hands, and threw it into the river. Then he pushed me in as I leaned over to try to save it.

The hat was ruined, of course. I had to make excuses to my aunt. She would never have believed anything bad of her son, so I made up the story about a swan."

"And was she . . . amused?"

Charlotte managed a weak smile. "Not enough."

He wished, suddenly, for some bit of magic that would wash the hurt of a joyless childhood from her eyes.

"If you stand perfectly still, the minnows will nibble at your toes."

She shot him one wide-eyed glance before inching her dripping skirts high enough that she could see her feet. "Really? Oh, there's one. And—oh—another, and . . . Oh!" Her chin lifted as she looked back at him. "It tickles."

He nodded encouragingly and watched as she wiggled her toes experimentally, trying to coax the tiny fish. The drowsy hum of insects filled the silence between them; in the distance, he heard Markham laugh.

When a cloud crossed the sun and cast the pond into shadow, the minnows once more flashed away. Edward took Charlotte by the elbow, led her back to shore, and sat down beside her as they dried themselves in the warm spring air. "So, your aunt punished you to keep you from telling stories."

Charlotte paused in the struggle to tug a surprisingly elegant silk stocking over her damp toes. "To keep me from telling lies," she corrected.

Her aunt's plan hadn't worked, of course. If anything, stifling her so-called lies had only forced her to get more creative with telling them.

Balling his stockings in his fist, he stood, stomped his feet into his boots, and strode back to the others, snatching his coat from the ground and stuffing the discarded hosiery into his pocket.

"Is everything all right, Mr. Edward?" Mari asked, springing almost guiltily to her feet. Beside her, Markham rose more slowly.

"Yes. No." He slapped his hat on his head and bent to pick up the basket, now laden with the used plates. In his haste, he knocked over Charlotte's half-empty glass. Wine spilled like blood across the ground.

As he passed her on his way back to the house, he nodded sharply. A gesture of apology? Or leave-taking? He could hardly say.

He tried to convince himself that the frustration building inside him was due to the heartlessness of Charlotte's family, who had exploited and distorted what once might have been a gift.

But something else was eating at him, too—something far more dangerous than a few curious minnows.

She'd just handed him more proof that he could never trust what she said. Yet he felt, somehow, as if he'd finally caught a glimpse of the real woman beneath her stories.

And what he'd seen only made him want to know more.

Chapter 10

Charlotte had always been skeptical of the notion of a "good" sort of tired. Exhaustion was exhaustion. But as she eased her body into the silky cool cambric of her—well, technically *Jane's*—night rail, she thought she finally understood. Her legs, her back, her hands—everything ached, but the dull pain of strained muscles and chapped skin faded beneath the glow of intense satisfaction that had swelled in her chest as she looked with pride at all she had accomplished in the last few days.

The dining room, the entry hall, the Great Room, and the gallery all gleamed with polished wood and sparkling glass. No more dust, no more cobwebs. No more draperies, either, and considerably less furniture and fewer broken knickknacks. Just the warm, sweet scent of beeswax, and beneath it, the sharper tang of vinegar. Perhaps, when—if—the Earl of Beckley ever returned to his estate, he would be displeased by what he saw. But she rather imagined he would think nothing of it. If her aunt was any indication, aristocrats knew very little about *how* their houses were kept clean, only demanded that they were.

Once dressed for sleep, she lifted a drowsy Noir from the seat of the chair and placed him on the bed instead. Stretching lazily, he looked for a moment as if he were considering protesting, but instead curled back into a ball, laid down his head, and closed his eyes. Only the tip of his tail twitched to reveal his feelings about the disruption of his nap.

Easing herself into the chair, she took up her hairbrush and peered into the piece of broken looking glass she had rescued from the gallery. Thanks to a few new blisters and her aching hands, her grip on the brush was tenuous, and she dropped it twice before managing to make a pass through just the ends of her hair, from not quite her shoulders to below her waist. Her arms did not seem to want to rise any higher, and when she attempted to make them submit to her command, pain knifed across her shoulders. Halfheartedly, she tried once more before twisting her lips in a grimace of both discomfort and annoyance. Laying the brush on the small table, she was about to give up and go to bed when the reflection of something behind her, the slightest movement, caught her eye. With a gasp, she spun around to see what it was.

She had left the door half open to allow Noir to come and go as he pleased. Now the once narrow gap had been widened to accommodate Edward's broad shoulders, one of which leaned casually against the jamb. He had been watching her, and nothing about his posture—arms folded over his chest and around a book, legs crossed at the ankles, the toe of one booted foot propped against the floor—suggested the slightest chagrin at having been caught in the act.

A nervous hiccup of laughter bubbled in her chest, and she turned back to the mirror to hide it, covering the handle of the hairbrush with trembling fingertips, as if its smooth ivory curves could be mustered in her defense. "*Bonsoir*, Mr. Cary," she said, eyeing his reflection. Days of breathing in dust had parched her throat, turning her words into a ragged whisper. "Did you—did you want something?"

For a long moment, he did not answer. Half shadowed by the door, his face revealed nothing. Nudging the door wider, he stepped into the room. "I have already found what I was looking for, thank you."

In the mirror, the square set of his jaw looked slightly ominous. At least, it raised her pulse a notch or two. He was fully clothed, of course, but every time she saw him, the mental image of him stripped to the waist seemed determined to interpose itself.

She forced herself to turn and face him, and he held out the small volume to her. Ah, *bien sûr*. That was all he had sought. A book. Flipping to the yellowing title page, she read, "*The Farmer's Kalendar; or, a Monthly Directory for All Sorts of Country Business: Containing, Plain Instructions for Performing the Work of Various Kinds of Farms, in Every Season of the Year.*" Her eyes darted up to meet his. "Are you having trouble sleeping, Mr. Cary?"

The jest caused one corner of his mouth to curve. "A West Indian sugar plantation is not an English farm. But as someone recently reminded me, if I once managed one, I can learn to manage the other," he said, lifting the book from her hands. A moment of awkward silence fell, then he cleared his throat. "The transformation you have wrought here is nothing short of miraculous."

"I did not do it alone. Mari helped, as you know. And Peg, the girl from the pub. Even Garrick—"

"Yes, I heard. He told me you stole the ladder and nearly stranded him in the stable loft." His smile crept higher, into his eyes.

She tipped her chin in acknowledgment. "It was the only way to reach the corners of those high-ceilinged rooms."

"I certainly did not intend to deprive the others of their due," he said, sliding the book into the pocket of his coat. "But I think we both know who deserves the credit."

Embarrassed, she turned to face the table again, refusing to meet his eyes even in the mirror.

"I am—" Edward continued, "that is, Lord Beckley will be pleased to see everything so well taken care of."

"I thought you said he had expressed no concern about the house."

"I said he had given no instruction about it," he corrected.

"Ah, well. It takes no great skill to sweep and polish." Absently, she tapped the ragged nail of her first finger against the brush before lifting it to resume her toilette, although she had no more success than before. She still could not raise her arms above her head to make a proper job of it.

"Why do you not ask Mari's help with that?" She saw him nod toward the brush. "She has never been a lady's maid, but I am sure she—"

"I will manage. Besides, Mari has gone out walking this evening. As she often does."

A rumble of acknowledgment escaped his throat; he looked vaguely surprised, or perhaps displeased, by the information, despite the fact that she had spared him the details of where she walked. Or with whom.

Then she heard—no, *felt* him step closer, close enough that when she dared to look in the mirror again, she could see nothing behind her but the checked pattern of his waistcoat, his loosened cravat, and dark stubble on his chin.

Leaning forward, he curved his fingers around the handle of the brush and drew it from her grasp. His touch was warm and soft, as she had known it would be. "Then allow me," he said.

"I really don't think—"

"Surely a husband can do as much for his wife, Mrs. Cary," he insisted, his voice gently teasing now. "A repayment, of sorts." Before she could reply, the boar's bristles tingled against her scalp, sending off little fireworks of ecstasy, followed by ripples of relaxation that seemed to flow from the top of her head through every limb, every vein, every cell. "Relax."

She had been without the gentle touch of another person for so long . . . forever, really. Though she craved it, she had schooled herself not to need it. Yet here she was, tormented daily by the touch of a man who was all but a stranger to her. She could still feel where his hand had circled her arm and jerked her to safety; where his arm had clutched her waist, brushing the underside of her breast with each bounce of the horse; where his fingertips had skated with care over her injured palms. And now, his deft hands, his long fingers, made her forget the pain of her own hands and the tightness in her shoulders, in favor of an entirely different ache, in a place no one had ever touched her. A place no one ever would.

Realizing it would be a terrible mistake to surrender to his command to relax, she kept her spine straight as ever. Still, her eyes drooped closed and a sigh escaped her lips as he dragged the brush downward, again and again, stroking its bristles through her hair until it crackled and shone.

Too soon, he laid the brush aside. Unwilling to let the moment of pure indulgence come to an end, she refused to open her eyes. When he gathered her hair in one hand and swept it to the side, over one of her shoulders, a few strands caught on his work-roughened fingers. Then she heard the tell-tale creak of leather as he shifted his weight. Caught the scent of him, wool and shaving soap and man. Felt the warmth of his body as he leaned closer still.

Please.

How did her body know to want the press of his lips against that curve of skin he had exposed, at the base of her neck where it joined her shoulder? Were those forbidden cravings a part of her blood, as everyone had always insisted? An instinct, prowling silently along the shadowy edges of her mind, like Noir in search of a mouse? Would she have a moment to react, to save herself, when the tension coiling tighter and tighter within her finally sprung?

"Where did you find this?"

Her eyes popped open, and the bubble of contentment burst. He had picked up the little toy soldier and was turning it this way and that in the candlelight, as if it were a priceless curiosity. Darting her gaze to the mirror, she watched his face, starkly lined with some emotion she could not identify.

"Where did you find this?" Louder this time, each word crisply enunciated, as though he suddenly doubted her understanding of English. As he spoke, his hand tightened into a fist around the little leaden man, driving its sharp metal points into his palm, and she winced for the pain it must be giving him.

"Upstairs. I—"

All at once, he straightened, depriving her of his heat and his scent, leaving her shockingly aware of what a fool she had almost been. Before she could finish her explanation, he lifted the candlestick in his other hand and turned toward the door. "Show me."

His footfalls were already ringing along the corridor, headed deeper into the house, before she caught up, her bare feet silent on the stone. The moonless night sky left all in utter darkness, and she was glad of the candle, though it drove back the looming shadows only a bit.

For all he had asked her to guide him, he walked like a man sure of his destination, or at least, one unaccustomed to being led. On the landing at the top of the stairs, however, he hesitated. She took the candle from his grasp and moved toward the small receiving room, feeling him follow in her wake. When she stopped before the door, his hand stretched for the knob, hovering over it for a moment before curling his fingers around the patterned brass oval and opening the door.

Candlelight struck the shattered mirror and bounced off it like a prism, casting bright beams in every direction, making the spatters on the wall look almost black, though they were still unmistakably blood. She had not thought it possible that the space could look worse than it had by daylight, and yet . . .

Before she could leave him to his explorations, his ruminations, she felt his hand searching for hers, first tangling with her fingertips, then gripping her like a drowning man. It hurt—her hands were sore from days of hard work. But she did not pull away.

Because when she looked up at his face, she saw unshed tears sparkling in his eyes.

"Here?" he asked, although his tone told her he already knew the answer.

"Oui." Turning her gaze on the room, she said, "I found the remains of a bird. He must have crashed through one of the windows, then injured himself further by struggling for some time to get out." Her explanation for the room's ramshackle state seemed to offer little in the way of comfort. At least, the pressure of his hand did not relent. "I will put it to rights first thing tomorrow, if you wish," she offered uncertainly.

"No."

The hard reply made her flinch, and the slight jerk of her arm seemed to bring him to his senses, enough to make him release his grip on her hand and step away from her side, at least. Grasping the high-backed sofa, he pushed it aside, almost overturning it, wrinkling the carpet that lay before it, and driving it into the little round table on which the broken pieces of the crystal lamp had lain. They slid onto the floor with a tinkle, but the sound of their fall was further muffled by the louder noise of Edward dropping to his knees in the place where the sofa had been, sweeping his hands blindly across the floor at the carpet's edge. When they found nothing more, he clutched his fists to his chest with a groan and rocked back onto his heels.

She wanted to ask how he knew his way around Ravenswood Manor so well. How he had known exactly where she had found the toy soldier.

But a woman who kept secrets was in no position to expect others to reveal theirs.

She placed the candlestick on the writing desk and made her way to his side with careful steps, mindful of the broken glass now scattered across the carpet. When she looked down, it was not at him but at the starlit garden, the trees, the very peak of the Rookery's roof. Despite the neglect, it was a fairy landscape, the stuff of one of Charles Perrault's tales.

Most of which came to a rather grim end for at least some of the parties involved.

Without touching him, without speaking, she simply stood and waited. If her presence was a comfort, she would stay. After all he had done for her, she could safely offer him that much.

Beside her, she felt him shift. Expecting every moment that he would rise to his feet, she could not contain the gasp of surprise that parted her lips when he instead turned toward her, wrapped his arms around her legs, and buried his face against her hip.

Even the thickest, most practical fabric would have no barrier to the heat of his touch, his breath, his tears. But the thin cotton of a night rail seemed to amplify every sensation. He shuddered against her with the effort of trying to fight off . . . something. The chill of the night air. Frustration at the impossible task he had been set. Grief.

A combination of all three, perhaps.

Or . . . none of them.

Strong, lean fingers kneaded the backs of her thighs, traveling slowly upward, cupping her bottom, drawing her more tightly to him, to his lips, which skated along her hipbone and nuzzled the swell of her belly. His every exhalation was another touch, warm fingers of air that traced across her skin and ruffled the thatch of curls at the joining of her thighs.

Feeling suddenly as if she might collapse—to her knees, into his arms, over some precipice from which there could be no return—she forced herself to stand tall, arms stiff, hands curled into fists at her sides. He rose still higher, following the curve of her ribcage upward until he reached her breast. Pillowing his cheek against its softness, he murmured formless words. A name, perhaps? Beneath the hot rush of his breath her nipple peaked, and in another moment it was between his lips.

As he sucked and nipped, a battle built inside her, and she tightened her grip until her fingernails carved ridges into her tender palms. She knew the proper thing would be to push him away, but oh, how she longed for the courage to draw him closer. Seeming to understand that she was on the verge of splintering into a thousand pieces, like the broken mirror behind her, he stood at last and settled his lips over her mouth instead.

A kiss. Just a kiss. He did not even try, as Mr. Sutherland had, to push his tongue past her teeth—though she now understood, with sudden, shocking clarity, why a woman might welcome the sensation. While his mouth moved over hers, his hands slid up her bare arms, over her shoulders, to cup the back of her head, his fingers slipping through her long, loose hair as they caressed her scalp.

She longed to reciprocate, to give back his touch, but whatever instinct she had possessed in such matters seemed to have flown. Her hands remained locked at her sides.

"Ah, Charlotte," he whispered when he at long last drew back. "I owe you an apology."

Her heart jerked in her chest. Of course he regretted what he had done. He had forgotten himself.

While he was kissing her, he had no doubt been thinking of someone else.

Her breath caught as she tried to respond, and in that dreadful moment of silence, he released her. "You must be freezing," he said, as if he had noticed for the first time her dishabille. He shrugged out of his coat and laid it around her shoulders. Its weight, its warmth was a second embrace.

From within its depths, she clutched the garment closer; the movement did not escape his shadowed eyes. "Have I frightened you?"

Still, no words would come. She shook her head, but the sharpness of the gesture seemed to persuade him of its opposite. "If it helps"—here, his voice broke on a sort of laugh—"I frightened myself a bit, too. But you needn't worry about a repetition of my bad behavior. I'm bound for London soon—tomorrow, if I can manage it."

London? Back to Mrs. Corrvan, she supposed, though she made herself ask, *"Pourquoi?"*

Ever since she had come to England, French had been a sort of refuge from thought, from reality. She had spoken it often in her mind, because her aunt had forbidden it to pass her lips. It had been a shield she could raise and lower at will.

Now, however, even spoken aloud, it no longer felt like adequate protection.

"A matter of business," he said. "Something I have waited too long to address." His hand rose, and though his explanation had brought little comfort, she closed her eyes, inviting the stroke of his fingertips across her cheek, brushing the hair from her face.

But the touch never came. In its place, another self-deprecating laugh. "You will be glad to see the back of me, I do not doubt."

Don't go. Don't leave me tomorrow. What would happen to her if he left her here? What would happen to her if he didn't?

Don't leave me tonight.

"*Au contraire*," she managed to say, after swallowing twice. "And I'm sure everyone at Ravenswood will be happy to see you return. *Bon voyage*, Mr. Cary." With a tremendous effort, she forced herself to dip in a halfhearted curtsy, then walked out the door.

With every step, she felt something heavy in the pocket of his coat bump against her thigh. Glancing over her shoulder, she saw no sign of Edward following her down, so on the landing, she paused to investigate.

The small volume on husbandry nearly filled the pocket. But alongside it was tucked the toy soldier. Possessively, she curled her fingers around the worn metal figure.

A child's plaything unearthed in a ruined room. That kiss. And now a hasty departure.

What did any of it mean?

Even with her capacity for invention, Charlotte could not put together the pieces of this puzzle in a way that made the picture clear.

When he could no longer hear Charlotte's footsteps on the stairs, when he felt certain she was safely back in her bed, Edward allowed himself to leave the room, taking one final look around before he blew out the candle and closed the door.

Had his mother died here?

It would have been unlike his father to strike Mama in her receiving room, whose door had always stood open to visitors, at his insistence—a sign that there was nothing to hide. But deep within the labyrinth of the family chambers, there had been other rooms, of course, more private spaces where he had often made his displeasure known. And if the rest of the house was any indication, something had snapped the thin cord by which the man's temper had been tethered.

Clearly, the outbreak of smallpox had been a fabrication, a story to cover up the terrible truth. Coming face-to-face with the evidence—her gravestone, her sitting room—forced Edward to confront the dire consequences of his decision to leave Ravenswood. His mother's blood was on his conscience, if not his hands. He should have been here to save her. Far from saving her, his actions had led directly to her death.

Perhaps, after all, he had turned out to be little better than his father.

Finding himself in the back of the house, he exited through the gallery and strode through the woods to the pond. By the time he had reached the water's edge, he had stripped off his waistcoat, his cravat, his shirt. Pausing only to toe off his boots and shuck his breeches, he dove headfirst into its depths.

There was a certain irony in coming here now, to the spot where his father taught him to swim. Why had Father insisted on taking that particular task to himself? The curate had tutored him in Latin and mathematics, though his father had excelled at both. His father had been a first-rate horseman, but a groom had taught Edward to ride. The prospect of any sort of lessons with his father, who was almost invariably stern and critical, had filled Edward with quiet dread. But here in this pond they had splashed and laughed together—unless Edward's memory was as untrustworthy as Charlotte's.

He did not want or need the reminder that his father was not always a bad man. Despite his sometimes sharp temper, his peers had generally thought well of him, his tenants had respected him, his son had . . . loved him.

Feared him, too. Every time some well-meaning person had insisted he was like his father—in looks, in abilities, in temperament—Edward had felt as if he were being torn in two. Though there had been much in his father to admire, Edward had been too well aware that he also possessed qualities no man ought to want to emulate. Lust, chief among them, although he would not have known to use that word then. Lust for power. And women—Edward's mother, the occasional housemaid, some girl from outside the village—had been his victims of choice.

It had never been quite as simple as vowing to do opposite of what his father had done, however, because his father's choices had not always been the wrong ones.

Edward prided himself on never having struck another person, though few would have thought less of him for it—and some had certainly deserved punishment for their actions. In the West Indies, his abhorrence of violence had been regarded as a peculiarity, a weakness, by almost everyone he knew.

With respect to women, Edward's path had been perfectly clear. He had contented himself with being treated as a brother. A friend. He held himself at a safe distance, because he feared that deep down, he might not be safe. He had grown adept at keeping his desires, his needs, his feelings ruthlessly in check.

But did that mean he had truly triumphed over his father's nature?

Protecting Charlotte had been the last thing on his mind tonight. The slightest encouragement and he would have rucked up her skirts, pressed her back to the wall, and sheathed himself inside her.

Fortunately, she had offered no encouragement. In his arms, she had been a marble statue, whose coolness had at last brought him to his senses.

She deserved better. Better than a man like him.

What woman did not?

Determined to distract himself from her, he had been working himself to the dropping point every day, until his muscles screamed. But every night, when sleep should have offered him respite, he tossed and turned through feverish dreams, and woke every morning achingly hard. Even now, the icy chill of the water had done little toward wilting his cockstand.

In the West Indies, most men had paid dockside whores to slake their lust, or more often, forced slaves to service their needs.

He was not most men.

Just as he was about to close his hand around his own flesh—though he generally disdained such weakness—he heard a rustle along the pond's edge. Silently, he slipped back into deeper water, treading slowly, stirring up ripples that made the starry sky reflected on the pond's surface shimmer and wink.

Mari was returning from her midnight stroll, dragging her lame leg behind her. She had been limping along that way the first time he had seen her, the smallest and weakest in a coffle of slaves bound for sale. By then, he had known enough about the Middle Passage to guess that, while a lame leg might have been the only visible injury slavery had inflicted on Mari, it was likely far from the worst.

Apparently without observing him, Mari passed by and into the house. What incredible strength it had required for her to brave that Atlantic crossing once more. But her disability had never interfered with her getting where she wanted to go. For all the imprecations he had heaped on Tempest's head for encouraging her to come here, he was glad Mari had made that choice. She was almost his only connection, now, to the world in which he had grown into a man, to the life that had been his for so long. It pleased him to see her enjoying the freedom he had always wanted for her, but which had never been his to give.

Edward leaned his head backward and let himself float on the water, although the heaviness beneath his breastbone threatened to sink him like a stone.

For many years, the gossips had insisted he was infatuated with Tempest Holderin. He had been her friend, her employee, her protector. He had loved her as a sister. And in other ways, too, if he was being honest with himself.

Precisely because he cared for her, he had sworn to himself he would never act on his feelings—a promise he had broken exactly twice. Once, with a clumsy kiss that had made her laugh in his face. And once with an even clumsier proposal of marriage.

His own interference had landed her in a dangerous situation, and the only protection he could think to offer her had been his name—dubious though such protection might be. He had written to her with a shaking hand, telling himself all the while that her upbringing in a vile, violent world had made her tough enough to withstand what he sometimes still feared he would become.

He had reassured himself with the certainty she would say no.

Which she had done in spectacular fashion: by sending as her reply to his offer the announcement that she had married another.

It was just as well. Tempest was right where she wanted, where she *needed* to be—with a man who was undoubtedly a bit of a rogue, but who knew from experience the folly of trying to tame the sea.

And he was where he needed to be, as well: at Ravenswood.

When Tempest had finally been able to free the slaves at Harper's Hill, she had set him free, too. Or perhaps it would be more accurate to say she had set him adrift—although he might have continued in her employ indefinitely, he supposed; might have stayed in Antigua for the rest of his life.

But once he had carried out her instructions regarding the plantation, he had realized that it was time for him to start a new chapter. Or, to be more precise, to pick up a very old book and see if he might begin again where he had left off many years ago. He had never expected it to be easy.

He had failed, however, to understand the precise ways in which resuming his life here would be difficult. Perhaps impossible.

Wanting Charlotte did not make things any easier.

He had glimpsed enough cracks in her alabaster façade—the nervous giggle, the occasional broken-English phrase, the hints of her troubled past—to know that something hid inside that shell. But he ought never to expect to be the one to discover what. Ought never to dream of becoming a Pygmalion to that lovely marble sculpture, to feel her come to life in his arms.

Like any work of art, she changed depending on the angle of the viewer. Even looking straight on, he could not be sure what he saw, who she was.

But if he did not trust her, it was at least in part because he did not trust himself.

He swam to the pond's edge, then hoisted himself onto the bank and sat there dripping in the cool night air. He was in no position to demand anything from her. Still less could he offer anything to her. Confronting his father, getting his affairs in order, restoring this estate—those needed to be the sole focus of his attention. He could not let desire for Charlotte distract him from what he had come back to England to do.

Gathering up his clothes and boots, he set off in the direction of the Rookery and another long, lonely night.

Chapter 11

At the first pink light of dawn, long before the hour for making calls, Charlotte set out for the little cottage in the woods to visit Tessie. No sense in pretending that sleep would come. A walk in the fresh air was her last, best hope for restoration.

Over her arm she carried a basket filled with food. No doubt Mari would raise a disapproving brow when she woke and discovered her pantry had been raided. Or perhaps not, especially once Charlotte explained. At present, Mari seemed to have other things on her mind.

Although Edward was likely far away by now, she gave the Rookery a wide berth, entering the woods on an unfamiliar path that seemed to point in the right direction. She fought her way along it until she was certain she was lost, then emerged at the edge of a field, where she could see Mr. Markham trudging to work in the distance. Following along the hedgerow, she made her way back to the clearing she sought. Smoke already rose from the cottage's chimney, and Tessie's strange, haunting song wove its notes among the cheerier melodies of the birds.

"Tessie?" Charlotte wished she knew another name to call out.

Noir was the first to offer a greeting, but Tessie soon followed, still wrapped in her dressing gown. "Is that you, Charlotte?"

"I'm sorry for calling so early, ma'am."

"It's quite all right. Come in. I was just about to pour some tea."

Ducking beneath the lintel, Charlotte entered the little stone hermitage, warmed this morning by a crackling fire. While Tessie busied herself with finding another cup and saucer, the tea kettle whistled merrily on the hob, competing like the birds with Tessie's habitual tune. Once Tessie had filled the teapot, Charlotte lifted the tray and carried it to the small, battered table that divided the single room between bedchamber and kitchen.

"How is your husband finding his work at Ravenswood?" Tessie tilted her head to fix Charlotte with her good eye.

"Challenging, I believe. The estate has fallen into disrepair."

"I know. Lord Beckley has not done his duty by the people here."

"I wonder at the sort of man who would allow this to happen." Charlotte poured tea into two cups, surprised by its strength. Tea was dear, and she had fully expected these leaves to have been washed more than once.

"As well you should," Tessie agreed, taking a cup from her hand. Only then did Charlotte recognize the pattern: the same as that on the broken fragments of china she had so recently swept from the floor of the dining room at Ravenswood. The dishes in Tessie's possession were chipped and faded. Had she gone through the abandoned house, scavenging for the best of what remained?

"Did you know him? Lord Beckley, I mean."

Tessie took a sip of tea, then returned her saucer to the table with a steady hand. "It's not very likely, is it, that an old woman such as I, a vagrant, would have ever met an earl?"

"No, I—I suppose not. I did not mean to be impertinent. It's just that—well, I must confess I am curious about why you seem to be hiding here—"

"Hiding?" Tessie drew herself upright, as much as her injuries would allow. "From what would I have to hide?"

"Why, nothing, ma'am. I only thought . . ."

"I prefer to think of myself as *surviving*." Lifting a spoon, she gave her tea a brisk stir. The silver, though tarnished, looked as if it had been made to accompany the china. Charlotte wondered that she had not thought to sell it. "We none of us know what hand we will be dealt in life. We have only the choice of how we will play our cards."

"But what will you do if the rightful owner comes back to Ravenswood and finds you here?" Charlotte cried. Would Tessie be driven away? Sent to the workhouse?

Tessie turned toward the light passing through a small square window, covered in oiled paper, not glass. "I have been waiting for that day." Her voice was quiet, and Charlotte could see only the scarred, expressionless side of her face. Still, to Charlotte's ear, she sounded almost . . . hopeful.

"Perhaps it will never come," Charlotte said, uncertain whether she was offering reassurance, or crushing a long-cherished dream.

For a moment, she wondered if Tessie had even heard her speak. Then she returned her half-blind gaze to Charlotte's face. "I begin to think you may be right."

Unable to choke down the last of her tea, Charlotte soon excused herself and returned to Ravenswood Manor, Noir at her feet. Although the visit had not exactly been a comfortable one, she was not sorry she had gone. Tessie was just what she had needed: living proof that people could make the best of bad situations.

Charlotte had lain awake all night, reliving those moments in the ruined room, wondering if she had made the wrong decision to come here, to stay here, to hide.

I am not hiding. I am surviving, Tessie had insisted.

Charlotte recognized that independent spirit. Once, she had claimed to share it.

There was safety in the seclusion she had found here. But if she truly intended to be free, she would have to nip her reckless desire for Edward Cary in the bud.

She might have inherited her mother's eyes, her hair, her nervous laugh. But she had *not* inherited her weakness where men were concerned. Yes, fire sparked in her blood every time Edward touched her. But fires died as long as no one put fuel to the flames.

By the time he returned from London, she would make sure that spark had been doused.

When she drew near the stables, she found them in an uproar. Garrick was scurrying to and fro, fetching water for strange horses. A man she had never seen was scraping flecks of foam from their sides, and an unfamiliar carriage, a hack by its looks, sat parked in the yard. In his separate stall, Samson watched everything with his ears pricked forward.

"Has Mr. Cary not left?"

Water sloshed onto Garrick's boot and across the straw-strewn stable floor as he thumped a bucket before one of the horses. "Left? An' where would he go?"

"He told me yesterday he was leaving for London at first light."

The two men exchanged a glance—of commiseration, she decided. Grooms likely did not appreciate being the last to learn of travel plans.

"Well, he's here yet. Jus' went into th' manor," he added with a jerk of his chin over his shoulder. "T' meet with Lord Beckley."

A few minutes later, and Edward would have missed him. He had been on the point of setting out for Marshfield, the village south of Little Norbury. The one from which he had left so many years ago. Through it passed a regular coaching route, and from there, he could make his way to London in little more than a day. Since he had elected not to leave with Dobbs when he'd had the chance, it was the best avenue of escape remaining to him.

When Garrick knocked on the door of the Rookery and told him about the earl's arrival, the better part of him had wanted to push past Garrick and race to the house.

Instead, he calmly said, "Please tell his lordship I shall make my way up to the manor shortly."

His excuse for getting away had come to him.

Forcing himself to wait—five minutes, fifteen, thirty—had not in the end made him feel more calm when he walked through the front door of Ravenswood Manor, which had been left standing open, no servants in sight. He stepped to the threshold of the Great Room, expecting to find his father within.

Instead, a man—his own age, not his father's—turned from inspecting the books on the shelf and stepped toward him without offering his hand. "You must be the steward." His hair was dark, a shade darker even than Charlotte's, and his olive complexion belonged more properly to some Mediterranean clime. In a few short strides he came to a stop before Edward and stood, as if waiting for something. When Edward did not bow, the man said, not a little impatiently, "I am Beckley."

No, no, no, thumped Edward's heart, while a single word—*how?*—screamed in his brain. "I was expecting . . . someone else. An older man."

"M' father, I suppose," the other said in an affected aristocratic drawl. "He died in early February."

Numbness crawled along Edward's limbs. Shock, not sadness. The stranger's words joined the others pulsing through his body. *Dead, dead, dead.* Was it true? It certainly fit with Markham's story about the change in the collection of rents.

"Ah," he managed to say. "And so you are . . . ? That is, I understood the heir to be—"

"Missing? For many years, yes. In fact," the man said, throwing himself easily onto the sofa in the center of the room, "I did not always realize I was he. When the late earl died, the story of his son's disappearance so many years ago began to circulate again. Abducted as a boy, they said. Hidden away. The more I read, the more I began to realize the child they described had been me."

With the scream still echoing inside his skull, Edward struggled to make sense of the man's words. He was a fraud, of course. Masquerading as . . . "Edward Cary."

The man tipped his head in acknowledgment. "Although the name is strange to me now. A child is a malleable thing, you know. Can be made to forget, or made to believe, almost anything. For the last twenty-two years, I've been called Jack."

"And did you—?" Edward stopped himself. He must proceed with caution. "You have assumed the title, then."

"Well . . ." Jack ran one hand through his overlong hair, disordering it. "Not exactly. I require more proof before I can make a claim. I thought perhaps if I came back to the place of my birth, I might find it."

"We were given no warning of your return, sir."

"No," he said, rising to resume his restless inspection of the room. "It was a spur-of-the-moment decision. I knew m' father left here a good many years ago, you see. I was not sure what I would find. It looks as if things have been left to rot."

"Conditions are less than ideal," Edward conceded.

"You're a younger fellow than I expected, Mr.—"

Edward hesitated. "Cary."

Jack's head jerked upright, and he twisted about to fix him with a curious stare. "Are we related?"

Meeting the man's dark gaze, Edward lifted one shoulder. "Perhaps." What was the best course of action? To continue his charade as steward until he could sort out what was going on? "This post was promised me by the late earl," he found himself reassuring the stranger who claimed to be he. "You'll find I have a great deal of experience with the management of property. I am recently returned from the West Indies, where for several years I had sole responsibility for a sizable estate."

"Ah." As it had done with Charlotte, that revelation about his past seemed to convey far more than the mere facts of his situation. The man looked him up and down, a mixture of emotions on his face. Disdain, and a hint of uncertainty. "And are those skills . . . transferable?"

"Some of them."

With one long-fingered hand, the man jerked the bell pull and waited. Nothing happened. Edward suspected the cord had long since been disconnected. Or had deteriorated into nothing. "The old place is rather thin on servants, it seems."

"There are no household servants. Only Garrick. A groom by training, although he has proved to be a fine man of all work." Edward felt no guilt at the slight exaggeration of Garrick's abilities.

"You have been doing your own cooking, then?" Idly, Jack swiped his index finger along the edge of a nearby table. "And cleaning?"

"I have a cook. She traveled with me from Antigua."

"A Negress?" Something more than mere curiosity edged his voice.

"Mari is African, yes."

The statement earned him another speculative look. "An African cook. Well, I suppose your time in the islands gave you a certain appreciation for a . . . well-spiced dish."

The implication could not have been clearer. Edward locked his jaw. "As for the cleaning of this house," he added when he had reined in his temper enough to keep it from his voice, "that was done under the direction of . . . my wife."

By rights, that lie ought to have been more difficult to tell. After last night, he ought to be especially reluctant to repeat it. Yet it was growing increasingly natural to think of Charlotte as a part of his life. Until he had seen the results, he had not realized how her efforts at restoring Ravenswood Manor would affect him. It was as if she had known what he most needed. She had returned to him something he had begun to think was lost forever. His home.

Some thanks he had given her.

"You are a married man, eh? Better you than I." Jack glanced around the cavernous room. "Well, well. Mrs. Cary has been quite industrious. I hope I shall have the opportunity to meet her, to thank her in person."

Something about those words slid uncomfortably along Edward's spine and caused his shoulders to tighten.

What would Charlotte do when she discovered this place was no longer a safe haven from the outside world? He had not forgotten her obvious worry that she might encounter someone here who could recognize her. And Jack's demeanor gave the distinct impression she might have more to fear from him than discovery. Almost as if he truly were Edward's father's son.

But then, Edward's appalling behavior had already shown her the dangers Ravenswood posed.

"Have you brought no servants of your own?"

"I did not expect to find the estate in need of them—in need of everything, Mr. Cary." His eyes darted to the corner of the room where a dark stain marred the ceiling and the plaster moldings had crumbled, a sign of needed repairs far beyond the scope of Charlotte's broom.

Edward could not argue. He knew too well what was lacking at Ravenswood. "I have already begun to make a few improvements."

"Hmm." He turned away then and said, in a tone that was clearly intended to convey his dismissal, "I shall wish to discuss your plans later."

Edward bristled. It had been many years since he had been required to defend his management decisions—and then only to those who had true authority over him. He mustered a curt, "Yes, sir," before spinning on his heel and leaving the room.

It was not that he felt powerless in the face of a challenge to what was rightfully his. He knew what powerlessness felt like. But with another man claiming to be the heir, Edward would have to proceed carefully. Nothing good could come from an abrupt announcement that he was the true Earl of Beckley.

Especially as there was now no one left alive who could help him prove it.

Chapter 12

When tangling her fingers together in her lap did not stop them from shaking, Charlotte sat on them instead. The illusion of security she had felt in this place had burst.

Beckley. Beckley. Had she ever heard the name before meeting Edward? Might the earl be an acquaintance of Aunt Penhurst's? Worse, a friend of the Duke of Langerton—either father or son? Would he recognize her, reveal her secret?

"Excuse me, missus." The earl's coachman stood in her doorway, shouldering a large trunk. "I don' suppose you could direct me—?"

"To the earl's chambers?" Beneath her, she curled her fingers more tightly into the tattered upholstery of the chair, then forced herself to rise. She could not hide in this room forever. "Yes, of course."

It had not been easily said, and was not easily done. Because the horrifying wreckage of the upstairs sitting room had blunted her enthusiasm for exploring the rest of the house, she was not entirely sure which rooms were which.

As she preceded him down the passageway and up the stairs, the man grunted his way behind her. His struggle gave her a moment to decide where to lead him next. Skirting the only familiar room, she peered through the next few doorways, heart thumping and eyes half-closed, more than a little wary of what she would find. Curiously, the rest of the rooms into which she looked were in far better shape than those downstairs. Dusty, yes. And damp. But it did not appear as if someone had turned loose a pack of wild dogs in any of them.

With a quick perusal, she was able to determine that fully half of the first floor of the house was taken up by a suite of rooms nested together like a rabbit's warren. The ruined sitting room was connected to a lady's bedchamber, and beside it was a second, larger bedchamber that must belong to the earl. Within that room, another door led to a dressing room, with quarters for his lordship's valet. It was there that she directed the driver to deposit the trunk.

"Much obliged, missus," he said, tugging a ragged handkerchief from the inside of his waistcoat and mopping his brow with it. "There's another like it to fetch, yet."

After he had gone, she stood at the window, trying to collect her thoughts.

The once bronze-colored draperies were thick with dust, but still sound, not having been exposed to the wind and rain like those in the sitting room, or to the sunlight that poured through the windows at the front of the house. Even now, at midday, this room was cool and dim, sheltered by the woodland behind. From this vantage point, she could almost see beyond the trees' uppermost branches: the hint of the roofline of the summer house, the sparkle of water in the pond. She flicked the hasp and pushed open one of the casements to let fresh air into the stale room.

The same wind that swept through the window stirred the bright new leaves on the trees and set them aflutter. Eventually their multiple shades of green—emerald and chartreuse and lime—would blend and mix to become the deeper, more uniform verdure of summer.

Every room, even the view from every room, brought with it a sense of sadness at the estate's neglect. But for the first time, that vague melancholy was heightened by the awareness that she might never know what would become of Ravenswood. As the earl's arrival had so forcibly reminded her, she could not stay here forever, and once she left, what excuse would she ever have to return? She would never see it restored and full of life. Would never gaze from its windows on the warm ochres and reds of an autumn landscape, or the bright promise of a snow-covered wood at Christmas.

Would not witness Edward's triumph at bringing this place back to life.

As she turned away from the window, her eyes trailed over the room's stately furnishings. Heavy, old-fashioned, but evocative of an ancient heritage that connected generations of one family to the land, this land, this house. Some man who had served bravely at the side of Henry V at Agincourt might once have slept in this massive bed. Someone strong and noble. Would the man who would be sleeping there tonight be lost in its proportions, indifferent to its history?

Ridiculous, she supposed, to think it would ever be otherwise. The earl had never known a different life; it was to be expected that he would take his surroundings for granted. Did she imagine her stepson, Robert, retired each night impressed with the weight of his forefathers' achievements, welcoming their ghostly presence into his bed? Of course not. If he cared one bit for the true legacy he had inherited, he would not be attempting to have his father declared mad.

There was a certain irony in the fact that only Edward seemed to revere this place and what it represented. His shoulders were broad enough to carry the weight of such illustrious ancestors. His frame would not be dwarfed to insignificance by such furnishings.

Treacherous to imagine him there, bare-chested as she had seen him once, his arm flung possessively across the bed's width, strong even in sleep.

Treasonous too, perhaps. This was not his birthright to claim. He was a mere steward. A nobody, like herself—

"You must be Mrs. Cary."

At the words, she jerked around to locate the speaker. A handsome stranger with a warm complexion stood just inside the doorway. He was slight of build, and half a head shorter than Edward, at least.

But he could only be the Earl of Beckley.

"Your lordship," she said, dipping automatically into the sort of curtsy that had been required of her in Aunt Penhurst's household.

But her previous fears were quickly put to rest. This man was too young, and too fashionable, to move in the circles of old men and women. She felt certain she had never seen him before.

"I am glad of the chance to meet you, ma'am. And to express my gratitude for your care of Ravenswood Manor in my absence."

"You are most welcome, my lord. It was nothing at all," she lied, still aware of her aching arms and back as she bent her knee once more.

"*Vous êtes française*."

Unlike Edward, this man spoke with the accent of a native. Although his eyes were heavy lidded, almost drowsy looking, she could tell he missed no detail of her appearance. She had had too many men look down the lengths of their Roman noses at her to have any doubt on that score. Steeling herself against the judgment that typically accompanied those words, she nodded. "Half-French, my lord.

Yes. Your driver brought up your things," she added quickly, hoping to divert his attention. "I had him put them in the dressing room. Your valet—"

"Haven't brought one." He crossed the room as he spoke, inspecting its dusty furnishings, drawing closer to her with every step. Carefully, she eased her back away from the window and sidled along the edge of the bed. Once he reached the window, he paused to look down at the landscape. "The steward's house is in better condition than this one, I hope?"

"Worse, I'm afraid," she said, shaking her head. "In fact, the condition of the Rookery is such that my husband felt it would be best if I stayed here—"

"In the manor?" His head turned sharply to look back at her.

She hesitated. "In the servants' quarters, yes."

Interest piqued, he grew suddenly still, like Noir when his prey was in sight. "Without your husband? I must say, it would take something worse than a bit of chipped plaster and shabby furniture to keep me away from my beautiful wife."

She backed another step toward the door, thankful he had not closed it when he entered. "I shall make other arrangements immediately. I would not wish to impose."

"Please," he said, tilting his head, "stay."

Something about the way in which the offer was tendered made her even more eager to leave. She did not know him. But she knew his type. Before she could pass into the corridor, however, he raised a hand to halt her. "Though I wonder if I might impose upon you in turn? Would you—? No, I cannot ask it . . ."

Expecting that he would find the words to make his request, despite his supposed reluctance, she held her tongue. And her breath.

"Might you be willing to tidy up my chambers and unpack my things? You have done such an excellent job downstairs." His voice was warm and rich, almost a purr.

How many women had he persuaded to do his bidding with it?

How could she refuse?

If she denied the earl's request, it might anger him, might even jeopardize Edward's position here. What would become of Tessie, Peg, and the others then? In the face of Ravenswood's desperate need, her own dignity was a matter of little significance.

Before she could make an answer, however, the coachman came

in, huffing under the burden of the second trunk. Lord Beckley's eyes flicked toward him. Seizing the opportunity provided by this momentary distraction, she curtsied once more and left without a backward glance.

In the kitchen she found Mari and told her what Lord Beckley had asked. "It will be the merest nothing," she insisted, ignoring Mari's skeptical glance. "The work of an afternoon."

Mari laid aside the pestle with which she had been grinding some aromatic seed into powder and dusted off her hands. "What would Mr. Edward say to that?"

He would tell her to refuse, of course. Would insist that she was not now a maid—if she ever had been.

For that reason, she had no intention of telling him anything about it.

Edward threw open the door to the Rookery and stormed inside, desperate for some means to vent his spleen, a part of him wishing he had had the time to set the little house to rights merely to give himself something to tear to pieces now.

As his father had done at Ravenswood Manor.

Horrified that his own frustration could have taken such a turn, he instead slapped his hat on his head and set out in the direction of Markham's farm. He would put his energy into something productive rather than destructive. A warm spring wind whipped at his duster as he strode across the field. "Put me to work," he shouted as soon as the farmer was within sight.

For a long moment, Markham said nothing, and Edward imagined he had not heard his words clearly across the distance and over the rattle of the horses' harness and the plow. But when Edward had come within a few rows of newly overturned ground, he stopped the team. "I thought you meant to be off today."

"A visitor arrived this morning."

"Oh?"

"Claims to be Lord Beckley. Not the man I expected," Edward added hastily, avoiding Markham's gaze. "Not the man your father would have known."

"An heir? But his son disappeared years ago."

"So they say."

After looking Edward up and down, Markham slipped himself

out of the loop created by the reins and held them out. "Plow, then, if you've a mind to. I'll follow along with the seed."

Gratefully, Edward took up the leather and slung it over his own shoulder, chirruping to the horses, whose ears turned forward and backwards as they investigated the change. Together, the two men made one pass across the breadth of the field without speaking.

Already, he could feel the strain of the task in his back and his legs, and he welcomed the discomfort, though it did little to distract his mind. Two more rows, and the field would be done. "Looks like rain." Edward nodded toward the horizon, where clouds were gathering.

"Aye."

"It won't flood the fields?" Where he had come from, the rains often were not gentle, and they could not afford the loss of the seed.

"Just a spring shower," Markham reassured him. "It'll pass and the sun'll be shining again before you know it."

But rather than brightening, the sky grew increasingly gray.

"It speaks well of the man that he came back to Ravenswood after his father abandoned the place all those years ago," Markham ventured.

"I . . . suppose." Edward knew better than to reveal too much, to encourage Markham to speak badly of the man he believed to be his landlord. But surely it would do no harm to inject a note of caution into the conversation. "I imagine he had some particular motive in doing so. Perhaps he hopes to investigate Ravenswood's income."

Markham's boot stomped the sprinklings of seeds into the ground with a heavy tread. "That'd do for us all."

An ambiguous phrase. Markham might have meant that everyone on the estate and in Little Norbury would be benefitted by greater attention to Ravenswood's profitability. Or he might have meant that if the new landlord was focused only on pounds and pence, they were all doomed.

It was difficult not to side with the latter interpretation when the skies opened. Rain came down in thick drops, heavy enough that the hedgerow he had been using to guide the horses and plow was little more than a darker blur in the distance. It felt like an ill omen.

Still, they kept moving. By the time the field was finished, Edward was soaked to the skin and his boots made a sucking sound with each step.

"Much obliged," said Markham when, at the end of the row, Edward laid the reins across the other man's palm, grateful for the ache in his forearms.

"I would say the same to you." The exertion had taken the edge off his temper, at least, though his head was no clearer. How had he found himself in such a predicament? Why had he not returned to England years ago, while his father was still alive, when he might have done something to set things right?

"Might I ask you a personal question, Cary?" Markham asked, waving off Edward's offer to help with unhooking the plow.

With more trepidation than he would care to admit, Edward tipped his head in assent. "What is it you want to know?"

"It's about Miss Harper, sir." Nervous fingers knotted and unknotted the harness as he spoke. "Mari."

Markham's unexpected answer succeeded in driving all thought of the imposter from his head. "What of her?"

"I wondered if she—that is, well . . . is she spoken for, sir?"

Edward had only just managed to bank the anger that had been stoked by the would-be earl, so Markham's words were like the puff of a bellows to glowing coals. In less time than it took the other man to blink, Edward faced him, toe to toe. The horses shied in alarm at the sudden movement.

"Do you mean to ask if she is mine?"

"I—" The reins slipped from his hands.

"My . . . mistress? My . . . *property*?" Stunned, Markham attempted no answer. The man who claimed to be Beckley had just insinuated as much, and Edward knew where his anger ought really to be directed, but he lashed out nonetheless. "Mari Harper is not now, nor ever was, 'mine' . . . in *any* sense of the word. Do I make myself clear?"

"Yes, sir." Markham dipped to snatch the reins from the muck at their feet.

Edward had jerked around and started to walk away before he thought to ask what perhaps ought to have been his first question. "Why do you ask?"

"I—well, she strikes me as a respectable woman—smart, a fine manager, a good cook. I thought I might—"

"Might what?"

"Well . . ."

"Are you suggesting you'd like to *court* Mari?" When had this happened? How? The two had less than a fortnight's acquaintance.

But had not his own experience shown him that a week or two was more than enough time to make one long for things that only a short while ago had been out of reach?

Where—in his case, at least—they ought to have stayed.

"I thought you said you could only afford to marry a woman of fortune," Edward recalled, fixing Markham with a stern look.

The younger man shifted awkwardly. "There's all kinds of fortunes, sir. Besides, I—" He broke off, obviously embarrassed. "Well, sir. I should think you'd know how a fellow feels, what might change his mind. Seeing as you're a married man yourself."

The very last thing Edward needed was to be reminded of his feelings where Charlotte was concerned . . . certainly not how she had felt in his arms. At first sight, she had roused his protective instincts; now, however, she roused something else in him entirely.

Reluctantly, Edward nodded.

He could hardly remember a time when he had not been aware of how others looked at Mari. With expressions ranging from indifference to curiosity. Sometimes with hunger, as if she were merely an exotic delicacy to be consumed—*a well-spiced dish*, in Jack's phrase. And sometimes with fear, as if she might devour them.

Anger, frustration, and yes, defensiveness, had blinded him to what was in Markham's eyes now, however. They held none of those familiar expressions. Just the look of a man who fancied a woman and hoped the feeling was returned.

"Mari is an extraordinary woman, sir. I only want to do what's proper by her, but . . . well, she hasn't—that is, I know it's not likely she has any notion of what's become of her family."

"No." She had arrived in the West Indies alone, and if he had to guess, her family was dead.

"Then is there anyone to whom I should speak—?"

"Mari's a free woman. You needn't ask anyone's permission but hers. But," he added, when a smile cracked Markham's rain-streaked face, "even if she agrees, you will still face opposition." Though there were no laws here against them marrying if they chose, Markham must know the resistance they would nonetheless meet.

Markham's chin jutted forward defiantly and he set his feet apart, the posture of a man spoiling for a fight. "Some, I suppose. But as long as she's for it, I don't much care who's against it."

It was difficult to imagine Mari tumbling headfirst into love with Matthew Markham over a few eggs and some seeds for her kitchen garden. He hated to see Mari do something rash, merely for—what? A sense of security? Of home?

Then he remembered Mari and Markham sitting together at the side of the pond, laughing. Recalled Charlotte telling him about Mari's late-night strolls.

Perhaps she had not been walking alone.

Who was he to presume to tell her which way happiness lay?

"I wish you luck," he said at last, extending his hand. Markham hesitated at first, then shook it vigorously. When Edward turned and walked away, he could guess that Markham would soon set off in search of Mari. He hoped the man was not destined to be disappointed.

In some ways, Charlotte reminded him of Mari. Slow to trust. Something of an enigma. As if whatever had happened in her past had given her reason to be chary and aloof and sometimes even afraid. Had some man—her husband—harmed her?

If so, and if she had placed herself under Edward's protection because of it, then the universe had a wicked sense of humor. He had brought her here with a promise of help and safety; now, he doubted his ability to provide such things to anyone. Whom had he ever really managed to protect?

Last night, she had given no sign that she wanted his touch, his kiss. And he certainly had not stopped to ask. Afterward, he had told himself that if she had not, she could have—almost certainly should have—slapped him across the face. But what if she felt she dared not?

She feared something that lay beyond Ravenswood's borders, that much he knew. What might she be willing to endure, what price would she be willing to pay, if it meant she did not have to leave?

Guilt oozed and bubbled in his gut like boiling sugarcane mash: thick and slow and dangerously hot.

He had set out for the field to work off his anger toward a man who called himself the Earl of Beckley. But what if the real danger came from the late earl's true son? Perhaps they would all be better off if Ravenswood were left in a stranger's hands.

Chapter 13

When rain began to spatter the window, Charlotte stretched an arm through the casement to close it, dampening her sleeve in the process, raising gooseflesh beneath.

"What about that fire, Garrick?"

As if in answer to her question, a bristly broom shot down the chimney and clattered onto the hearth, bringing with it a cloud of soot and the remains of a bird's nest or two, streaking Garrick's face with black and leaving him sputtering. Sykes, the earl's coachman, had agreed to be the one to ascend to the roof, and until that moment, Garrick had been quietly guffawing at his willingness to take the less desirable task.

"Right on it, missus," he said when he had scrubbed his face with his handkerchief, which only made matters worse.

Of course, the room was large, and damp even before the rain had begun, so it was going to take some time to warm it, even though the fireplace was nearly as big as the one in the kitchen. Charlotte, who had been dusting and polishing, paused to frown sharply at the mess surrounding Garrick. With a shiver, she retreated into the dressing room, where the earl's trunks sat, and knelt to unpack them instead.

His clothes—as smooth and sensual and sinfully rich as he—ought not to have come as a surprise. In London, they must have drawn the eye of every woman he passed, perhaps even the touch of a few of them. Here, however, they felt not just out of place, but somehow almost an affront, for every fiber that had gone into their making felt as if it had been thoughtlessly ripped from Ravenswood, leaving holes and tatters.

Despite being tempted to abandon the task—she was not, after all, the earl's servant—she slid her fingers into the garments and began to put them where they belonged: hanging coats and waistcoats, stacking folded breeches on the shelves, tucking rolled cravats into a shallow drawer. Small wonder Sykes had struggled under the trunks' weight. They contained more clothes than a man would need for a six months' stay, although she doubted a young man would be content to pass anywhere near that much time in the country. The scent of sandalwood competed with camphor and made her head ache.

At last reaching the bottom, she bent to close the lid and realized the trunk was not quite empty. What her fingertips had felt, what she had imagined to be the bottom of the trunk, was in fact a large case of some sort, a portfolio tied shut in several places with frayed silk ribbon. Should she leave it there? She wanted to do nothing that might be misunderstood, felt no curiosity about his private papers.

Curious or not, however, she was not to be spared from discovering what the case held. Deciding at last to lay it on a shelf so that the empty trunks could be stored away, she lifted the heavy, leather-covered boards, one hand over the hinged side, the other between two ties on the side opposite. She failed to notice that the single tie at the bottom of the portfolio—or perhaps the top—had come undone, either during its travels or through the carelessness of her own fingers as she had scooped up the clothing lying atop it. A sheaf of heavy, deckle-edged paper slid out and scattered across the floor at her feet.

There were dozens of pictures, some rough sketches, some carefully finished to the last detail, most of women. The artist's skill was undeniable. In one, the woman's blushing cheeks looked as if they might be hot to the touch. In another, the tears welling from troubled green eyes threatened to spill off the page.

Although beautifully executed, the pictures made her uncomfortable, though she could not quite put her finger on why. The expressions of the subjects—sorrow, embarrassment, fear—were human emotions. *Mon Dieu!* Had she not felt them often enough herself?

Perhaps that was the reason for the disquiet she felt. Because it was evident that the artist intended for the images to draw the viewer's eye. And she could not be at ease with the notion of using one person's obvious distress for another's pleasure. Who was the artist? Some friend of the earl, perhaps?

The chill that passed through her had nothing to do with the cold, damp room. She would never want to meet such a man, with a gift for making art of others' suffering.

"Tell me, what do you think?" The earl's voice.

Charlotte jumped and hastily stuffed the sketches into the case, although there was no hiding what she had seen. "I don't—that is, I am no judge of art, my lord," she managed to say as she turned, smoothing a hand over her hair, feeling her own cheeks flame like those in one of the pictures.

"Come, now," he said, filling the doorframe so that there was no way past. She took some comfort from the fact that Garrick and Sykes were merely in the next room. "You must have had some reaction."

Had he expected her to find the pictures?

"They are . . . the artist clearly has a gift." A gift for what, she would not venture to say. "Is he known to you?"

"Intimately." She could by no means call the curl of his lip a smile. As he looked her up and down again, he took a step closer. "Your husband is a fortunate man."

Surely he did not intend to flirt with her? The very notion almost forced a giggle past her lips. But it really was no laughing matter. Men like him, possessed of wealth and power, had no occasion for anything as subtle as flirtation. In her experience, they simply took what they wanted. An accident of birth became a ready excuse for base behavior.

"The estate is fortunate to have him here, my lord." The prim answer brought a spark of amusement to his eyes, making her wish she had not spoken quite so hastily. "If I may be so bold. He is determined to see Ravenswood restored to its former glory."

"Restored? Does he have some familiarity with the estate's history, then? Was he ever here before?"

"No," she said quickly, before recalling Edward's inexplicable knowledge of the house. "That is, I do not know."

"If he had, one presumes he would have told his wife." Surely she had imagined the sardonic note in his voice, the almost imperceptible stress he had laid on the final word.

She gestured toward the doorway. "If you would be so good as to excuse me, my lord. I'll just see that Garrick and Sykes have finished their tasks, and the room will be yours."

He grinned. "I do believe it's already mine, is it not, Mrs. Cary? And as those fine fellows had already done with their work, I sent them on their way when I came in."

Panic tingled through every limb. As frantic and unthinking as that poor bird in the sitting room, she dashed toward the door, though it meant coming closer to him. His sandalwood cologne filled her nostrils. Did he intend to hold her, keep her here against her will? And if so, would anyone hear her struggle to get free?

To her surprise, he made no move to stay her. "Duty calls, I suppose?" Turning slightly to the side, he let her pass. Only the hem of her skirt brushed against him, but she felt it nonetheless, the way a cat's whiskers might sense a narrow escape.

"Still raining, is it?"

Standing just inside the doorway of the Great Room, Edward felt Jack's dark, hooded eyes look him up and down, pausing at the boots caked in an aromatic layer of mud that was not solely dirt.

"This late spring has given us a chance to plant another field of barley. I was helping Mr. Markham, Ravenswood's chief tenant, to see the crop in the ground when the storm started." He was trying hard not to envision trenches washing through the freshly plowed ground and sweeping away seed they could not afford to lose.

The young man lazily swirled the wine in his glass but did not drink it, instead resting the foot of the goblet against his knee. "I could wish you had consulted with me before making such an expenditure, Mr. Cary. That money might have been needed elsewhere."

"I used my own money to pay for it."

Surprise sketched across the other man's face. "Well, the planting will be for the best in the long run, I don't doubt," Jack acknowledged, sitting more upright. "But it doesn't change the fact that things are deuced uncomfortable in the here and now."

Edward withdrew a sheaf of papers and a small rectangular book from inside his coat and tossed them on the table between them. "As you requested, I have brought you what accounts I have been able to make of the rents, the expenditures." He had been tempted at first to refuse, but he knew of no better way to prove to this man that there was nothing for him at Ravenswood.

Jack glanced at the pile. "I don't suppose there's anything in them I'll wish to see?"

When Edward did not answer, the younger man polished off the contents of his glass with an expression half smile, half grimace, then stood and began to pace the room. "The rumors about the state of m' father's finances were not promising. I look to you for some good news, Mr. Cary."

Edward shook his head. "I have none to give, I'm afraid. Things here are as they seem. Decades of neglect can hardly be expected to produce a profitable estate."

Over the course of the day, he had pieced together what must have happened. More than twenty years ago, his father had left Ravenswood in a fit of pique. The estate was entailed—but that would not have prevented his father from mortgaging to the hilt. After his father's death, it would have fallen into the hands of trustees, charged with maintaining it in the unlikely event of Edward's return. But those trustees must have taken one look at how things stood and washed their hands of the whole mess—clearing the way for an imposter like Jack to stake his claim.

"If I weren't in a bit of a tight spot myself, you see," Jack said, "it wouldn't matter so much."

Edward could not keep his jaw from setting stiffly, though he knew this man who called himself an earl would not think it his steward's place to scowl at him.

Jack returned to the table to tip the bottle toward his glass once more. Only a few blood-red drops tricked out. Tugging at his cravat, as if the mere mention of his debts had left him parched, he strode toward the bell pull, apparently having forgotten both that it was broken, and that there were no servants to answer it, if it were not. "Do you know, I begin to think there's something to this notion of our being related."

"Oh?"

"Yes. I fancy there's something familiar about you. Your eyes perhaps. They remind me of m' father's."

Fighting the impulse to cut his gaze away, Edward held the other man's scrutiny for a long moment. The color of his eyes had never been the point of resemblance to his father that concerned him.

Would something as simple, as common, as a pair of blue eyes be the undoing of his masquerade here?

Or could it be a piece of the proof he needed?

He ought to have told everyone who he was from the start. Including Charlotte. Instead, he had jumped into this morass without thinking of how he was to get out of it. If he put an end to the charade and claimed his true identity now, it would sound like the kind of tale his supposed wife was prone to telling.

Perhaps he never would get things set straight. Doomed to be a steward on the estate that was meant to be his. Believed to be married to a mysterious marble statue who would never be his to touch.

And perhaps he deserved no better.

Impatient, the pretender threw himself onto the sofa to wait. "There's one thing I need you to understand, Mr. Cary. I don't fancy a stay in debtor's prison. Coming here was my last hope. So you'll just have to find some way to make Ravenswood pay," he said, twirling the stem of his empty glass between his fingers. "If you can't, I'll be forced to remove you from your post."

Late in the afternoon, Mr. Markham had burst into the kitchen with the news that Peg had been injured when one of the pigs she was charged with feeding decided the girl looked more appetizing than the slops she carried. There was no medical man in the village, not even an apothecary. Immediately, Mari had snatched up that little wooden box of hers and offered to help.

Now, several hours later, Mari still had not returned, and Charlotte stood at the sink cleaning up the half-charred, half-underdone remains of the dinner she had prepared for Garrick and Sykes, which they had valiantly pushed about their plates for a quarter of an hour before deciding to return to the stables for the night. Well, she had never claimed to be a cook.

The quiet of the kitchen was broken by something clanging harshly behind her. A little scream of surprise caught in her throat. She jerked around just in time to see one of the bells on the board that hung near the door clatter to rest. For a moment, she watched it, waiting to see if it would ring again. It drooped, still and silent.

Just as she allowed herself to breathe a sigh of relief, it jangled again. Squaring her shoulders and wiping damp palms down her skirt, she set off down the corridor to see what the earl wanted, uncertain even to which room the bell was connected.

The dining room was empty, the gallery dark. She glanced up the wide staircase, reluctant to enter his bedchamber again. Then she saw a thin seam of light around the heavy, curved door of the Great Room. She knocked, then pushed it open without waiting for a reply.

The earl was stretched along a sofa, the foot of an empty wine glass resting on his chest. As she entered, he greeted her with a lazy smile and rose. "See, the bell *does* work, Cary."

Her eyes darted to Edward, who stood closer to the window, cloaked in shadow.

When he stepped forward, she was shocked by the state of his clothes. How long had he been out in the rain? If she had not sent Garrick to return his other coat, she might have offered it to him now. She longed, even so, to go to him and slip the wet coat from his shoulders. She was believed to be his wife, after all. It would be only proper.

But after last night she no longer wanted the proper things where Edward was concerned.

"I confess I was not expecting *you* to answer my summons, ma'am," the earl said, stepping closer and drawing her attention back to him. He was studying her expression carefully, his gaze moving between her and Edward with obvious interest.

"You've met, then." Edward's voice was sharp with disapproval.

"Your wife was so kind as to see to things in my bedchamber this afternoon," he explained to Edward.

Surely her eyes were playing tricks on her. Surely she had imagined the way Edward's brow furrowed at the other man's words.

"Do you know, Mrs. Cary, that your husband and I are related? Cousins, or some such thing." The earl tilted his head in the light, offering himself for her inspection. "Do you not fancy a family resemblance?"

The two men's features, their coloring, their . . . demeanor were all too dissimilar. Charlotte dropped her gaze to the carpet and shook her head—or tried.

"You will excuse us." Edward's firm voice managed to penetrate over the clatter of her pulse and the rattle of the windows. "The weather seems to be growing worse. You must allow me to return my wife to the comfort of our own fireside."

The earl snapped his gaze to Edward. "I understood from Mrs. Cary that the steward's cottage is almost uninhabitable."

"*Was*," Edward corrected mildly. "As I said earlier, I've made some improvements."

Resentment radiated from Lord Beckley's posture. Too pampered, too used to having his own way to know how to respond to Edward's self-assurance.

After a long moment had passed, Edward held out his arm. "Come, Charlotte." With obvious reluctance, the earl bowed his head to excuse them.

"Good evening, my lord." Charlotte made her curtsy and laid her fingertips on Edward's damp sleeve. The forearm beneath was every bit as hard as it had been the last time she had touched him there, the morning she had suspected he was about to knock Garrick down.

"Wait." Beckley's sharp command made her stumble at the threshold, forcing Edward to yield as well. "Take these things away with you," he said, waving a hand at the table before him. "I don't care where you find the money. Just see that you find it."

"Sir." Feeling the sharp edge in Edward's voice, she readily released his arm so that he could gather the papers the earl had indicated. Lord Beckley, too, looked perturbed—and not only by his steward's tone. The man must be having money troubles. No doubt it was what had brought him to Ravenswood. She could not say she was surprised. It was how these young noblemen lived, from debt to debt. Was not Roderick forever begging Aunt Penhurst for something to supplement his allowance? Had not George told her that Robert had been much the same?

Well, from what she had seen and what Edward had said, Lord Beckley was bound to be disappointed.

When Edward returned to her side, the papers tucked securely beneath his greatcoat, she slipped her hand through the crook of his elbow. Once through the door, she turned automatically toward the rear of the house, the quickest route to the servants' quarters and her own room.

Edward pulled her in the opposite direction.

In another few steps, she found herself on the other side of the front door, in the pouring rain, without even the meager protection of Jane's mantle, hurrying to keep pace with him as he set out on the stone path that led away from the manor. "Where are we going?"

Edward did not answer.

Farther along, they met Mr. Markham and Mari hurrying along the mud-slick path as quickly as Mari's lame leg would allow. Despite the rain, Edward stopped them. "Don't go back to the house, Mari."

Something in his voice—instinctively, she would have called it anger, although it seemed uncharacteristic of him—rooted her to the spot. She recalled what Mari had said of the fear deep within him. And she wondered again, *fear of what?*

"And why not, I'd like to know?" Mari said, stepping past him. "Maybe your English blood has learned not to mind this cold rain, but I—"

With his free hand, he caught Markham's shoulder. "Take her back to the village, and keep her there."

The whites of Mari's eyes shone in the murky evening light as she looked first at Charlotte, then at Edward. When she would have turned to Mr. Markham, her gaze seemed to falter.

"Why?" Markham asked. "What's happened?"

"Nothing. And I'm determined that nothing will. If *he*"—Edward tipped his head toward the manor to indicate Lord Beckley—"wishes to travel without servants, then let him see to his own comforts."

So it was as she had feared. She had angered him by agreeing to tidy the earl's chambers, and perhaps had involved Mari in his displeasure.

Markham nodded his understanding and, taking Mari by the hand, turned her back in the direction they had come, but not before she could cast one bewildered glance over her shoulder at Charlotte. Charlotte could only shrug in response.

A few more steps and she was once more entering the Rookery. On either side of the entry was a small, square room: one cold and dark, the other—the one where she had stood and begged him to allow her to stay at Ravenswood—lit and warmed by a crackling fire. It was cleaner than when she had seen it last, the dust of disintegrating plaster and years of neglect having been swept away. But it would be a stretch to call it improved, to say nothing of comfortable. The furnishings had been pared down to a single chair and small table before the hearth. And the poor state of the rest of the house was confirmed by the presence of a straw-filled mattress in one corner, as neatly made as its lumpy, misshapen form would allow.

"Come in," he said, before withdrawing the papers from inside his coat and spreading them across the mantel to dry, then squatting to stoke the fire.

"I—"

Why did she hesitate? It was not as if she regretted the loss of the dingy butler's room. Nor had she been particularly eager to spend even one night under the same roof as the Earl of Beckley.

Still, she lingered in the doorway. Sharing this house with Edward would pose an entirely different sort of danger. Not to her reputation, since he was believed to be her husband. Not to her physical safety—unless the roof really did collapse.

No, the danger was all to her heart.

She stepped toward the fireplace, feeling as if she were leaping into the flames.

Chapter 14

When he rose and turned away from the hearth, he realized Charlotte still stood too far away to feel its warmth. She looked much as she had the first time he saw her: her face pale, her hair and skin damp, the hem of her dress caked with mud. Automatically, he reached out a hand to her. "Come! Warm yourself."

"*M-m-mer . . .*" The rest of her expression of gratitude was lost when her teeth chattered and she shivered violently. She seemed unable to move.

Without a moment's hesitation, he went to her and lifted her carefully into his arms. For once, she did not grow rigid at his touch, but clung to his neck with an eager whimper, her body pressed against his chest, as if determined to soak up his heat and his strength.

When she showed no sign of letting go, he carried her to his chair by the fire and held her curled on his lap. He ought never to have brought her out on a night like this. But what might have happened if he had left her alone for the night in Jack's company?

What might happen if she spent the night here instead? Guilt rose like bile into his throat.

Gradually her trembling lessened, and after a time, she lifted her head. "I'm sorry." Her lip wobbled. "I don't know what came over me."

"Charlotte," he murmured reprovingly, as he shifted beneath her so he could rise and leave her alone in the chair. "It's my fault for dragging you out in the rain."

As he shrugged out of his coat and reached around her to hang it over the back of the chair, her wide, dark eyes followed his movement. "I do think, however, that you would be more comfortable if you would get out of those wet things, my dear."

My dear.

When had she become dear to him? That was a question he could not answer. He only knew that what he felt for her was something more than the old protective instinct that always flared in the presence of someone who needed help.

She was not some nameless damsel in distress. She was Charlotte.

His Charlotte.

No, he thought, recalling what had happened the night before, *never his*.

When she nodded her cautious agreement with his suggestion, he helped her to rise, then grabbed one of the blankets from his bed, held it up, and turned his head away while she undressed. Expecting any moment to hear the sound of wet fabric slithering to the floor, what he heard instead was a huff of exasperation. "Oh, I cannot!"

Hesitantly, he lowered the meager shield between them and saw her cold fingers fumbling and failing to unpin her bodice. "May I—?" *Dangerous question*. He ought not dare to ask it. "May I be of some assistance?"

Unwilling, or unable, to meet his eyes, she kept her gaze fixed on the floor as she nodded once more and dropped her hands to her sides. He tossed the blanket over the arm of the chair, and with fingers he feared would tremble as much as hers, he helped her to undress, tugging the pins free and sliding damp fabric over her shoulders, revealing a shift that was somewhat drier than her dress, but far more transparent. Once her dress and petticoat slithered over her hips and puddled at her feet, she snatched up the blanket, wrapped it around herself, and retreated once more to the chair.

Kneeling at her feet, he gathered up the discarded items and spread them before the fire to dry, then turned his attention to removing her mud-caked shoes, first the left, then the right. "The stockings should come off, too," he said. She nodded, fumbled beneath the blanket to untie her garters, then rolled her stockings down to her calves. Rubbing his hands together to warm them first, he slipped the ruined silk over her delicate ankles and off her feet. If he had ever allowed himself to imagine Charlotte in her shift, the feel of her skin as he skated his fingertips along her bare leg, this had not exactly been the fantasy his mind had conjured.

"Now," he said, rising. "Rest there. I'll make tea." Any excuse to put a bit of distance between them. A wool blanket was no barrier to his imagination.

But what sort of man would allow his eyes, his mind, any part of him, to wander in that direction under the circumstances?

Without waiting for her reply, he turned and walked toward the kitchen. After he filled the kettle, he gathered a few things on a tray and carried them back to the sitting room. She had tipped her head against one wing of the chair and lay now with her eyes closed, curled beneath the blanket. The top of one bare shoulder glowed in the firelight.

God, he was sunk. Not just because he wanted her. That particular realization had been coming over him for days now—in truth, since that long, cold ride, warmed only by the feel of her pressed against him.

But this was more than wanting. Or another kind of wanting altogether. It was the sudden realization that he wished all their lies were truth. He wanted simply to push aside their hidden, horrible pasts and imagine a future in which they grew old together. In this very cottage if need be, curled companionably before the fire. He had seen how she could make a broken-down place a home. The home he had been longing for all his life. *She* would be his home. *Mrs. Cary.*

There was, of course, the complicating factor of his being Beckley. His father's son.

After placing the tray on the floor near the hearth, he drew the blanket over her shoulder. She stirred slightly, burrowing into its warmth, but her eyes did not open. For a moment, he simply watched her sleep, knowing that, despite the fantasies of their future his mind seemed intent on conjuring, he was unlikely ever to have the chance again. When her lips parted on a soft sigh, he dragged his gaze away.

As quietly as he could, he placed the kettle on the hob, then spooned tea into the pot. Since he kept no sugar in the house, he added a splash of brandy—marginally better, at least, than that served by roadside inns near Chippenham—to the bottom of each cup. While he worked, he hummed a song he had not thought of for years, a haunting melody his mother had often sung to him.

"The cuckoo is a pretty bird,
She sings as she flies;
She bringeth good tidings,

She telleth no lies;
She sucketh sweet flowers
To keep her voice clear,
And when she sings Cuckoo,
The summer draweth near."

Strange that he should think of that old song now. Or perhaps not so strange, really. Surely the last time he had heard it had been the last time he had sat by a crackling hearth and felt something like domestic comfort. Once, he had asked Mama about the other verses, but she had told him they were too sad to be sung—about false loves and partings and deceit.

When the kettle boiled, the sound roused her. "Is that—?" She shifted more upright in the chair. "Is that toast?"

He nodded. "And cheese."

A treat for a child, but her eyes did not disguise her eagerness. "*Merci*," she murmured, taking a plate from his hands, devouring the first morsels quickly and sipping tea while he sat with one leg tucked under him—half turned toward her, half turned toward the fire—and made more. It was a pleasure to watch her eat—a pleasure he had denied himself, even when they took meals together. The way her plump lips drew up in the most delightful pout as she blew impatiently to cool her food, the way she closed her eyes when she swallowed, the way she kissed the last crumbs from her fingertips.

He could not disguise his smile when she held out the plate for the third time. "More?"

She blushed, such that he almost regretted teasing her about her appetite. But he could not regret the sudden color in her cheeks. "No. I couldn't possibly—"

But he was already sliding the last of the toasted bread and cheese off the fork and onto her plate. After taking two bites in rapid succession, she pinched the remaining cube between finger and thumb and held it up as if she were going to pop it into her mouth, then smiled, not seductively, not coquettishly, but sweetly, and held it out to him instead.

As he leaned forward to accept the gift, she placed the morsel into his open mouth and her fingertips brushed across his lips. Intimate as a kiss. More so. He was tempted, almost, to close his eyes.

If he had, perhaps he would not have noticed that the blanket had slipped from her shoulder again, baring the soft curve of her upper arm, the sharper angle of her collarbone. Without conscious thought, he reached to cover her once more, this time allowing his fingers to caress her skin. As pale as marble. As smooth, too.

But not cold. How could he ever have thought her cold?

At his touch, she shifted slightly—not a flinch, not a cringe, but hesitation, nonetheless.

He withdrew his hand. "Ah, my dear. I am sor—"

"No." Her voice cut across his, forestalling his apology.

When he searched her face, her eyes darted to her lap, watched her thumb trace the edge of the empty plate. "It will not happen again," he promised.

"Please don't say that." Still, she did not lift her head.

He had to remind himself to breathe, and when he drew air into his lungs, the ragged sound was loud to his ears, even over the crackle and hiss of the fire. "Why not?" *It ought to be true.*

In place of an answer, another shake of her head. Fighting the impulse to gather her into his arms once more, he rocked back on his haunches and sat on the floor instead. She laid the empty plate aside and drew her arm beneath the blanket, so that no inch of skin remained exposed. "Lord Beckley is not the man you were expecting, is he?"

If only she knew. "No." He lifted his cup to his lips and drank deeply, wishing he had foregone the tea entirely in favor of the brandy. "It would seem that the man with whom my . . . arrangement was made has been some months in the grave."

"Will the current earl honor his commitment?"

Edward mustered something he hoped might pass for a smile. "The current earl has many decisions to make."

"But he must keep you on. Ravenswood needs you," she insisted, leaning toward him. Her dark eyes flickered over his face. "The late earl was your father, wasn't he?" she said, the words coming slowly as she pieced the story together. "And your mother was . . . some innocent girl from the village, I suppose." She paused, and he thought for a moment about seizing that momentary silence, correcting her, setting her straight. But she was not as far wrong as she might have been, and as before, he gave in to the temptation of her gift for spinning tales. "We are two of a kind, you and I. My mother, too, was not my father's wife."

Ought he to be shocked by the revelation—or rather, the confirmation of his suspicions? Mostly, he found himself imagining the ways in which her illegitimacy must have shaped her childhood, must have affected the woman she had become.

"I suppose you favored him—and she could not bear the resemblance, the reminder of what he had done," Charlotte suggested, drawing surely from her own history. The French uncle, disapproving of his sister's choices. The English aunt, resentful of her very existence. "So you were sent away. But he promised you the post of steward on his estate if you survived to return."

Slowly and deliberately, Edward returned his cup and saucer to the tray and raised his eyes to her face. "And here I am."

A quick shake of her head. "Here *we* are." Her gaze flitted around the small room before returning to him. "Why did you bring me to the Rookery?"

Shifting uncomfortably on the hard floor, he drew one knee almost to his chest. "Because I suspect our new arrival is something of a libertine. And I promised you that you would be safe in Gloucestershire."

With a faraway look, she nodded. "That's why you sent Mari away as well. But you and I, at least, are believed to be married. She cannot stay with Mr. Markham all night."

"I imagine they'll make do." At her quick frown of uncertainty, he explained. "They have formed an . . . attachment."

"Oh. That is . . ."

. . . scandalous? . . . shocking?

". . . sudden."

A part of him had hoped Charlotte would be swayed by the romance of it—enough to throw caution to the wind herself. He brushed at the mud speckling his breeches. "It's been known to happen."

"Yes. It has. But I thought . . ." A pause. "I have often wondered . . . if you and she ever . . . ?"

"No."

She flinched a little at the abruptness of his reply, although he had tried to keep his voice soft. A gentler response, at least, than Markham had earned earlier, to his similar question.

How to explain something that lies so far outside Charlotte's experience? "If Markham asks her to go out walking, to kiss him, to marry him, even, and she says yes—or no—he will have the comfort of knowing she speaks her own mind. Her own heart. But for all the years I have known her, she was a slave. Not my slave, but a slave nonetheless. Even if I had wanted some sort of relationship with her . . ." He paused, seeking the right words. "If I had asked, she might have said yes. But I would always have feared that, circumstanced as she was, she might have felt she dared not say no. I would not want a woman who could not freely choose."

Charlotte listened, wide-eyed. He almost envied her ignorance of what went on in places like Antigua. But perhaps it was not all bad to have learned what he had learned. Perhaps it was true that the meaning of freedom became more evident in a world of slavery.

"Some men seem to," she said at last.

And he realized that she understood much more than he realized.

He had spoken firmly of Mari's right to choose, but what of Charlotte's?

"What do *you* want, Charlotte?" He pushed the question past lips that were suddenly dry, despite the tea he had drunk.

Moments ticked past as she considered her answer. "All my life, people have behaved as if it was only a matter of time until I showed myself my mother's daughter. Until I took up with some man and—" In place of words, she lifted one shoulder. The blanket slid down once more. "I grew up determined to prove them wrong. Then people said my English blood had made me cold, and I prayed they were right." There was no mistaking the note of defiance in her voice, the note of pride.

"You *were* married, though?"

"Oh, yes. I was married." The little laugh that bubbled up was nothing short of bitter.

The sound chilled his blood. "Was your husband a cruel man?"

"Just the opposite," she insisted, stretching out one hand from beneath the blanket to reassure him, though in the end, she did not reach far enough to touch him. Her ring winked in the firelight. "He was kind to a fault. He married me to protect me with his name, to banish those cruel whispers once and for all. But he was an old man. We never—that is, he could not . . ." Her voice fell.

"Ah." Privately, he had to wonder if the man's eyesight had been failing as well as his heart. Good God. One glimpse of Charlotte's bare shoulder was enough to raise him from the dead.

"I told him I did not mind. I never wanted, never *allowed* myself to want that," she corrected. "Yet . . ."

"You are human."

"Perhaps they were right about me," she continued as if she had not heard him—or as if she meant to deny what he said. "Perhaps I *am* more French than English. Because in the end . . ."

"What do you want, Charlotte?" The question was a whisper now, but he would keep asking until she answered.

"I don't have words to tell you," she insisted with a small shake of her head.

"*En anglais? Alors, parle français.*"

"No. I do not believe speaking French would help me now—if it ever has." Once more, her gaze dipped to the floor. "I want . . . you."

That single word fell on him like an answer to prayer. A prayer he had not even been aware of making. A selfish, sinful sort of prayer.

But, oh, he wanted her too.

Which was the reason he forced himself to ask her, "Why?"

"Because I have always been afraid. And you make me feel safe."

It was hardly a declaration of love. Not that he had expected one. God knew he had no business wanting one. This could not be about the future, about forever. But for one night, he would not let his fears keep him from giving her everything they both desired. Only her own fear stood in their way now.

"Of what have you been so frightened?" he asked.

"Of myself."

Rising to his knees before her, he rested his hands on the arms of the chair, one on either side of her body. And waited until she faced him once more.

"The words you seek are simple enough," he said when she had raised her eyes to his. "Yes or no. In French or in English. It does not matter. I will ask, and you need say just one word in reply."

"Yes or no . . ." she echoed on a whisper. "And you will heed that one word?"

"Always." It would be torture. The sweetest torture imaginable.

"But what if—what if I am not sure?"

"Then say no. You can change your mind later. You are always free to choose . . ."

Her dark eyes widened, framed by spiky black lashes and a few damp tendrils of hair that had escaped their pins. Freedom was a revelation.

He had seen enough men and women in chains, both real and imagined, to know the value of freedom. But he did not know if he had ever met another soul who had built those chains, link by link, to imprison her true self.

For all his failures, he at last had in his hands the power to set someone free.

The distance between the arm of the chair and her face, the distance his trembling hand had to travel, stretched for miles. At last, however, he reached her. He dragged the tip of one finger over her lips.

"May I kiss you here?"

He felt her warm breath before he heard her answer. "Yes."

Softly, slowly, he brushed his mouth over hers. Gentle. Sweet. Anticipation was an almost painful pleasure, building with each sensation, the way her lips parted ever so slightly, then began to respond, moving beneath his, giving back—lightly, tentatively—what they received.

Next, he brushed aside a loose lock of hair with his fingertips and traced the delicate shell of her ear. "May I kiss you here?"

The surprise in her eyes made his heart flip in his chest. What had he done, that she should entrust him with the honor of introducing her to these delights? To say nothing of the delights yet to come.

"Yes."

He allowed himself to do little more than brush her ear with his lips, to breathe in her scent, to breathe out her name. "*Charlotte.*" Trailing his fingers down the soft curve of her neck, he paused at the ridge of her collarbone. "Here?"

Beneath his touch, she swallowed. "Yes."

With a string of kisses, he traced the same path, sucking the pulse point at the base of her throat, then nibbling his way back to her ear to trace its graceful whorl with his tongue.

"*Yes.*" More exhalation than speech.

Smiling into her neck, he murmured, "Best not give me carte blanche just yet."

Some of the familiar stiffness returned to her frame, and she drew back. "I did not mean—"

"I know." She was not ready to be teased. At least, not with words. He returned his hands to the arms of the chair. Held his mouth over hers, almost, but not quite touching. And waited. Counted to ten, while she ventured closer by fractions that would defy measurement. Knew, felt when she wetted her lips with the very tip of her tongue right before she reached him, before their mouths met in a kiss so cautious it hardly deserved the name. Still, it sparked along his skin, made him dig his fingers into the worn upholstery to quell a shudder of need. At this pace, the night would slip away and leave them both unsatisfied.

What better excuse did he need to turn one night into many nights? Into forever.

She leaned closer, increased the pressure of her mouth against his, more eager, but still obviously uncertain. It was his turn to whisper "Yes," to breathe that word of encouragement across her trembling lips, which parted, although no word passed them. Merely a kiss. Innocent, sweet. The sort that would bring a hardened rake to his knees.

Well, he was already on his knees, but certainly no rake—in truth, his experience was so limited as to be laughable. In this moment he hardly knew whether that was something to be celebrated or regretted. He could almost wish himself as perfectly innocent as she. But also, somehow, skilled enough to feel certain he could bring her perfect pleasure.

Out of their shared uncertainty, they built the kiss with care. Instinctively, she tipped one way, he the other. The soft brush of lips grew firm. The tentative flick of one tongue became a slick tangle of two. Deeper. Longer. Until the air they drew was nothing more or less than one another's breath, leaving them both light-headed and panting.

When he drew back, her plump lips released him with obvious reluctance. Gradually, her eyes opened, as if she were awakening from an enchanted slumber. What expression did he hope to see in their depths?

He was not fortunate enough to find out. Her lids lifted only far enough to discover that the blanket in which she had been wrapped had slipped to her waist, revealing her shift. With a quick movement, she grabbed it in both hands and tugged it firmly up to her chin, then winced.

"What's wrong?"

"My—my—" One finger creeped out of its hiding place enough to gesture at the point where her neck and shoulder met.

He recalled her struggle to brush her own hair. "Still sore from all that cleaning you shouldn't have done?"

A tiny, guilty nod. Two more of her fingers slipped free to work at the knotted muscle.

"Will you let me do that?"

Her dark brows dipped together. "I—I suppose."

He laid his hand on her shoulder, firmly ran his thumb over the point she had indicated, kneading her soft skin. A gasp parted her lips. When he repeated the motion, her eyes drooped closed and some of the tension began to ebb from her body. On the third pass he leaned in, just to brush her mouth with his, and in another moment, all his ministrations were for her sweet, coaxing lips. Her aching neck and shoulders had been forgotten.

Until he cupped her head with his hand to draw her closer, and her answering whimper spoke more of pain than pleasure.

Chiding himself for his selfishness, he broke the kiss. *First things first.* After a momentary study of the best way to proceed, he rose and dragged his makeshift bed closer to the fire. "Here," he said, patting the center. "Sit."

Hesitantly, she uncurled from the chair, rose, and did as he asked, arranging herself with her legs crossed beneath her, facing the fire. The blanket she wrapped around herself, shawl fashion, allowing it to sag just enough that the tops of her shoulders showed. He sat behind her, his back propped against the chair she had abandoned. "This way, I won't be tempted to kiss you instead."

True, the position hid her face from him. But he had not reckoned on the temptations every other part of her seemed to provide. The way a few loose tendrils of hair curled along her neck, marking out winding paths to all the other places he longed to kiss. The curve of her throat, the plump lobe of her ear. Well, the rest of him was simply going to have to be as strong as years of hard work had made his hands. With care, he began to massage her shoulders with long, even strokes that moved steadily upward and outward, drawing her discomfort away. Each touch was rewarded with a moan or a murmur that seemed designed to direct his fingers where she most wanted them to go. *Harder. Higher. Here—just here.* With each sound, he felt an answering thickening in his groin.

Still, he held his desire in check. Seeking the tender spot behind one shoulder blade, he met the edge of her shift and prepared to pass over it, when the tightly gathered fabric seemed all at once to loosen and let his fingers slip beneath instead. Charlotte must have untied the bow between her breasts. With the sweep of his palms, her shift slid lower, and then there was nothing between his hands and the silky skin of her upper back. Gently—as gently as he could manage—he eased every knot, every ache, every twinge he could find, each one set free with a gasp or a sigh that settled over him like a touch.

On one pass upward, almost to her hairline, the tip of his thumb brushed against something rough. The scratch from her fall the morning after they arrived. "Does that still hurt?"

"No." As if she had not spoken for days, her voice was husky, too low almost to be heard. She shook her head, too, making the firelight shimmer over her skin.

He sat more upright, desperate, suddenly, for the power to heal all her hurts.

"May I kiss you there?"

This time she did not speak, merely tipped her head forward in a nod of assent that bared the back of her neck to his lips.

"Better?" he asked, when he lifted his head.

"Yes."

Reluctantly, he withdrew his hands and raised the blanket to cover her again. Her shoulders sloped beneath the woolen fabric, more relaxed than he had ever seen her. "Would you like me to take down your hair so it can dry?"

"Please."

Tugging loose her hairpins, one by one, he deposited them in an empty teacup. When her dark hair tumbled free, he spread it over her shoulders, a curtain of coffee-colored silk that smelled like spring rain.

"This reminds me of the ride to Ravenswood," she said.

A huff of laughter escaped him. "Cold and wet?" Then, more serious, he added, "You were frightened then."

"At first. Then I realized that with you behind me, holding me, I was secure. Safe. Free." Her chin lifted as she turned her head, not quite looking over her shoulder. "Will you hold me that way again?"

If he pressed tight to her, she would discover how aroused he was. How would she react? Was it possible she already knew?

He drew another ragged breath and eased closer. When he tightened his thighs around hers, he expected to feel her stiffen and pull away.

Instead, she wiggled more securely into the vee of his spread legs. As he had the afternoon of their rainy ride, he snaked his left arm around her waist. Only the sturdy fabric of the blanket, bunched now around her middle, offered a meager barrier between his hand and the soft weight of her breast, between the plump globes of her bottom and his hardness.

Until, that was, she tugged the blanket loose and tossed it aside. "I'm not cold anymore."

"Indeed not," he managed to say. She was perilously close to setting him on fire.

A log shifted in the fireplace, sending up a plume of sparks. "What comes next?" she asked.

You do.

He bit down, hard, upon his lower lip to keep himself from speaking that answer aloud. *Steady.* Until tonight, he had always imagined himself a patient man.

"That's up to you," he said instead.

She had told him she wanted him, but could he really be certain what those words meant? Coming from a widow, a woman of experience, who found herself missing the sort of companionship to which her marriage had accustomed her, their meaning had been clear enough. He—and perhaps every other clerk at the shipping warehouse where he had been apprenticed—had known such a widow once, in the buxom person of Mrs. Amelia Tate-Wetheby.

But such words might mean something else entirely from a woman of no experience who seemed wary of desire—her own as well as others'.

While his mind raced, her right hand crept to cover his where it lay spread on his own thigh, the better to keep it from wandering where it ought not. Slowly she entwined her fingers with his, then lifted his hand toward the firelight. With the fingers of her other hand, she traced the breadth of his palm, around his calluses, inscribing a circle on his palm. "I don't know—"

"I think you do. Trust yourself," he urged. "Close your eyes. Feel what you need. Breathe . . ."

Carefully, she drew his hand to her breast.

Was she truly ready? He was going to have to trust her, too. Cupping her breast, he allowed himself a moment simply to revel in its fullness before brushing his thumb along the edge of her puckered areola. She sucked in a breath and her chest rose, but she did not pull away.

"Yes?" He hissed the hopeful question into the sharp peak of her shoulder blade before turning it into a kiss.

"Yes."

Her nipple pebbled against his palm, and remembering how it had felt between his lips, he longed for her to turn around, that he might watch her face while he stroked her, might set his tongue to that firm bud. But their current position had been her request. She felt safe in his arms, she had said. So he held her tighter still, as his fingers fondled and played over the silky fabric of her shift and his lips skated over every inch of her neck and back he could reach.

When her whimper of longing grew almost fretful, he allowed the hand wrapped around her waist to slide lower, over the curve of her belly. "Let me touch you here." No longer a question. He wanted, *needed* to feel her shatter in his arms.

An almost imperceptible hesitation. *Perhaps not really hesitation at all . . .*

He stopped. "No?"

"I—" He saw her lashes flutter down. Had she closed her eyes? Or was she watching his hand, making sure it stayed put? "Are you certain?"

Certain of his desire for her? *God, yes.* It was a wild thing snapping at the bars of its flimsy cage. He could not remember ever wanting anyone, *anything* with such intensity.

Certain that acting on his desire was the right thing to do? *By no means.*

"I want you, Charlotte. Make no mistake about that. But if you are not certain, that is all that matters."

"It's just that everything suddenly feels so . . . strange." Her head tipped forward. "Down there."

In the nick of time, he buried his smile in her damp hair. It was really a matter for pity, when he thought about it. She had been so determined to prove the gossips wrong about her moral character, she had never even let herself experience arousal. As he smoothed his palms over her hipbones and down her thighs, he urged them gently apart. Her shift, already hitched above her knees, inched higher. "Open your legs," he whispered. "Feel the cool night air. Feel the heat of the fire against your skin."

When he had given her a moment to accustom herself to the sensations, he spoke what he hoped were words of reassurance. "You're wet. And I'm hard. That's just our bodies' way of saying they are ready for each other." Another pause. "But we don't have to listen to them." God knew his cock oughtn't to be trusted with making decisions right now.

She brought her legs together again, shuffling backward so her body was tight against his. "I feel you."

"And am I—?" He swallowed hard and began again. "Am I to be accorded a similar pleasure?"

Slowly, she parted her thighs once more. "*Oui*."

In the part of his brain not fogged with lust, her answer registered. Had the French word been a deliberate choice? It felt, somehow, like a sign that she was giving him her truest self.

With a palm laid against each of her legs, he swept his hands upward again and again, over her shift at first, then under, caressing the soft, delicate skin of her inner thighs, stopping always at the crease where her legs joined her body. When it seemed to him that the tension in those muscles spoke more of eagerness than uncertainty, he allowed himself to play over her dark, silky curls, his touch at first feather light, then firmer, until her fingers, which had been spread on his thighs, began to curl and knead, a silent plea for more.

At last, he dipped into her wetness. "Ah, Charlotte. So good. You feel so good." He whispered reassurance at her ear, though she no longer seemed to require it. Her breath hitched as his fingertips slid higher, brushed against her pearl. Vaguely, he considered what her answer might be if he asked to kiss her there.

While one hand played below, the other rose to tease and pluck her nipples. Her spine arced and before he could wonder whether she would struggle to find release, after holding it at bay for so long, she was shuddering in his arms, swallowing a little cry of ecstasy. Easing her down onto his bed, he curled his body around hers and held her until she stopped trembling.

Just when he thought she had fallen asleep, she stirred again and turned in his arms to face him. "I—I didn't know." Tears streaked her cheeks. He kissed them away, hoping she would never have cause to regret her newfound knowledge.

In this position, there was no disguising his need. The swell of her belly cradled his erection, which nudged against her as if it had a mind of its own. But she did not shy from it.

The hand that had wrapped itself around his ribs slid upward to loosen his cravat, unwound the streamer of linen from his throat, then found its way beneath the collar of his shirt. Her fingertips swirled mesmerizing patterns in the smattering of hair on his chest; her fingernails lightly scored his skin. With whisper-soft lips, she kissed the hollow at the base of his throat.

"Will it hurt?"

In truth, he did not know. Deflowering virgins lay far outside his experience. He'd heard stories, of course, and expected she had, too. No doubt the disapproving voices who had found it necessary to keep her in the dark about the pleasures of intimacy had been only too happy to warn her about its pains.

He only knew he could not bear to hurt her.

"No." A rash promise. How would he find a way to keep it?

By being careful, gentle, slow—the very opposite of everything his body demanded. The vision of her lying beside him—the glow of the firelight across her skin; her dark, wild hair streaming across his bed; her shift loose and bunched so as to hide almost no part of her—did nothing to help his case. Far from offering any resistance when he touched the hem of her meager garment and made as if to strip it from her, she rose to her knees and lifted it over her head for him.

Ah, but she was beautiful, from her deep brown eyes, to her large dusky nipples, to the lush curve of her thighs. Rising to his own knees, he tugged his shirt from the band of his breeches, eager to join her in her nakedness. Before his hands were free of his cuffs, her hands were running over his shoulders and down his arms with undisguised eagerness.

He tossed aside his shirt and caught her fingers in his before they could travel lower. Something about the position—kneeling together, hands clasped—made his heart leap. He wanted this moment, yes, but now that he was on the verge of experiencing it, he found he wanted the promise of something more along with it.

But an offer of marriage was out of the question. Had he learned nothing from the first rash proposal he had made? Was he willing to tempt fate again? He could not count on her to refuse him. And he was not sure he wanted her to.

He had come here intending to put an end to his father's legacy. He had imagined himself prepared to allow the family line to die out, for the title to pass to someone else's hands.

He hadn't counted on Jack.

Or Charlotte.

As he raised their joined fingers to his lips, she lifted her face to his, waiting.

But what else did he have to offer her? Just himself. And beyond what he could give her tonight, he was still not certain he was a gift worth having.

At his hesitation, her gaze flickered anxiously over his face. "Have you—have you changed your mind?"

Which answer was she hoping to hear: *yes* or *no*?

Dipping his head, he avoided her question. "There's something I need to say."

He could not give her only part of himself. She deserved more.

She deserved the truth.

Chapter 15

Although she knew it was a childish response, Charlotte caught herself holding her breath. If she had not, she might have stuck her fingers in her ears. She did not want to hear what she knew he was going to say.

Her father had abandoned her. No one in her family had ever shown her affection. Even George had been unable to muster the enthusiasm to perform his husbandly duty.

Now, she had shocked Edward with her eagerness. Disgusted him. And as a result, he was about to add himself to the long list of people she had loved who could not bring themselves to love her.

Love? How could she claim to have loved her father, when she had never met the man, and likely never would? And as for her family . . . well, there had been a sense of obligation to them, certainly. A few, very few, moments of affection between them. But *amour*? *Non*.

On the short list of people who held a place in her heart, the only person who had some right to be there was her late husband, and if what she had felt for him had been love, then how could she use that same word to describe—?

Bah! Had she really been so unutterably *stupide* as to have fallen in love with Edward Cary? And for what? Because he had snatched her from harm's way on a cold, rainy day, brought her to this run-down estate on the edge of nowhere, and then touched her—

Her heart. He had touched her heart with those big, strong hands of his.

And now, he was about to break it.

She shuddered, giving him an excuse to snatch up the blanket from the floor beside them and wrap it around her, looking all the while at the fire rather than at her, as if he could not bear the sight of her. When he sat back on his heels, she did too.

"You are better than I am at telling stories, Charlotte," he said, after a moment. The words, not at all what she had expected, caught her reluctant attention. "I have not your gift for inventiveness. I lack your cleverness." *Inventive? Clever?* No one had ever applied such words to her or her tales—her *lies*. "Any other time, I would far rather listen to you, but this time, I must do the talking. Your version of my childhood was interesting. But not . . . quite accurate, I'm afraid."

As he spoke, he fiddled with the hem of the blanket where it lay between them. Just moments ago, those long, calloused fingers had been stroking her with such heart-stopping gentleness. It felt now almost as if he still were.

She fought the impulse to jerk the blanket from his reach.

"You were right about one thing," he said, turning his blazing blue eyes on her at last. "I was born here."

"In Little Norbury?"

A shake of his head. "At Ravenswood."

At Ravenswood? How? She clenched the blanket more tightly around her, remembering his strange behavior the night before, still feeling the cold weight of that mysterious toy soldier in her hand.

"But my father did not send me away. I ran."

So far, their pasts were still more similar than different. "I ran once too," she confessed quietly. Afterward, while doling out her punishment for that display of base ingratitude, her uncle had insisted she ought to be ashamed. But Charlotte had only ever been ashamed that she had failed to get away. "You were more successful than I."

"That, my dear, depends on your definition of success," he said with a humorless sort of laugh. Though he was still looking in her direction, his gaze drifted until she felt as if he were far away. "I was just nine years old, but I got from here to Bristol without much trouble, and I had no difficulty at all finding a ship's captain to take me on. I was tall for my age, and strong. Captain Keswick told me I'd make a fine addition to his crew, and I—I believed him. Like most boys, I suppose, I was eager for adventure. But I had never been to sea before. I was so ill at first, that I did not realize where we were headed."

"To the West Indies, you mean."

Another shake of his dark head. "To Africa. The *Pearl* was a slave ship."

"*Quel malheur!*" she breathed, drawing backward without conscious thought.

The movement did not escape his notice. "You needn't fear that I am about to regale you with its horrors. Even if I wanted to, I—I haven't the words. It was a long, gruesome voyage. Sometimes, I still have nightmares . . ." A shudder passed through him. "Suffice it to say that more than a year later, I found myself in Antigua, tied by the neck to a hitching post outside some vile tavern." His hand crept to his throat, as if the sensation of rough hemp rope abrading his flesh had not faded, even after all those years. "It's not uncommon for the captains of slavers to abandon a portion of their crew in those port towns; it takes fewer men to sail the ship back to Britain, and there are always unlucky souls who can be made to sail out again. But Keswick had no intention of leaving me behind. In a fit of despair, I had told him who my father was, you see. I hinted there would be a sizeable reward for my safe return."

From what Charlotte could tell, Edward's criticism of his abilities as a storyteller had been too self-deprecating. He seemed, at the very least, to have managed to convince this Captain Keswick that a man who had carelessly fathered a bastard would be interested in whether he lived or died.

"What happened?"

"Thomas Holderin found me there. A religious man would call it providential, I suppose. I learned later that it was not a part of St. John's he typically frequented. When he approached, offered to help, I was skeptical. He looked like a planter, and I had already seen enough to know that there's usually not much difference between the men who sell slaves and the men who buy them. But his eyes were kind. And he had his daughter with him, a fiery-haired thing not half my age. I learned later that Mrs. Holderin had died not long before, and so he took his little girl everywhere with him. She—Tempest took my hand, though I was filthy and ragged. She chattered at me while her father worked at the knot around my neck. He had almost—"

His fingers fidgeted absently at his throat. That emotion she had sometimes glimpsed in his eyes gleamed there now, and she understood why Mari called it fear. At last, she understood of what Edward had once been afraid, and why he had never fully recovered.

"Another moment, and he would have succeeded in getting me loose, I think, but someone must have alerted Keswick, for half the *Pearl*'s crew came pouring out of that pub, knives drawn, and surrounded us."

In his words, she could feel the heat of the tropical sun, smell the stench of those villainous men. Despite herself, she leaned toward him, reminded him of what he seemed to be in danger of forgetting. "You got away."

"Yes. Mr. Holderin stepped between me and them. Ugly words flew back and forth. While her father talked, Tempest worked at that knot with her clumsy little fingers. I didn't know it then, but as I soon discovered, she never fails at what she sets out to do. Once I was free, Mr. Holderin reached into his pocket, took out a handful of coins, and scattered them on the cobblestones at the men's feet. While they scrambled after them, Mr. Holderin grabbed my hand, picked up his daughter, and we ran."

Her heart raced as if she had made the narrow escape with them. "He took you in?"

"More than that. He raised me like a son. A year or so later, he apprenticed me to a shipping company. Showed me how to take care of property. Taught me things. A bit of law—enough to make a sound contract and spot a bad one. Doctoring of one sort or another, when the need arose. Even," he added, mustering something like a smile as he settled his gaze squarely on her for the first time in what felt like hours, "a smattering of French. And many years later, when he grew ill, he arranged to have me take over as manager of his father-in-law's plantation, Harper's Hill."

"I understand that you felt you owed this man a great deal—"

"*Everything*," Edward corrected. "I owed him my life."

"But even so . . . twenty years? Why did you not try to come home, in all that time?"

She had not expected her question to strike a nerve. Pushing himself up from the makeshift bed, he strode to the rain-spattered window and stood looking out. When the firelight flickered over his skin, she saw the cross-hatched pattern of old scars on his back—a permanent reminder of his days aboard the *Pearl*, she could only guess. Certainly, she would never dare to ask.

"I couldn't. You . . . you must understand. My father could be a vicious man, particularly to women. I sometimes thought, when I was in Antigua, that he would have fit in well there. He—he beat my mother. Many, many times. And one day, I overheard her telling the vicar's wife that when I finally left home, went to school, she would leave too, would go live with her sister. I decided not to wait. I ran away the next day. I—I thought I was saving her life. I thought if I stayed away, she would be safe."

She strained to catch every broken, whispered word. From the way his shoulders lifted and sank, she thought he must be fighting back sobs, but she hesitated to go to him. Would he even want her comfort?

"But he killed her just the same. And you have seen the proof."

Mon Dieu. The room. The blood. *No wonder . . .*

She felt hot tears sting her eyes, the back of her throat. Struggling to her feet, she made her way to him, the blanket tangled around her body and trailing behind. When she stopped beside him, she stood in silence for a long moment before freeing one hand to lay it on his back. Beneath her fingertips, the old scars were faint ridges and valleys. Did they pain him still? What if—*ah, c'est pas vrai*—what if they had been made by his father?

Although everything beyond the window was black, he was staring fixedly in the direction of Little Norbury. "*Was* your mother a girl from the village?" she asked.

"No. She was his wife. And Jack is not the Earl of Beckley." He shrugged away her touch and turned burning eyes on her. "I am."

Truth be told, it was the least shocking of his many revelations, the last piece of a complicated puzzle falling into place. She managed, somehow, to nod.

A searing, searching look. "You would be well within your rights to doubt me. I have no proof. But before I—that is, before we—" His eyes darted uncertainly toward the rumpled bed and back again. "I wanted you to know the truth. Who I am. *What* I am." Slowly, he raised his hands to cup her face. "Ah, Charlotte."

Just as his palms were about to caress her cheeks, he froze. "In my veins runs the blood of a man who . . . who raped. And—killed. How dare I touch you with these hands?" With wild eyes, he inspected his work-roughened palms, as if aware, like Lady Macbeth, of the damned spots they bore, invisible though they might be to others. "I threw myself into the crucible of the West Indies, hoping to burn away the taint. *If you can survive this place without being tempted to violence,* I told myself, *surely that will prove you have risen above your father's nature.* But what if it's not been enough? What if—?" He clenched his hands into fists, the strain cording the muscles of his forearms and streaking his face with anguish. His voice dropped to a hoarse whisper. "What if I hurt you?"

Releasing her hold on the blanket, though she was still naked beneath it, she put her hands over his, gently coaxing his fingers to relent, until she could press his palms to either side of her face and hold them there. "These are the hands Thomas Holderin and his daughter took in theirs. Mari has told me what a kind, gentle man he was. It sounds to me as if *he* was the one responsible for shaping you into the man you have become. These are strong hands, capable hands," she insisted, though they trembled now, like those of a man burning with fever. "For twenty years, you have been using them to keep others safe. I am not afraid of them. I am not afraid of you."

He lowered his head and dragged her closer for a crushing kiss—fueled, she would have said, by a very different sort of passion than his earlier kisses had been. But was it? The pieces and parts of his life, of him—once scattered from the West Country to the West Indies—seemed suddenly to have coalesced into a single point, the place where their lips met. Yes, he could be gentle, careful, tender.

But this hardness—this desperate need—was him, too.

He dropped his hands to her shoulders—her bare shoulders, for the blanket had slithered unnoticed to the floor between their feet—and held her at not quite arm's length, breaking the kiss. "Understand, Charlotte, that I may never be able to claim my title. And even if I can . . . well, you've seen Ravenswood." His fingers slid higher, caressed her throat, tangled in her hair. "I wish—oh, how I wish—I could offer you something more . . ."

Something more? She did not want more, did she? Certainly not an offer of marriage. She had come here with the idea of testing her independence, of living for herself.

Drawing her closer, he leaned in as if for a kiss and whispered across her lips, "But perhaps you do not want anything at all from me, knowing what you do now."

"I want what I asked for," she said, pushing aside her doubt, slipping soft kisses between her words. "You."

A wrinkle etched his brow, and he gave one slow, incredulous shake of his head, before lifting her into his arms and bearing her back to his bed.

The straw-filled mattress rustled beneath her weight, and before she could form a wish for the blanket to cover herself, he was lowering himself onto her, kissing her, skimming one hand over her hip, along her ribs, to her breast. The coy game of question and answer had been abandoned. Neither spoke, the room's silence broken only by the occasional wordless murmur, gasps and groans of delight, and the pop and hiss of a dying fire.

His kiss was firm, hungry—his touch, more so. After ravaging her mouth, his lips descended to her breast, sucking her as he had the night before. Only this time there was no barrier between them. Then, she had been bewildered by the spark of sensation that had leapt from her nipple to the secret place between her legs. Now, last night's mystery came clear. She shifted beneath him, ran one hand up his arm, craving his touch.

And he obliged. One nimble finger slipped between her legs, circling that most sensitive spot, then sliding easily into her core. When a second finger joined the first, he raised his head up to kiss her lips, swallowing her gasp—of surprise, not pain. She felt stretched, full, and this was only the beginning.

She moaned her loss when he drew his hands and his mouth away to shuck off his breeches and drawers. Longing to touch the skin he had bared, but suddenly shy, she contented herself with allowing her eyes to graze over him . . . his lean, muscled legs, his firm buttocks, his—oh. How—?

Tucking one finger beneath her chin, he lifted her gaze to his and broke the silence with one whispered word.

"Yes?"

Trying and failing to produce a sound, she could only nod. *Yes*. With one hand, she reached up to pull his mouth down to hers, letting him kiss away her worry. In another moment, he was easing her thighs apart, kneeling between them, and she could feel his sex at the entrance of her body. Instinctively, she exhaled as he entered her. She expected it to be over in one hard, quick thrust—and painful, despite his promise.

But he moved now with exquisite care, easing them together with tenderness that made her feel strangely like weeping. It was too much, too much. And, oh, so much more than the mere joining of bodies. Then he was right inside her, filling her, surrounding her. No pain at all. His arms trembled and his head came to rest against her shoulder. Spearing her fingers into his dark, wavy hair, she pressed herself against him, needing somehow to be closer still.

Slowly, he began to move, and her body caught the rhythm almost effortlessly, their hips meeting and retreating as the pace grew more frantic, their breathing more ragged. In that moment, it felt as though everything she had thought she was, everything she had thought she understood, was being cast out to make room for something new.

All at once, his head lifted, exposing his neck corded with strain. He pressed deeper and went still as his seed spilled from him on a groan, its heat branding her as his.

While he slept, Charlotte listened to the rain slow, then stop. Gradually the sky began to lighten—first gray, then white, then streaks of pink, hints of blue. The storm was over. The morning light showed her Edward's face, stubbled with more than a day's growth of dark beard, but peaceful. Did he always sleep so soundly?

"*Je t'aime*," she whispered as she swept a dark lock of hair away from his eyes. The words felt strange on her tongue. But they felt true, nonetheless—even if she could not expect to hear them spoken to her in reply. Perhaps, given the life he had led, those words were not part of his vocabulary. In any language.

At the first merry notes of the birds, she slipped out from beneath the warmth and weight of his arm, collected her shift, her dress, her hairpins. As she braided and coiled her hair, she caught herself humming Tessie's song. But why should those sad notes be in her heart this morning? It felt somehow as if she had heard them recently, as if they hung on the air in this very room . . .

With a quiet gasp, she turned toward Edward's sleeping form. *He* had been humming that song last night while he made tea. The sound of it had called her back from the edge of sleep.

It might have been a coincidence, of course. Perhaps everyone in Gloucestershire knew that old folk song. Perhaps mothers sang it to their babes in their cradles.

And went right on singing it when their children were gone.

What was it Mr. Markham had said? *People thought she put on airs . . . Said she acted more high and mighty than the Countess of Beckley herself, God rest her soul.*

The Countess of Beckley. The Countess. Tessie.

She thought of that horrible bloodstained room. The terrible crime of which Edward had accused his father.

And she thought of the pattern on the china. The silver. The scars. That poor woman hiding in the hermitage couldn't possibly be . . .

But what if she were?

Hastily, Charlotte tugged on her stockings and shoes, though both were stiff with mud. She would go to Tessie, and say—what? It would be cruel indeed if her suspicions were wrong. But if she could convince Tessie to leave the hermitage, to come as far as the Rookery, they would see each other. And if Charlotte's suspicions were right, they would recognize each other.

Hugging the surprise to herself, she slipped out the door with one backward glance at Edward, his sleeping form flung across the narrow mattress. If she hurried, she might be back before he awoke.

Just a few steps down the path, however, she met Mari, returning from the village, similarly rumpled and mud-stained and . . . smiling to herself.

"Good morning," Charlotte called.

Mari started. "Good morning, Mrs. Cary."

At the end of every branch, every blade of grass, raindrops turned into prisms at the touch of the rising sun. "That was quite a storm last night."

"Was it?"

Tilting her head to the side, Charlotte studied the other woman's expression. "You didn't notice?"

"I—" Mari's chin tipped, a little defiantly. "I think the walls of the pub must be very thick."

"So, you stayed at the Rose and Raven all night."

"Peg offered to share her room," Mari explained, "but Mr. Markham and I were talking, and . . . before we realized it, it was dawn."

"I suppose he had to set out for his farm at first light. But I am surprised he would leave you to return to Ravenswood alone."

Mari's expression shifted slightly; Charlotte might have called it sly. "I think he expected I would stay where I was. But I had to do something." Together, they walked a few steps before she added, "He didn't go back to his farm. He set out in search of the curate. About . . .

about the reading of banns. He—he's asked me to marry him, and I—I've said yes." Her hesitation suggested she expected not to be believed, or could not quite believe it herself.

But Charlotte did not mistake Mari's uncertainty for unhappiness. "That's marvelous. Mr. Cary told me last night that you and Mr. Markham had formed an attachment, but I did not realize . . ." She extended her hand, and after a moment, Mari took it. "I wish you both well. I think you will be very happy."

"Yes. We are. Mr. Markham is so . . . so very . . ." But adjectives seemed to fail her. For the first time, Charlotte wondered if Mari, too, sometimes struggled to find words in a language that was not the language of her heart. "It was not what I was expecting when I came here. I would have said it wasn't what I wanted. But, now . . ." Mari's eyes darted back in the direction of the village. "I'm glad I came."

Although it was not her intended destination, Charlotte allowed Mari's limping stride to lead her farther in the direction of Ravenswood Manor.

"Did the storm keep you awake last night?" Mari asked after a moment, her tone cautious.

"We—" Charlotte began, "that is, I—" But she was saved from having to give any answer at all by their arrival at the back of the manor. She recalled Edward's insistence on keeping both Mari and her away from Jack last night. "Is it safe to go in, do you think?"

Mari reached for the door. "I'm not afraid of *him*."

After her various encounters with the supposed earl and last evening's revelation, Charlotte was not willing to say the same. But she did not think it was her place to tell Mari that Jack was not Lord Beckley—or that Edward was.

Fortunately, the kitchen was empty. Mari turned to go to the housekeeper's apartment, while Charlotte headed farther down the corridor toward the butler's room. It was still very early. As long as she was here, she might as well freshen up and change her dress before going to Edward's mother.

Then, once she had revealed them to each other, she would muster the courage to reveal herself. And once she and Edward had been completely open with one another, was it too much to hope that last night might lead to—?

Her ruminations were brought up short by the discovery that Jack blocked her way.

He gave her a somewhat lopsided smile in greeting. "Ah, Mrs. Cary. Good morning." Based on appearances, he had managed to find a second bottle of wine last night. Perhaps a third. His eyes were shadowed, his hair mussed, his clothes unchanged.

She half curtsied, half sidestepped back in the direction of the kitchen. "Good morning."

The knowledge that he was an imposter did not make him any less threatening. Desperate men did desperate things.

"Wait." She froze as he took a step closer, his dark eyes sweeping over her with the same interest they had shown in his dressing room yesterday. "I've been thinking. You look rather familiar to me. Might we have met once? In town, perhaps?"

"No."

The hastily spoken denial produced quite the opposite of the desired effect. Clearly intrigued, he ran one hand through his hair, mussing it further as he pulled a pencil from behind his ear. Reaching into his breast pocket, he withdrew a folded scrap of newspaper. "Mind if I—?" Without waiting for an answer, without even finishing his question, he pinned the paper to the wall and began to sketch. The pencil swept across the paper in practiced strokes, its scratch loud in the quiet corridor.

Instead of giggling nervously, as she was wont to do, she felt herself blush under his scrutiny, just like the model for that strange portrait she had found upstairs. Those drawings must be his work. The mere thought of someone stumbling upon her own face and form in that portfolio made her want to clutch her arms around her body, to shield herself from his gaze, from the gaze of strangers.

But she forced herself to keep her hands at her sides as she took a step in the direction of the housekeeper's rooms, where she could hear Mari bustling about.

Then he stopped abruptly and extended the paper to her.

It was a rough sketch, hasty, unfinished, but unquestionably her face. And unquestionably the product of the same hand that had drawn the others she had seen.

He stood so close that she could smell the wine he had drunk. She longed to step back. But whatever remained of her good sense warned her that movement would be a mistake, the final act of some frantic creature before the predator struck.

Making no move to take the picture from him, she lifted her gaze from the paper just enough to glimpse the loose knot of his cravat, one of those she had earlier unpacked and placed in a drawer. How she wished she had refused to see to the arrangement of his room. Had left his trunks untouched where they sat.

"Oh, how careless of me." He snatched the picture back. "Such a striking portrait deserves a title, don't you agree?" Using the palm of one hand for his easel this time, he scribbled down a few hasty words at the top of the sheet. "There."

She shook her head, refusing to look. But earl or not, the man was unaccustomed to taking no for an answer.

Slowly, she raised her eyes and took the paper into her hands.

The Disappearing Duchess.

"I don't—"

Before she could claim ignorance, he pointed at a spot beneath his sketch, directing her attention to what was printed there: last week's society gossip. The print had been smudged by his pencil and by his hand, but the words were still legible:

> *Our newest duke was seen in Town yesterday, sporting the latest fashion, though we recommend he dismiss his tailor, for this particular suit—half Chancery, half ecclesiastical—seems to have more than a few loose threads. Meanwhile, the Disappearing Duchess*

A fold in the paper hid the rest of the item from her eyes. For that, she felt oddly grateful.

Our newest duke. It could only be a reference to Robert. So, he had gone ahead with his plans to challenge his father's will, even if it meant annulling her marriage.

Although the paper trembled in her fingertips, she lifted her chin and met Jack's eyes. "It sounds to me as if this particular writer, at least, seems to think the duke's suit frivolous."

But Jack's sardonic expression wiped even that meager reassurance away.

Convulsively, her fingers tightened, crumpling the paper into a tight ball that fell from her nerveless hand and onto the floor between them. "Wh-what do you w-want?" Fear was a chestnut burr in her throat. Trying to swallow it, to speak past it, was torture.

"Your . . . cooperation." An unpleasant smile curved his lips. "The

Duke of Langerton has offered a substantial reward to anyone with information that leads to your return. You've seen the state of this place. I could use the money, Your Grace." Charcoal- and ink-stained fingers reached out to curl around her upper arm.

"You're right. I am the Duchess of Langerton. But you're not the Earl of Beckley."

Her charge was nothing more than a whisper, but it was enough to make him drop his hand, to drive him back a step. In his less-than-sober state, he stumbled, lost his footing, and wound up on the floor.

Seizing the opportunity, Charlotte raced along the corridor, through the empty kitchen, and into the blinding morning sun. Instinct told her to get far away from him. Until she saw Sykes's horses harnessed and Garrick leading them toward the drive, however, she did not realize how far she could go.

"Wait!" She waved a frantic hand. The carriage wheels creaked as they came to a halt. "You are returning to London, Mr. Sykes?"

About to leap onto the driver's perch, he paused with one foot on the step. "Aye, missus. This moment."

She had been a fool to run from one stranger in a dark coat. How many desperate men were now chasing her, hoping for a reward? Her days of hiding must be at an end. Robert would run her to ground like a fox and stand by while the dogs of Society ripped her to shreds. It was past time for her to meet him face-to-face, answer his accusations with dignity, and hope that the resolution of the matter would bring lasting peace, and with it, freedom.

"Will you take me with you, Mr. Sykes?"

A wrinkle of surprise flickered across his brow. "No baggage, missus?"

She shook her head.

For a moment, she thought he meant to refuse. Glancing over her shoulder, she scanned the yard, fearing to see Jack on her heels. When she turned back, Sykes gave a nod. "All right."

As she hurried forward, Garrick sprang to open the carriage door. "I'm afraid I have nothing to offer you for your trouble, Mr. Sykes."

From the coachman's box, he called down, "No trouble, missus. Jus' don' keep the horses standin', if you please."

"Oh. Oh, no. I wouldn't." She clambered in with a nod of thanks to Garrick. "*Merci.*"

Only as Sykes chirruped to the horses and the carriage lurched forward did Charlotte consider what Edward would think when he discovered she had gone. And from there, her mind did not have far to go to wonder what he would say if—or when—Jack told him who she was.

Would he forgive her for not telling him the whole truth?

Last night, her words had felt like all the truth that ever needed to be told. She had bared her soul to him, had explained who she was in every way that mattered. In every way but one. And really, how much did a title signify? After all, she was a duchess in name only, as Robert was so desperate to prove. And she certainly bore Edward no ill will for keeping his title a secret.

She glanced out the window at the scenery that had already begun to slide past. In leaving Ravenswood she was leaving half her heart behind. But she couldn't go back. If she did, she might soon find herself headed to London in Jack's company instead. And if anyone was going to claim some sort of a reward for her return, it would be she.

Only this time, she was not thinking of the money.

With fumbling fingers, she dropped the window in the carriage door and leaned out. "Garrick!"

Sykes checked the horses, but did not stop them. Garrick came loping to the side of the carriage, out of breath. "Aye?"

"Tell—" she began as the carriage rolled slowly forward and Garrick jogged alongside. "Tell Mr. Cary—" But the words that came to her tired, anxious mind were a jumble of French and English. They could not be entrusted to another to relay. As Sykes's spry horses leaned into the bit, Garrick struggled to keep up. In another moment, he would be too far away to hear her words. "Tell Mr. Cary I'm sorry."

Once she'd dealt with Robert, she would come back to Ravenswood, explain everything in person. She would make Edward understand how she felt.

In the meantime, however, there was one parting gift she could give.

"And go to the hermitage," she shouted to Garrick. "Tell Tessie that the one she has been waiting for has finally come home."

Chapter 16

A beam of morning light slanted across the room, chasing away the last fragments of Edward's dream. In it, he had been fifteen or sixteen again, listening with half an ear to Tempest practicing her conjugations, the rest of him lost in some book her father had lent him.

"To love. *Aimer.*" A giggle, which he had ignored. "*J'aime. Il, elle, on aime. Nous aimons. Vous . . . vous aimerez*?" She rattled through the forms quickly, with little regard to accuracy or accent.

"*Vous aimez,*" he had corrected automatically.

"No, no. You misunderstood. I was asking. Do you think you will ever fall in love, Edward?"

The question had succeeded in capturing his full attention. Snapping shut his book, he had dropped to one knee beside the chair across which she had carelessly draped herself, caught up her slight, girlish hand, and said, with exaggerated passion, "*Mais oui, ma chérie. Je t'aime.*"

And, as he had hoped, she had squealed in protest, jumped up, and left him to his reading.

A dirty trick, of course. One of many they had played on one another, growing up together as they had. It would be years before the thought of anything more than brotherly love would cross his mind in regards to Tempest Holderin, and when it had, she had rebuffed his overtures just as thoroughly as she had that day.

Je t'aime. I love you. The words every young man with a passable command of French dreamed a beautiful woman would someday speak to him.

But why had that particular memory come back to him this morning?

As he brushed his hair away from his face and rubbed the heel of one hand against his eyes, he remembered. *Charlotte.*

He shifted on the lumpy mattress, half turned, expecting to find her still curled beside him. But the other half of the bed was cool and empty. Bright light flooded the room. It must be an hour or more past dawn. For the first time since returning to England, he had slept like the dead. She must have woken early, grown restless, gone out.

Not back to the manor? Hurrying to his feet, he found his scattered clothes and tugged them on. *Surely she knew better than that.*

When he could see no sign of Charlotte around the Rookery or walking in the nearby wood, he made his way to the manor house, entering through the kitchen, expecting to find it unoccupied. Instead, Mari was within, lighting a fire. A lithe black cat—*Noir*, had Charlotte called it?—was playing at her feet, swatting a balled-up piece of paper.

It was on the tip of his tongue to scold Mari for returning, but this was not the time. "Have you seen Charlotte?"

"This morning?" Mari turned away from the hearth, a curious slant to her head. "Yes. I met her just leaving the Rookery, and we walked back here together. She's in her room, resting, I believe." Something like a smile played around her lips. "She looked . . . tired."

Before he could muster a reply, Jack stumbled into the room, looking—and smelling—the worse for a night of drinking. He rubbed a hand over the back of his head as he sat down heavily on one of the benches and grunted, "Coffee."

Stone-faced, Mari shot a look at Edward before moving to follow the surly order.

"She's gone," Jack mumbled, half slumped over the servants' table. "Sykes was meant to take the coach back to Town this morning. I 'spect you'll find she was on it."

"Gone? Town?" Unable to restrain himself, Edward grabbed Jack by the hair and lifted the man's head high enough that their eyes met.

Jack winced. "Hey, now. Easy. She gave me quite a knock already."

"What the hell are you talking about?"

One dark eye squinted closed, as if he struggled to remember. "Now that I think on it, she only gave me a shove. Must've hit my head on the wall when I fell."

"And what did you do to her to earn that shove?" Edward ground out.

Jack only laughed.

Letting the man's head drop back onto the tabletop with a thud, Edward strode out of the kitchen and down the corridor. Though his feet, and his heart, wanted to race, he would not give in to the impulse. He would find her safe and sound in her room. He would.

But his knock received no answer; the old butler's room was empty. With quicker steps, he moved back through the kitchen and out the door. In the stable yard, he could see the grooves of carriage wheels and the rounded outlines left by the hooves of Sykes's horses, though the mud was too soft to hold much of an impression. In the stable itself, Samson whickered softly at him. Garrick was nowhere to be seen.

Back in the kitchen, Edward reached across the table and caught Jack by the cravat this time, yanking him to his feet. The bench tipped behind him and clattered to the floor. "Mind telling me what happened here this morning to drive her off?"

Despite his position, Jack managed a leer. "Seems to me the real story is what happened last night. Did she get you to swive her before she ran off?"

For answer, Edward dragged him away from the table and pinned him against the wall. Above his head, the servants' call bells jingled quietly on their plank. "Have a care," Edward warned as his grip tightened. He'd never yet hit a man, but Jack didn't know that.

Jack's eyes rolled upward, showing their whites. "I just gave her a bit of a fright, I swear."

"A fright?" Edward hitched him higher. Now, only the toes of Jack's boots scuffed impotently against the floor. "Why?"

"T-told her I know who she is."

"And who is that?"

"Charlotte Blakemore," he rasped out. "Dowager Duchess of Langerton."

Shock made Edward relax his grip. *A duchess?*

Gasping, Jack sank to the floor.

The rest of the story came more easily, once he had caught his breath. "She disappeared from Bath a fortnight or so ago. Her husband left her a whacking great fortune, they say, but her stepson, the current duke, means to have his late father's will voided—and the marriage, too, if it can be done."

"On what grounds?"

"Claims the old man had already gone round the twist before they were wed."

Mad? That was a serious allegation indeed.

In his mind, Edward tried to reconcile what he knew of her—her cheap clothes, her knowledge of housekeeping matters, what she'd told him of her origins—with the notion of her as a duchess. Only her impossibly erect carriage seemed to fit the person Jack had identified.

Of course, she might just as easily have told the same sad stories to some soft-in-the-head, elderly duke, won his pity, and then his fortune.

Almost.

Out of the corner of his eye, Edward saw Noir arch his back and pounce. The wad of paper with which he had been playing popped from between his paws. For a moment, the draft of the fire caught and held it, threatening to devour it before whirling it out into the room instead.

Edward snatched the cat's plaything out of the air. "What's this?" he asked, righting the bench and sitting down. When he smoothed the paper against the tabletop, Charlotte's worried eyes stared up at him from the tattered page, drawn by a hand with some skill, although the pencil lines were smudged. *The Disappearing Duchess* was scrawled above her head.

"Proof," said Jack, hoisting himself to his feet and joining Edward at the table.

As he stared, snatches of print surrounding the sketch came into focus. *Our newest duke . . . a suit . . . more than a few loose threads.* When he came to the crease in the paper, he unfolded it and read on.

> *Meanwhile, the Disappearing Duchess was last seen headed west in the company of a dark-haired stranger. No doubt she hopes he is possessed of a cure for her late husband's "infirmities."*

"Rumor has it the marriage was never consummated," Jack explained. "When it came out she might lose everything if Langerton could prove she hadn't been plucked, she scampered off—in search of some chap who'd do the deed the old man couldn't, they say. The new duke put up a pretty penny to anyone who brought her back before she succeeded. And when I recognized her, well, I figured I could use that money as well as anybody. But it seems," he added, casting shrewd eyes over Edward's rumpled clothes and making a show of straightening his own collar, "I'm too late."

"Have a care," Edward ground out. "You're speaking of my—" He broke off before the word passed his lips; that particular lie was no longer required, it seemed.

But the omission did not go unnoticed. "Your wife?" Jack gave a wry laugh.

Edward made no answer. The details of the gossip column, and Jack's tale, fit with what he knew. He had met Charlotte not far from Bath. She'd worn a wedding ring and claimed to be a widow. And last night, he'd taken a virgin to his bed.

Mari stepped to the table, almost tripping over Noir. Muttering, she poured steaming liquid into an empty cup and handed it to Jack.

"Bah, that's bitter stuff," he said, pulling a face at the first swallow of Mari's coffee.

Edward recalled Charlotte's anguished account of feeling torn between two worlds: French desire and English sangfroid. He could see her coy smile. Hear her beguiling accent: *I want . . . you.*

Well, he'd known almost from the moment they met that she was a storyteller.

His thoughts were dragged back to the present when Jack slapped his palm on the table. "Woman, what are you about? Why are you staring at me like that? Are you trying to curse me?" His eyes darted from Mari to the black cat and back again. "Are you some kind of witch?"

"Witch? Ah, no suh," Mari insisted with a shake of her turbaned head, her normally flawless English turned suddenly into the singsong patois of the islands. "No speak de curse. Me no obeah woman."

Jack appeared to take little comfort in her reassurance. Beads of sweat sprang up on his forehead.

Edward glanced back at Mari. "What have you done?"

She looked at him for a long moment, as if weighing whether or not to reveal her secret. "Sure now, you remember hearin' 'bout bad massahs what got struck sudden by de megrims or de cramp or de flux?"

"Well . . . yes, of course." Disease of every sort was rampant in the islands.

"Slave women talk in de market, you know," she said with a pointed look. "Give advice. Swap recipes. I knows how to make a cruel man suffer."

"What did you give him?"

"Jus' plain p'ison," she said, nodding toward the half-empty cup. "Dat's all."

Until that moment, Edward had never actually seen a man turn green; he had always imagined it nothing more than a fanciful expression. "P-poison? In the c-coffee?" Jack managed to stammer before he clutched at his stomach and collapsed forward onto the table.

Edward grasped one of Jack's shoulders and shook him, hard, but he could not be roused. Slowly, he raised horrified eyes to Mari.

"Settle yourself, Mr. Edward," she said, her voice her own again. "If I set out to poison a man, he'd never know until it was too late." With calm, deliberate motions, she poured a cup of coffee for herself and took a sip. "For some men, there's nothing scarier than the sight of a woman who knows her own power—the more so, I suppose, if her skin is black. I saw that fear in his eyes. So I decided to play with him a bit, pretended to be what he imagined I am. I didn't suspect he was weak enough to frighten himself into a faint."

Still surprised by Mari's performance, Edward could not deny that her game seemed a fitting punishment for the way Jack had frightened Charlotte.

Mari snatched up the paper with one hand. Her dark eyes took in the hasty sketch and the circled words. "Well, we all knew she was hiding something. Any fool could see she was scared."

"Or shrewd. God, Mari . . . I begin to wish I had never come home."

"Home? To England, you mean." When he did not answer, she pressed further. "It wasn't the promise of a job that brought you here, was it? You're from this part of the country. Gloucestershire, Little Norbury . . ."

"Ravenswood." He could see no point in denying it to Mari. Frankly, he was surprised it had taken her this long to piece it together. "I was born here. My father was Lord Beckley."

Mari looked from him to Jack and back again, her face a perfect blank. If she was surprised, she seemed determined not to show it. "And now . . . ?"

"I am."

Her gaze dropped to the picture, and she studied it for another moment before crumpling it and tossing it onto the floor for Noir, who pretended to ignore it, though the tip of his tail flicked. She jerked her chin toward Jack. "Don't you listen to him."

"Even if he's right?"

"He can't know the whole truth," she insisted. "He doesn't know what's in her heart."

A scoffing laugh pushed past his lips. "Her heart? She lied to us, Mari. She made me think she cared. Cared for the fate of Ravenswood. Cared for me. But in the end, it was all just another one of her stories."

"It seems to me she wasn't the only one telling stories. M'lord."

Edward opened his mouth to retort, but stopped when he realized Mari's attention had been caught by something on the other side of the room. He turned and looked toward the still-open kitchen door. An old woman stood there, stoop-shouldered, her knobby fingers clutching a walking stick. When she lifted her head, he could see the scars on her face and one blind, milky eye.

"May I help you, ma'am?" he asked, rising.

She twisted her head awkwardly to fix him with her other eye, then drew in a sharp breath.

Her exhalation brought with it one whispered word: "*Neddy?*"

Chapter 17

When the woman tried to step up into the kitchen, she tottered unsteadily on her feet. Garrick appeared in the doorway behind her, ready to help, but Edward was at her side first. Gently, he drew her arm through his, led her to the bench, and knelt to bring his face level with hers. Afraid even to blink, for fear that if his eyes dropped closed he would awake to find it had been a dream, he studied her face, looking past the mask of scars to see familiar features untouched by time.

Surely his memory was playing tricks on him. His heart hammered in his chest.

"M-mama?"

Her soft blue eye fixed him in return. "And to think," she murmured, "I worried all this time that I might not know you when you came home."

Though he longed to wrap his arms around her, she looked so fragile that he contented himself with lifting the hand that rested on the bench and pressing it first to his trembling lips, then to his cheek. He had no words to describe the sensation of his mother's touch—after so many years, when he had thought never to feel it again.

"Oh, Mama, Mama. I thought—I thought you were dead."

"I feared you were, as well. Oh, my darling, where have you been all this time?"

He brushed aside the question. "It does not matter. I'm here with you now."

"He has been in the West Indies, ma'am," Mari said, stepping forward.

Surprise flared in his mother's clear eye as she took in Mari's appearance. "Oh." Part exclamation, part question, the sound left her lips on a gasp.

"Are you the one they call Tessie?" Mari asked, undaunted. Mama nodded.

"You—you have—you are the one who has been living in the hermitage?" Edward sputtered. Markham had mentioned something about an old vagrant woman to him, but he had brushed the concern aside. At the time, other matters had seemed more pressing. *My God.* If he'd listened, he might have found his mother that much sooner. "Oh, Mama. That was no life for you. No life for anyone. Why didn't you go to your sister, as you said you would?"

"As I said—?"

At last, he broke her gaze, embarrassed at the memory, at his childishness. "I was hiding—playing soldiers in your sitting room. Mrs. Henderson came. I overheard you tell her that you could leave Father when I went away to school. I was afraid of what might happen if you waited that long. So I . . . I ran away."

"Neddy."

The almost-forgotten gentleness of even her scold brought tears to his eyes, and he dropped his head to her lap to hide them from her. Leaning her walking stick against the edge of the bench, she laid her other hand on his head and began to smooth his hair with gnarled fingers.

"Oh, Mama," he whispered into her skirts. "Why did you stay?"

"I did not have a choice."

It took all the strength he possessed, but he raised his head once more and forced himself to see the truth: her faded brown hair with its streak of white, how thin she was, the scars she bore. Suffering had made her old before her time. "What did he do to you?"

Her head darted a refusal, but he did not break his gaze.

"He convinced himself I knew where you had gone," she said at last, sounding resigned. "Even if I really *had* known, though, nothing he said or did could have made me tell him. One day, after you had been gone about a fortnight, he—" She broke off, steeled herself, began again. "He sent for a physician from Stroud. I caught bits and pieces of their conversation. He told the man to say I had the smallpox. But I was never examined. I daresay money exchanged hands. Afterward, your father locked me in my room and dismissed the staff—for their safety, he told them. He wanted no witnesses to his cruelty. Word of the supposed infection spread like wildfire, and people fled. A few days later, I watched some men carry out a coffin. Full of rocks, I imagine. But who would dare to investigate and risk spreading the contagion? Or worse, risk angering your father? Mr. Henderson was gone, having taken his dear wife to safety, and poor Mr. Cummings must have been harried near to death by the chaos in the village."

"There is a gravestone in the churchyard," Edward said, his voice as rough as the slab of granite that loomed in his mind.

"I know. I have seen it." She spoke the words softly, but firmly. "Your father left Ravenswood that afternoon. I was . . . badly injured. Very weak. Why he left me alive, I cannot say. I'm sure he meant for me to die in that room. But I suppose he did not like to think of himself as a murderer. Or perhaps he felt that putting me out of my misery would have been too great a kindness."

Edward, on the other hand, felt certain if his father were still alive he could have dispatched him with his bare hands, and without a twinge of conscience—and he was no longer sure whether that made him a monster, or a hero.

"Eventually, I made it out of my prison, as you see, although I feared for a time that I might never find the strength. By the time I escaped, everything was . . . well, much as you see it. People had scattered. The house had been abandoned. I did not know if he would return. But I hoped with all my heart that *you* might," she said, stroking his cheek with cool fingertips. "So I stayed. I made my way, somehow, to the old hermitage. And I have been living there ever since. The mad old woman everyone knew only as Tessie."

"Did no one help you?"

She nodded. "Oh, certainly, now and again. On occasion, a man on the tramp happened by and chopped firewood in exchange for a meal or shelter. Mostly, though, I helped myself. I took food and whatever else I could manage from this house, and I had been putting by bits of my pin money for years, just in case. Pennies here and there; never so much that your father would notice. In time, I grew bold enough to venture into the village to buy more supplies, but by then most of the familiar faces were gone. And if those who remained ever suspected who I was," she added with an uncertain glance toward Garrick, "they never said a word."

"You should have gone to the magistrate, Mama," he said. "You should have denounced what my father did."

Her expression shifted. For the first time, he could hear a note of anger in her voice. "Wives have no recourse under the law, Edward. That would have brought down his wrath, nothing more."

With a creak of boot leather, he rose and sat beside his mother on the bench, one arm around her stooped shoulders. "I should've been here to help you."

"You were a child, Edward."

"I have not been a child for many years, Mama."

"I can see that." A smile creased her face. "My boy has become a man."

"Be proud of him," Mari urged from over his shoulder. "He has been a part of making something terrible into something bearable."

"A very small part," he protested.

"You survived, Mr. Edward," Mari insisted, folding her arms over her chest. "And you helped others do the same. Your mother has a right to know the sort of man her son has turned out to be. I'll not let you make your work seem less than it was—not to her, and not to yourself."

Mama still watched her with wide eyes.

"Thank you, Mari," Edward said, brushing aside her praise. "But I still don't understand how you knew who Tessie really was—did you suspect, somehow? Did you ask her to come here this morning?"

When Mari shook her head in surprised denial, Garrick stepped forward and mumbled, "No, sir," crumbs spraying from his lips as he spoke. He had been watching the reunion from the doorway, gnawing on a roll he had snatched from a nearby basket. "Mrs. Cary tol' me t' fetch her, right afore she left."

At the same moment, his mother said, "It was Charlotte who guessed."

"You've met Charlotte?"

"Mrs. Cary?" Mama's eyes were bewildered. "She told me she was the steward's wife."

The cross talk, each voice louder than the last, succeeded in rousing Jack from his faint. When he groaned behind them, Mama twisted slightly to bring him into her line of sight. "And who is that young man?"

"I'm not perfectly sure," Edward said, shoving the table so that it pushed Jack more upright. "But he's been telling everyone he's the long lost son of the Earl of Beckley."

Slowly, Jack lifted his head and cracked open one eye with a groan that owed more to last night's drinking than to Mari's supposed witchcraft. "I am. His eldest son, in point of fact."

"No." Mama's voice was firm, but there was uncertainty in her face. "This is my son," she said, placing her hand over Edward's where it lay on the table.

"I don't doubt it." Jack gave a bitter-sounding laugh. "That's been my luck, over the years." After sending Mari a sidelong glance, he rubbed the back of his head and said, "My name is Jacques Revard."

Edward felt, rather than heard, his mother's sharp intake of breath. "Revard?"

"You remember my mother, then?" Anger mingled with surprise in his expression.

"Yes. Of course. Louise Revard was my maid," she explained to Edward. "When I married, my papa told me I could take her with me to my new home. I was so relieved to have her by. Afterward, I—I wished I had not been so selfish. I wished I had left her behind. Once I fully understood the sort of man I had married . . ." Slowly, she shook her head. "It was too late. She came to me, and she told me she was with child . . . Your father dismissed her, of course. I did not know whether to plead for her, or whether it would only make things worse. And by then I had discovered I was expecting you . . ."

"The heir," Jack sneered.

"Yes."

Mari slipped into the chair closest to her, listening unabashedly, and after snagging the entire basket of rolls to himself, Garrick sank into the chair opposite and followed suit. "What became of her?" Mama asked in a whisper.

"She was forced to . . . hard times," Jack replied. Edward found himself almost glad when he did not elaborate. "When I grew old enough, I was apprenticed to a printer, who couldn't, or wouldn't, wrap his tongue around *Jacques*. That's how I became Jack. Once he discovered I had a knack for making a picture as a person described a scene or a face, he found a way to make a pretty penny off me. I drew charcoal sketches of people who'd died, for loved ones who couldn't afford a portrait. And a time or two, when there was a hunt for a wanted man, the constable brought me in to draw the face on the poster."

"That's how you knew about Charlotte," Edward said.

"Yes. Her stepson wanted her picture splashed about. I made the first sketch from his secretary's description . . . and when I saw her here, I knew."

"Knew what?" Mama asked. "Where is she? And what is this about her being Mrs. Cary?"

"She's gone, Mama. She left early this morning. And she is not Mrs. Cary. She was . . . *is* the Dowager Duchess of Langerton, apparently."

"Though a nobody by birth," Jack inserted. "Half French, like me."

"And caught up in quite a mess—"

Jack laughed. "You could say that."

"Though I did not know the extent of it until now," Edward finished, speaking over him. "When I first met her, it seemed clear to me that she needed a safe place to stay. I brought her to Ravenswood. But things here were in such a state of uncertainty that I was reluctant to announce who I was—even to her. So I told everyone I was the new steward. And to keep from raising further suspicions, we decided to claim we were man and wife."

As if she suspected all that their ruse might have entailed, Mama said, "All the more reason you should help her now, Neddy."

One of Jack's dark eyebrows arched, giving his face a sardonic cast. "He already has."

"Continue with your story, Revard," Edward demanded. "How is it you came to claim my name?"

"When Lord Beckley died a few months ago—"

Mama gasped. "He's dead?"

"So he says, Mama. I have not confirmed it, but from the state of things here, it would seem—"

"It's the truth," Jack insisted.

At his words, some of the pain and fear leached from his mother's face, leaving her looking years younger.

"When he died, the story was in the papers again . . . how his son had disappeared, how the loss had almost driven him mad with grief. He spent most of the last twenty years in London, living the quiet life of a respectable gentleman. Or so they say. Occasionally, a servant would escape to tell another tale," he added grimly.

"You'd always known he was your father, I suppose."

"Oh, yes. My mother made sure I knew. When she was gone, I set out to find him. I never got close enough to speak with him, but now and again, I caught a glimpse. I guessed who you were almost from the moment we met."

At that reminder of his resemblance to his father, Edward cut his gaze away.

"But when I read about the son who'd been missing for years, believed kidnapped, the title that would simply be tucked away and forgotten, the estate that would likely revert to the Crown . . . Well, none of it seemed fair. He had another son, one who was alive and well."

"And in need of ready cash."

"How was I to know anyone would be hurt by it?" he cried. "Everyone thought you were dead. So I hired a coach to bring me to Ravenswood, just to see what was what. Expected to find a few servants around. Not this. Not you. And certainly not the Disappearing Duchess."

"I'm sure she was not expecting you, either," said Edward. "That's why she ran."

"I am sorry for frightening her. But I could see there was nothing else here to help me. I needed that reward." He folded his arms on the table and his head drooped forward once more. "Now that's come to naught, too."

"A reward?" Mama asked. "For what?"

"Her return. The old duke left her something well beyond her dower," Edward explained. "And his son means not to stand for it. He hopes to have the will voided, and the marriage, too, if he can."

"Will he succeed?"

Jack shrugged. "There's folks that say the duke will do what he must to keep the money out of her hands."

A memory washed over Edward: Charlotte in the inn, glancing over his shoulder, terror filling her dark eyes. Had she been fleeing more than gossip? "Is she in danger?"

"She could be," Jack said. "Having met Langerton's servants, I'd say he's a man more feared than liked."

"What now?" Mama asked.

"I'll take the necessary steps to claim my title, then do whatever I must to bring Ravenswood back from the brink," Edward declared firmly. "No more sleeping in cold stone cottages for you."

At his words, an edge of bitterness crept into Jack's expression. Perhaps he was recalling his own mother's struggles. Edward's mother had spoken of Louise Revard with such affection. *Perhaps a good woman's blood was enough to temper the worst of his father's qualities*, Edward thought, glancing toward his own mother. He could not like Jack's behavior, but he was his brother, and he had been raised in a hard school. Under similar circumstances—without the gentle, guiding hand of Thomas Holderin—might he not have turned out much the same?

"And you're right, Jack. It's not fair. Your mother suffered through no fault of her own. You, too, have paid a steep price for what my—what *our* father did."

"It's a poor excuse for the way I've behaved these last days," Jack replied, sounding unexpectedly contrite. Then his shoulders sagged as the weight of it all seemed to hit him again. "But there's still my debts."

"How much?"

"Almost two hundred. Mostly doctor's bills, and what's owed to my mother's landlord. And the fee for her grave. I couldn't . . . I couldn't let her be buried as a pauper." When Edward gave a grim nod of understanding, Jack's expression grew sheepish. "There's also the tailor's bill, and the bootmaker's, of course—I knew I had to look the part, if I was to convince anyone I was Beckley."

Two hundred pounds. A paltry sum to force a man to play such a dangerous game. "I think some arrangement can be made to keep you out of debtor's prison," Edward said.

"Thank you." Jack's spine straightened, and some of the despair left his eyes. "Lord Beckley. And I hope I will have a chance to make amends with the lady someday. I owe you an apology, too, ma'am," he added, with a glance at Mari, who granted him reluctant forgiveness with the slightest tip of her head.

Edward felt as if he was seeing the real man for the first time, rather than the mask Jack had put on for a performance, a role part of him must have detested. Perhaps there was hope yet for Jacques Revard.

"Once things are settled," Edward said, "I'll do what I can to help you. Set you up in a business that would suit. Your own printmaker's shop, perhaps?"

Jack's eyes brightened further, though they still looked wary. "You'd do that? After what I've done?"

Edward smiled. "I've had a sister or two, over the years," he said, extending his hand toward Jack with a sideways glance for Mari. "But never a brother." Stunned, Jack took his hand, shook it. "But no more drinking to excess," he cautioned. "No more lies."

"No, sir!" Jack exclaimed, then pulled him into a hearty hug. At first, Edward did not know how to respond, but after a moment, he gave in and returned the embrace, slapping his brother on his back.

"That's all well and good, Neddy," Mama said, smiling, when they broke apart. "But when I asked what was next, I meant, what are you going to do about Charlotte?"

"Do? What can I do? If she wanted my help, she had an odd way of asking for it."

"Hmm. Did she say anything else before she left, Mr. Garrick?" Mama asked politely.

"'S-sorry,'" the man sputtered, spewing bread crumbs across the table. "She said *tell Mr. Cary I'm sorry*."

"Sorry for what?" *Deceiving him? Leaving him?* It would be nothing less than hypocrisy if he refused to forgive her for the former. But the latter required some explanation he was not sure he would ever get. And he could not say for certain that she had made the wrong choice, given what he had revealed to her.

Garrick's reply was delayed by another bout of coughing, followed by a shrug. "Don' know. Didn't ask."

Edward eyed the man for a long moment before glancing up at Mari. "Go on. Fetch Garrick a cup of coffee, won't you?"

One corner of Mari's mouth lifted in a smile. At the far end of the table, Jack gave a laughing sort of groan.

"Sometimes," his mother said gently, patting Edward's hand, "the people who need help the most are also the ones most determined not to involve others in their struggle. There must be an explanation. You mustn't just let her go," she insisted. "I like her."

"As do I," Mari chimed in.

His mother's assertion was hardly surprising. She had always had a warm heart. But Mari? Slow to trust, quick to judge . . . Her approval he had never expected.

"I—I like her, too," he said. A dreadful lie. What he felt for Charlotte was so much more. "But . . ."

But she had left him. After what they had shared. Without a word of explanation. What if the rumors about her motives were right? What if she had taken all she wanted from him?

"What if she doesn't want to be found?"

Mama only smiled. "She does. We all do."

Chapter 18

Mr. Sykes drove at a punishing pace, pausing only to change horses and stopping to sleep only for the few hours when the moon had set and the roads were too dark to continue.

"My livelihood's in Lon'on," he explained as he rousted himself from the driver's perch before dawn the next morning to hitch the horses to the coach. "I can't afford to dally." Uncurling herself from the musty coach seat that had served as her bed, Charlotte prepared to set out once more.

But beyond the headache and backache it gave her, Charlotte had no complaints to make about the speed of their journey. At just past noon, she caught the first glimpse of the great city on the horizon. The sight filled her with sudden dread. She was exhausted, faint with hunger, filthy—again. If she arrived at Blakemore House in this state, she would only be giving support to Robert's case.

She slid open the panel behind the driver's seat. "Mr. Sykes?"

"Aye, missus?"

"If it's not too much trouble, I wish to go to Clerkenwell."

Without slowing the horses, Sykes craned around and peered down into the narrow opening. "You sure 'bout that, missus?"

"I have a—a friend there. Sister to a butcher."

Disbelief sketched across his face, but he shrugged and turned back to his team. "Whatever you say, missus."

Clerkenwell was a part of town through which she had never traveled, and she had no idea, really, what she was looking for. It was, at least, a more respectable area than she had been led to believe. Mostly the cramped but decent homes of craftspeople and men of business, with shops—a watchmaker, a milliner, a bookstore—scattered about. Aunt Penhurst would have called it noisy and crowded.

To Charlotte, it looked like the sort of place in which a person might simply disappear, for better or worse.

On the edge of the district, as they drew closer to Smithfield, the wares in the storefronts were no less eye-catching, albeit slightly more stomach churning. An array of bulging-eyed sturgeon were spread out beneath the fishmonger's sign. Hastily plucked geese hung by their scrawny, web-toed feet at the poulterer's.

"Here's your shop, maybe, missus," Sykes called out, stopping the coach at the mouth of a narrow alleyway that must lead down to the shambles. Here, the metallic tang of blood was so sharp in the air she could almost taste it when she stepped uncertainly from the coach. "Leastways, I can't take you no further." Before she could protest, he had chirruped to his horses and was rattling away down the street.

With a heavy heart, she entered a butcher's shop and asked after the family of Jane Hamilton. Her question was met with a cold stare from the woman behind the counter, whether for her now shabby dress or for the accent with which she spoke, Charlotte could not be certain. The only reply was a prim shake of the head.

She emerged into the midday heat of the alley, shook the sawdust from her hems, and marched farther down the street. Around her, voices jabbered in something that might as well have been another language.

"Coo. Where to, ma'am?" The boy who spoke at her elbow couldn't have been more than seven or eight, scrawny, with a dirt-smudged face. But he tugged respectfully at his woolen cap.

She knew his offer of help might well disguise a plan to lead her down a blind alley to rob her. Well, he had chosen his victim poorly, then, for she had nothing. "I'm looking for the family of Jane Hamilton," she said, doing her best to disguise her accent. "They have a butcher shop."

He gave an eager nod. "Aye. This way, ma'am."

And, as she was out of options, she followed.

By the time he had led her down two more streets and around several corners, her feet ached and she was thoroughly disoriented. Why had she ever imagined this would be better, safer, than going to Blakemore House? If that gossip columnist could see the Disappearing Duchess now, he would certainly have a story to tell.

"Your Grace?"

Although she heard the words, they did not immediately register as being addressed to her. She was so intent on not losing sight of the boy, she brushed aside the hand that had touched her arm, to hurry after him.

But the hand was persistent. "Your Grace? Is that you?"

Charlotte turned and by some miracle found herself face-to-face with Jane.

"Why, ma'am! You're white as a sheet. Are you harmed?"

"No, Jane. No. Is there—is there somewhere I could sit down?"

Jane led her a few yards farther, to a short flight of soot-stained steps, and Charlotte sank gratefully onto the middle one. "My sister's house is just here, ma'am. Come up, once you've caught your breath."

The boy was leaning against the area railing. "There y' are, Miss Jane."

"An' what mischief are you up to this fine day, Jem?"

"Why, none 't all," he insisted, laying his hand across his chest as if swearing an oath. "Jus' helpin' this 'ere lady what's been lookin' for you."

"Yes," Charlotte managed to say. "That's right. Thank you. But I'm afraid I haven't anything with which to pay you for your assistance."

"Cor, missus. Tweren't nothin'," he said with a wide grin and went scampering on his way.

Jane put a hand beneath Charlotte's elbow and helped her to rise. "Do come inside, Your Grace, or people will begin to wonder."

Far from eager to draw more attention her way, Charlotte followed Jane into the house. "It really isn't necessary for you to keep calling me Your Grace." It would only add to the speculation.

"But, ma'am! It's only proper. That wicked duke hasn't succeeded in taking away your due just yet. Sally, fetch your mother." The last remark was addressed to a girl of perhaps four or five who was staring wide-eyed at Charlotte from around the newel post. When she didn't immediately move, Jane spoke more sharply. "Sally!"

"Yes, Aunt Jane." With a toss of her dark ringlets, the child swung onto the stairs and ascended them with frequent backward glances.

In a few moments, she returned, clutching the hand of a woman with the same brown hair and eyes as Jane. "What's happened? Sally said—"

"Your Grace, may I present my sister, Catherine Yates? Kitty, this"—she accented the word with a sweep of her arm, as if Charlotte were an item on display—"is the Duchess of Langerton."

"Oh." Mrs. Yates grew pale. "Oh, my."

The curtsy into which she lowered herself was so deep she required her sister's aid to rise again, and the absurdity of the situation—a clean, well-dressed, respectable woman prostrating herself to the dirty, disheveled daughter of nobody—made Charlotte begin to giggle. And once she had begun, she found she could not stop. The hiccups of laughter soon gave way to tears, which made the good Mrs. Yates even more frantic.

"Here, my lady—er, no, that's not right, is it?—here's a chair, ma'am. Should I fetch some smelling salts?" she asked, turning away, then back again. "I don't—I don't believe I have any smelling salts, now that I think of it. I've never been prone to fainting, myself. Maybe an onion? Or a—uh—"

"Kitty! Just let her breathe for a moment," Jane said, handing Charlotte a handkerchief. "Can't you see she's had a difficult time of it?" At that moment, two boys whooped through the hall from the back and ran up the stairs, the elder gripping some prize snatched from the kitchen, the younger trying and failing to get his share. "Boys! Richard, Charles! Stop your tomfoolery this instant!"

Charlotte waved the handkerchief in a feeble hand, trying to forestall Jane's protest. The tears became laughter again. It was good to see Jane among the loving chaos of her family.

"Would you—that is, do you think you could manage the stairs, my—er, Your Grace?" Mrs. Yates asked.

Jane added, "There's a proper sitting room upstairs, if the children haven't made a toss of it."

"You're too kind," Charlotte said, and surrendered herself to their care. Curious children were shooed from the best parlor, though they persisted in peeking through the crack in the door at the visitor. A maid brought tea, which Charlotte fell upon with such unladylike eagerness that an invitation to dinner soon followed. Finally, after a great deal of whispering with her sister and the maid in the corridor, Mrs. Yates extended the offer of a room for the night.

"*Merci*," said Charlotte, which resulted in a surreptitious exchange of glances.

Perhaps an hour later, when the bustle of interest surrounding her arrival had died down, when Mrs. Yates had gone to urge the cook to her best efforts, and the maid had fetched up hot water, Charlotte and Jane were left alone in the bedroom Charlotte had been given.

"I didn't think I'd ever see you again, ma'am." Jane poured the water in the basin and made as if to help Charlotte out of her dress.

Too tired to protest, Charlotte lifted her arms like a child and allowed herself to be washed and dressed and combed and tressed. "It really was not my intention to come here, to inconvenience your family. But I—I did not know where else to turn."

"Don't you worry about Kitty and the rest," Jane mumbled around a mouthful of hairpins. "This will give them conversation for the rest of the year."

"Oh, but they mustn't! What if Robert—what if the Duke of Langerton finds out and makes trouble for them?"

Jane smiled indulgently. "He's not often spotted in Clerkenwell, ma'am, truth be told."

"Well, no. I don't suppose . . ."

"And Kitty'll have the name mixed up. One side of the street will hear that Lady Somesuch came to call, and the other side will be sayin' it was the Queen herself."

Charlotte wrinkled her brow, uncertain whether Jane was teasing. "You weren't . . . he did not cause you any difficulty, then?"

"Pshaw. He's enough to do, what with disappearin' duchesses an' the like," she said with a wink. "He had his secretary out to yell at me one morning, told me lyin' was a sin, and stealin' too—"

"Stealing?"

"Your trunk went on to Blakemore House, 'course, but I kept your bag right with me. Told 'im it was mine and he hadn't any cause to go poking his nose in it. Well, eventually, he gave up, and I haven't heard another peep, 'cept a note sent round with my last quarter's wages. See for yourself."

Reaching around, she fumbled through a small drawer in the top of the dressing table, and Charlotte realized the room they were in belonged to Jane. "I can't—you mustn't give up your room for me, Jane."

"Don't think anything of it, ma'am. I'm up and down the stairs to the nursery so many times of an evening, I might as well sleep there as here," she insisted, laughing. "Now, see." She extended the paper for Charlotte's inspection. "Ten pounds, minus one pound six for missing bag and contents," she read, and laughed again.

"Do you—?" Charlotte hardly dared hope. "Do you still have the bag?"

"'Course. I hung the dresses in the press, but everything else is just as you left it." This necessitated rummaging through the bottom of a corner cupboard, but when Jane reemerged, she bore a small carpet-sided satchel in her arms and laid it easily in Charlotte's lap. "La, ma'am. There you be. Safe and sound."

With one trembling finger, Charlotte traced a pattern in the rough nap of the fabric. Inside, she could feel the sharp corners of what could only be a book. "Thank you, Jane. I'm afraid I left your bag behind in Gloucestershire."

"Gloucestershire. That's west, ain't it?" Jane asked. Charlotte nodded. "And is the bit about the man true, too, then?"

"Man?"

Jane slid her fingers into her drawer once more and this time withdrew a folded newspaper whose print was distressingly familiar to Charlotte. When Jane held it out for her to see, Charlotte read once more the words about Robert's suit. But this time, her eyes traveled farther down the page.

> *Meanwhile, the Disappearing Duchess was last seen headed west in the company of a dark-haired stranger. No doubt she hopes he is possessed of a cure for her late husband's "infirmities."*

Licking suddenly dry lips, she tried to find an answer to Jane's question. "I—I—"

That stammering syllable seemed to be all the confirmation Jane required. "Well, I hope he was handsome, ma'am," she said, with a sly smile. "For your sake."

Charlotte recalled Jane hinting, none too gently, that Charlotte was now free to use a widow's license and take a lover. Could indulge in a carefree *affaire*. Of course Jane would not have been the only one to leap to that conclusion.

By leaving to avoid one scandal, Charlotte had created another: She had become the Disappearing Duchess, who had escaped to taste the forbidden fruits wedded life had denied her. Or at least hoped to deceive the courts into believing her marriage had been consummated.

By giving in to her desire for Edward, she had turned terrible gossip into truth.

With trembling fingers, Charlotte laid aside the newspaper clipping. "He was."

"Are you all right, ma'am?" Jane asked.

"Yes," she lied. "Just tired."

"I'll leave you to rest up a bit before dinner, ma'am. Shall I?"

"Please, Jane. You're not my servant now. You—well, you've been a better friend to me than even you know. And I hope you'll consider me your friend, too."

With a bright smile, Jane turned to leave. "Ooh, la. Fancy me, friends with a duchess." But she sounded pleased by the suggestion, nonetheless.

Hardly had the door latched before Charlotte reached into the bag to withdraw the battered old book, brushing with one trembling fingertip the cracked spine that had once been touched with gilt, broken when her uncle had thrown it at her with words he had intended to sting. *Tu es exactement comme ta mère.* You are just like your mother.

When Edward learned what she was believed to have done, would he, too, see things in just that light? Would he think she had gone to his bed merely in hopes of preserving her fortune?

Slowly, she opened the volume to find the rest of her dearly bought legacy untouched. Between the book's worn pages lay banknotes. Scores of them. Several hundred pounds in all, almost as if George had anticipated that she might have need of ready money.

If she had never been separated from this book and its contents, she would be living alone, somewhere far from the watchful eyes of Society. Even here, in Clerkenwell, the eyes were rather too intent for her tastes.

But if she had never been separated from this book and its contents, she would never have met Edward. Would have gone on believing that men like him—men who were not afraid to get their hands dirty, who faced adversity and were willing to do anything to save others from a similar fate—only existed in stories meant for children and fools.

A fat teardrop splatted onto the book, temporarily restoring one small circle of its faded vermillion leather cover to a deeper luster. Two more tears followed in rapid succession. With the hem of her sleeve, she tried to wipe away the evidence of her foolishness.

By now, Edward must know all about the Disappearing Duchess. And she felt certain the Earl of Beckley wasn't sitting somewhere mooning and crying over his loss. More likely, he was breathing a sigh of relief that she was gone.

One night together. For a woman who claimed to crave her independence, it ought to have been enough.

How could she have let herself hope there might be more?

Gathering the book to her chest, she curled atop the coverlet on the narrow bed and wept until sleep claimed her.

Chapter 19

Although Edward had known it would involve a deal of discomfort and a little bit of luck, he had hoped to be in London late the next day. Instead—with none of the luck, but all of the discomfort, including a broken carriage wheel, a lame horse, and a drunk for a driver—he did not arrive until the morning after that.

Further proof that the supposedly romantic quest on which his mother, brother, and Mari had urged him would likely turn out to have been nothing more than a fool's errand.

The livery where Jack had hired Sykes and his coach could provide no leads as to his whereabouts. One man claimed Sykes had not yet returned, while another insisted he had already gone out again. Charlotte might be anywhere in London. If she had exited Sykes's coach somewhere along the journey, as Edward half suspected, she might be anywhere.

Though it was the last place he expected to find her, he found himself wandering through the quiet streets of Mayfair to clear his head. Near Grosvenor Square, he paused before the town house belonging to the Earl of Beckley.

In it, according to Jack, their father had lived a quiet, respectable life. His parlor maids and kitchen girls had probably not been so lucky. Edward knew better than to be deceived by an elegant façade. Father had always preferred to indulge his darkest impulses behind closed doors.

Edward had no desire to see inside.

A pair of smartly dressed ladies eyed him uncertainly as they passed. In desperate need of a wash and shave, he did not look as if he belonged here. Not now, certainly. Perhaps not ever. At Ravenswood, at least, he felt he had some purpose, could do some good. But live the life of a Town dandy? Never.

Except, of course, he would have responsibilities here, too. A house and its staff. Service in the House of Lords. In London, he could build the connections that ought already to have been forged at Eton or Oxford, cemented in the coffee room at White's.

Or attempt to build them, at least. Without an ally from among his own class, it would be at best a difficult task to find his way in the world that was his by birth. Perhaps impossible. And rather than enlist an ally, he had entangled himself with the Disappearing Duchess. Linking his ancient family name to her tarnished reputation would double his burden on this uphill climb.

Surely the wisest thing would be to return to Ravenswood and say she had eluded his pursuit.

But when, with respect to Charlotte, had he ever done what was wise?

Something thumped against his knee. When he looked down, he saw a tiny perambulator, of the sort a child might use for a doll. Except this one contained a gray cat, its striped face framed by the frill of a baby's bonnet, one white paw poking from the top of the blanket in which it had been swaddled. He could not imagine the creature was pleased by the predicament in which it found itself, although its green eyes were remarkably unperturbed as it blinked up at him. It seemed to be accustomed to such travails.

Pattering footsteps made him look up. A girl with golden-brown curls, her own bonnet nowhere in sight, was chasing after the escaped pram. He expected tears, but instead, a fierce frown lined her little face. "Now, Thomas," she scolded, "I told you to stay put."

A second set of footsteps—most certainly not those of a child—came running after. "Rissa, my pet, what did I say about holding on tight? I beg your pardon, sir, we—Cary?"

At the familiar voice, Edward froze. He lifted his gaze higher yet. Surely his ears were playing tricks on him. "Fairfax?"

But it was he: the fair-haired man with the mysterious past who had shown up one day at Harper's Hill looking for work—though Edward had been quite certain the fellow had never done a day's work in his life—and stayed there for nearly three years. Almost as if he had been looking for a place to hide. In those years, he had assisted Edward in whatever had needed to be done, and as he had arrived shortly after the death of Mr. Holderin, his help had been invaluable. But as much as he had helped them, Edward sometimes had felt as though Fairfax had needed them more. Edward had been sorry to see the man leave, but equally certain he had had good reason for returning home at last.

"It *is* you," Fairfax said and clapped him heartily on the back. "I never thought you'd leave Antigua. Or rather, I never thought Miss Holderin would allow it."

"She is here now. In England. And—and married."

Fairfax's pale eyes lit with surprise. "Fancy that."

Edward felt a tug on the hem of his coat and glanced down. The little girl was staring up at him. "Who're you?" she demanded. "An' how do you know my papa?"

"Your—?" Edward looked from Fairfax to the girl, who must be three or four years old, born—though presumably not conceived—while Fairfax had been in Antigua. "I'm Edward Cary, Miss Fairfax," he said with a tip of his hat. "At your service."

"I'm Lady Clarissa Sutliffe," she corrected primly as she curtsied.

Sutliffe? Not Fairfax? And *Lady*?

"I'm afraid there were more than a few secrets being kept all those years ago, Cary," Fairfax said, sounding somewhat abashed. "Please, meet my daughter. And allow me to introduce myself properly, as well. St. John Sutliffe. Viscount Fairfax."

Before Edward could rise from his formal bow of greeting, Fairfax had clasped his hand firmly between his own in a hearty handshake, a warmer gesture than he had grown to expect from the generally reserved man. Looking at the little girl by his side, it was not difficult to imagine what had produced the change in him.

"Yes," Edward agreed, with a faint smile. "There were a few secrets."

There must be—or have been—a Lady Fairfaix, too, he supposed. Had she played some role in Fairfax's decision to fly to the West Indies? Although Fairfax was cool by nature, Edward had never imagined him the sort of man who would abandon his wife or neglect his duty to his child.

"My wife is at home in Hampshire, I'm afraid. You must come visit us there when you have the time. After listening to all my tales, Sarah has expressed a great interest in meeting you, but I told her you weren't likely to return to England. She's—"

"She's going to give me a baby brother soon," Lady Clarissa proclaimed, with something very like a scowl.

"Or a sister," Fairfax reminded her.

Edward could not entirely stifle the laugh that rose to his already upturned lips. "You've been busy since you left the West Indies."

Fairfax laughed, too. "More than you know. Come, come. Sutliffe House is just the other side of the square. Won't you visit with us? Regrettably, my father is away—"

"Your . . . father?" But Fairfax had called himself a viscount. That could only mean . . .

"The Marquess of Estley, yes. He's in Hampshire with Sarah."

Edward had never really been one to stand on ceremony. And he had long ago ceased to think of the fact that he was the son of an earl with anything like pride of place. When the crisis of harvest had been upon them, he had often worked in the field alongside the other men. But . . . "Do you mean to say, I once ordered the son of a marquess to cut sugarcane?"

"No," Fairfax countered, gesturing for Edward to walk with him, while Lady Clarissa pushed the miniature pram ahead. "You once showed the son of a marquess what it means to be involved with the property one is charged with managing. You never stood to the side when there was work to be done. There's many a nobleman who could learn from your example—and when you come to Lynscombe, I hope you'll find it's a lesson I learned well."

Rounding another corner, they stopped in front of a set of wide steps. Fairfax handed the cat to his daughter with one hand and hoisted the pram with the other. "We're short a nursery maid," he explained, slightly abashed, as a footman bowed them into the marble-tiled entry and relieved him of his burden. "I brought Clarissa to town to stay with Sarah's parents for a few weeks. What brings you to London?"

Edward hesitated. "A matter of business. Is there somewhere we could talk?"

"Of course." Once a maid had come to take Clarissa and her preternaturally patient cat upstairs, Fairfax invited Edward into what must be his father's study. "I know it's early, but"—his eyes scanned Edward's travel-weary shabbiness—"you look as if you could use a drink." He waved one hand in the direction of a sideboard topped with an array of decanters.

"Thank you, yes." Edward eased himself into a deep leather chair. The room was warm and darkly furnished, a thoroughly masculine domain; its appointments oozed privilege and wealth. No doubt, a visitor would find a similar room in every house on this square. Rooms from which men of power orchestrated their lives. Including the one in which his father had debauched himself to an early death.

He took a sip from the glass Fairfax offered. Real French brandy. Nothing like that served in roadside inns near Chippenham.

What had inspired Fairfax to leave all this behind, even for a time? But that was, given his own choices, rather a ridiculous question to be asking. And despite the time spent in a far different world, Fairfax looked right at home in this one, every inch the English aristocrat.

Could he be the ally Edward needed?

"Fairfax," he said, setting aside the tumbler and leaning forward, elbows propped on his knees, "I have something to confess."

"What's that?"

After weighing his words for a moment, he told him. All of it. About his father. Why he had left England. What was left of the home to which he had returned. The woman who had made him believe it could be made whole again.

The woman who had made him believe *he* could be made whole again.

And then had left him, and shown him the folly of such a belief.

As he listened to Edward's story, Fairfax twirled the bottle stopper between his fingers, watching its facets catch the light. When Edward finished speaking, he expected his friend to ask about the Beckley title, or his plans for claiming it. Instead, he asked, "Does the lady have a name?"

The answer required another sip of fortitude from his glass. "Charlotte Blakemore."

"The Disappearing Duchess?" The heavy glass knob slipped from his fingers and landed on the plush-carpeted floor with a thud.

"Yes."

For a long moment, Fairfax said nothing more, though Edward suspected him of fighting the impulse to say a great deal. His words, when they came, were restrained to a simple observation. "I believe her aunt resides nearby. On Brook Street."

"I cannot think she would go there," Edward said, recalling the stories Charlotte had told.

"No," Fairfax agreed. "Certainly not if she had any inkling of the sorts of things Lady Penhurst has been saying since her niece's disappearance."

Edward started. "*Lady* Penhurst?"

"Mm, yes. Very poor *ton*. But then, she's been trying for years to distance herself from her brother's gadabout ways. You know, of course, that your duchess is the Earl of Belmont's daughter—his *natural* daughter," he added in a softer tone, as if he feared to impart unpleasant information.

This time, Edward tried to mask his surprise. He failed, but Fairfax was too much of a gentleman to remark upon it. Why would Charlotte have left out that crucial detail of her parentage? In terms of her social standing, it ought to have made an important distinction, despite her illegitimacy. Apparently, however, it had not. People had, no doubt, taken their cues from the behavior of her aunt.

"And of course Blakemore House—the Duke of Langerton's residence—is just a few doors away. She was meant to have the use of it, according to her husband's will. Would she go there, do you think?"

"And challenge her stepson?" He shook his head. "I can't imagine she would." Or perhaps he simply didn't want to believe she would do anything so foolhardy. "The truth is, I haven't the faintest idea where to begin looking for her. I suspect she does not want to be found—at least, not by me."

Fairfax's brows quirked as he looked Edward up and down.

"I suppose I don't look much like the heir to an earldom," Edward acknowledged, wondering if his friend doubted the truth of his story.

"No. You look like a man who feared any delay would cost him something far more important. Come," he said, rising. "While you freshen up, I'll see what I can learn. Our housekeeper always seems to know the latest gossip."

As they climbed the stairs, Fairfax laid a hand on his shoulder and said, "Just remember, you ran away once. As did I. Maybe everyone does, at some point."

"I ran because I felt helpless," Edward protested. "Because I believed someone I loved would be better off if I left."

"Exactly." Fairfax's toe paused on the next step, giving that single word a moment to sink in. "But in the end," he added, not looking back as he resumed his ascent, "the most important thing was finding your way home."

Charlotte woke early the next morning—not refreshed, exactly, but resolved. Rising, she went to the washbasin to splash her face, then pressed cool fingertips to her eyelids. Her eyes felt as if she had stepped in the path of someone sweeping and caught a broomfull of dust in the face. Nevertheless, she smoothed her hair and pulled one of her own gowns from the cupboard.

The black crape made her think of George, as it was of course intended to do. How much had happened in the short time since he had died. How much had changed. Had she betrayed her husband's memory by giving herself to Edward? Certainly, Society would see it that way. But she rather thought that George would have winked and told her to be happy.

Pray God she had not destroyed her best chance at happiness by concealing part of the truth.

Although it was early, the house was stirring. Footsteps thundered above her head—what she judged as the likely location of the nursery. Once she had packed her few things in her valise, nestling the book and its contents carefully among them, she peered up the empty staircase and then ventured one floor higher, in search of Jane.

She found her tying the younger boy's shoes, while the other eyed the lace-edged handkerchief he had been given, as if its use was unfamiliar to him. "Now, boys, you mustn't—oh! Your Grace." Jane tugged on the older boy's wrist to draw him down into a bow. Sally wandered in, covered head to toe in jam, and the baby chose that moment to begin crying. Beneath the ruckus, she heard Jane sigh.

"Here," Charlotte said, snatching the unused handkerchief from the older boy and applying it to Sally's sticky hands. "Let me tell you a story while your aunt Jane tends the baby."

The elder boy—Richard, wasn't it?—shot her a doubtful look, but Sally and Charles gamely came to her side as she wedged herself into one of the tiny chairs at the nursery table. She knew lots of stories, had regaled her younger French cousins with them time and again. But she had never told one aloud in English. Her stumbling start seemed to reward Richard's skepticism, but a few moments in, she had all three of them at her feet, rapt. Even the baby stopped crying as Jane came to the edge of the circle and stood, rocking and bouncing her, as she listened.

"Another!" Sally demanded when she had finished, and before Jane could admonish her niece, Charlotte launched into a second. At the request for a third, however, she shook her head. "I cannot. I have something I must attend to this morning."

There was some grumbling, but Jane prompted them to remember their manners. "Thank you, ma'am," they each mumbled, with obvious reluctance.

"No, thank *you*." She smiled down at them. "It has been too long since I told those stories." She had almost forgotten their magic.

At a nod from their aunt, the three eldest scurried downstairs to greet their parents for the day. "Where did you learn those marvelous tales, ma'am?" Jane asked when they had gone. "Did you read them in a book?"

"Why, no. They came from my own head."

Jane's lips quirked in surprise. "I'd no idea you've a way with children, ma'am. You ought to write those stories down."

With a small smile, Charlotte accepted the compliment, exaggerated though it was. Perhaps it was possible her wild imagination wasn't entirely a curse, as Aunt Penhurst had always claimed. What was it Edward had called it? Her *gift for inventiveness*.

Would he call it that still?

"Now, what was that urgent business you spoke of?" Jane asked.

Charlotte stood and smoothed her inky skirts. "I have to say goodbye, Jane."

"Where are you going?" she demanded with wide eyes. "To your aunt? Back to France?"

"If I tell you this time, Jane, you must promise not to try to stop me."

"Not to—*him*?"

"I'm afraid I must."

After a long moment, in which Jane struggled valiantly to contain her impulse to argue, she at last nodded and turned to go call a cab. "Are you sure, ma'am?" she asked, pausing on the threshold.

Blinking away a prickle of tears, Charlotte managed a steadying breath. "Not in the least, Jane. But I really haven't any choice."

She would never be free if she did not confront Robert—and perhaps not even if she did.

Chapter 20

Though it was far too early for a social call, the door of Blakemore House opened promptly to her knock, almost as if she had been expected. She had not, of course. That much was clear when the butler, an unfamiliar man with droopy features, actually gasped when she lifted her dark veil to reveal her face.

"You're—Your Grace," he corrected with a bow so abrupt it threatened to snap him neatly in two.

"I wish to speak with the duke." From whence this sudden show of firmness had come, she did not know. She felt certain the driver of the hackney must have been able to hear her knees knocking together.

"I shall inform His Grace you are here," he said, offering no practiced pretense that the duke might not be at home.

"No." She stepped up beside him as he turned to ascend the stairs. "I do not wish to be announced. Take me to him."

Something like panic flickered behind the man's sad eyes. Was she condemning him to lose his place over this? But he jerked his head in a stiff nod. "Very good, ma'am. Right this way."

He led her through the unfamiliar house that was to have been hers. In a small study, which must adjoin the duke's private chambers, Robert sat in his dressing gown perusing a freshly pressed newspaper. "Have I not made myself clear, Aimes?" he said without looking up. "I do not wish to be disturbed in this room."

The answering sound that issued from Aimes—an attempt, Charlotte thought, to clear his throat, though it sounded as if the man had tied his cravat too tightly—at last caused Robert to lift his eyes.

She had succeeded in catching him off guard, at least, though he recovered quickly. He flicked a dismissive hand in Aimes's direction, causing the butler to scuttle from the room. He did not rise.

"Well, well. So you've decided to come out of hiding."

"I was not hiding," Charlotte said, thinking of Tessie. "I was surviving. How dare you set men to watch me, to follow me, to *hunt* me."

Robert pressed four fingers to his chest. "I? I did no such thing. I was quite worried for your safety. I offered a suitable recompense if anyone could supply any . . . reassuring information."

"Information useful to your suit, you mean."

When he lowered his hand and smoothed his palm over the newspaper, his father's signet ring winked. She was not deceived by the calmness of his movements. "Why have you come, Charlotte?"

"To ask you to drop your suit. For your father's sake," she added, though it seemed futile to try to prick his conscience. She had seen few signs of mourning in the house. "I am not so naïve as to imagine you would do it for mine."

At last he stood and moved two steps closer. "And I suppose in exchange you'll give up your claim on my father's estate," he sneered.

"Yes."

She watched as he absorbed the word. His lips parted, his eyes widened, and some of his sneer melted away. "*Yes?*"

Refusing to repeat what she knew he had heard, she simply met his still-contemptuous gaze with a steady one of her own.

It was confirmation enough.

In a series of quick movements, he brought pen, ink, and paper from his desk and rang the bell for his valet, who was instructed to fetch Aimes. When Robert handed her the quill, she scratched out a few words and began to sign her name.

"Wait."

Once the servants had been assembled as witnesses to her signature, she gave it, then handed the paper to Robert. Once the butler and the valet had been dismissed, he held the document up to the window for more light by which to study her words. "Yes," he murmured, more to himself than to her. "Yes, I think this will serve."

How could dear, sweet George's child be so greedy? But fathers and sons were not always cut from the same cloth.

Edward was proof of that.

"I did not marry your father for his money, Robert."

"Mm?" He did not lift his eyes from the all-important paper. She doubted he was even listening. But after a moment, he asked, "Why, then?"

"Because he cared. About me. Had he been a ditch-digger instead of a duke, I could not have refused his offer. But that was not the most important gift he gave me."

Those words caught Robert's attention. "Something not in the will?"

She almost laughed. "No. Something quite intangible. He believed I deserved happiness." Beneath her glove, she twisted her wedding band. *Amore digna.* Worthy of love. "I realize now, he was trying to teach me to believe it, too. And I do. Now, you have what you wanted, so call off your dogs. Leave me in peace."

Then she turned and marched from the room, wondering as the door latched behind her if he would accede to that simple wish.

In the entryway, Aimes held the door, then followed her to her waiting cab. "I was honored to serve the late duke, Your Grace. May I make so bold as to offer my condolences?"

"Thank you, Mr. Aimes." She dropped her black veil back into place.

"I understood Blakemore House was to be your home."

"No."

"Ah." Aimes bowed and opened the carriage door. "Then I am sorry for that, too, ma'am."

These unexpected expressions of regret, of sympathy, almost caused her to stumble on the steps. Perhaps not everyone thought Robert was in the right, after all.

"Where to, ma'am?" the driver called down.

Somewhat self-consciously, she jingled her reticule. She had sufficient funds to last for quite some time, if she was frugal. Enough to take her anywhere. She thought fleetingly of France, and the little cottage in the Lake District of which she had once dreamed—had it been only two weeks ago?

But those were no longer the destination she had in mind.

Fairfax was as good as his word. Edward had just finished scraping the last flecks of shaving foam from his jaw and was donning a fresh shirt when his friend knocked on the door.

"We're going to Blakemore House."

Edward's fingers fumbled the knot of his cravat. "Why?"

"She's been sighted."

"By whom?"

"Langerton's valet," Fairfax explained as they hurried down the stairs. "I assumed he was hanging about the kitchen to flirt with the new parlor maid. He's a preening dandy—probably has girls in every servants' attic in Mayfair dreaming of him." Out the door and onto the square, without even stopping for their hats. "But this time, he was fit to burst with real news: The Disappearing Duchess just paid a call on the duke."

"Is she there still?" His own breathlessness alarmed him. It had nothing to do with their hurried pace.

"He didn't know," Fairfax said as he rapped on the door.

The man who answered his knock replied to their inquiry with a butler's typical restraint. "I'll see if His Grace is receiving callers."

Then he held out a salver for their cards, and Edward was brought up short.

Fairfax, however, quickly withdrew one of his own and dropped it on the tray. "Accompanied by Lord Beckley," he instructed the butler to add, and in another moment they were alone in the entry, which was every bit as stately as that of Sutliffe House—more so, perhaps, as there were no precocious little girls, or costumed cats, or toy perambulators in sight. In fact, Edward might be tempted to call the space cold. Difficult to imagine Charlotte here, in a mud-spattered dress with her hair half tumbling down. But perhaps that had only been her country costume. No doubt she had worn quite a different one as Duchess of Langerton.

Still unsure as to why she had left Ravenswood, he could invent no explanation for why she had come here, of all places. Unless, of course, she intended to boast to her stepson of how she had taken a lover and thwarted his plan.

"Don't worry, my friend," Fairfax said, misinterpreting his expression of uncertainty. "If Langerton knows where she's gone, we'll get it out of him."

Before Edward could reply, the butler had returned to show them upstairs. Behind a door opened by a footman, Langerton sat at breakfast, dressed for riding, the day's post spread around him. With a nod to dismiss another servant standing by the sideboard, Langerton peered over his table at them with shrewd eyes. "Lord Fairfax," he said with a nod. "I believe I've seen you around town." Fairfax bowed. "And . . ." The duke fingered the edge of Fairfax's card as he studied Edward.

"Edward Cary, Duke. Heir to the Earl of Beckley."

"The one who's been missing for twenty-odd years?"

"The same."

With a skeptical twitch of his lips, Langerton resumed eating. "What can I do for you gentlemen this morning? I know nothing of the late earl's estate, or any claimants to it."

Shaking his head at Edward, whose expression had deepened into a scowl, Fairfax said, "We came to inquire about the duchess."

"My wife is well. In general, however, she does not see callers at this hour."

"Not your wife," Edward explained, drawing something like patience from the steadier presence of his friend, but unable to keep the edge from his voice. "Your stepmother. The one they call the Disappearing Duchess."

Langerton ceased to chew, although he did not lower his fork. "You'll not find her here."

"Do you know where might we find her?" Fairfax asked, all politeness.

But Edward spoke at the same time. "Did not the terms of your father's will name this house as her place of residence?"

If the table had not been solid mahogany, the force with which Langerton pushed away from it would have sent it scraping across the floor. "What do you know of my father's will, *Mr. Cary*?" he demanded as he rose and stepped toward him. He was not an especially tall man, but he was wiry, and fit enough to stand his ground.

Edward did not back down. "Only as much as everyone else." Between what Jack had told him and the information Fairfax had added, he had formed a far more complete picture of the difficult situation into which Charlotte had been thrust by her late husband's demise—and the bequest to which the man's son objected so strenuously. "It's been in all the papers. As you know."

"Yes, well . . ." Mustering a calmer air, Langerton tugged his coat sleeve into place. "My father's health was regrettably poor. If you have read the papers, then you know that he was in no condition to be making decisions about the disposition of his property, near the end."

"I know that's your position." Fairfax sounded remarkably unperturbed. "But from what I've heard, his friends object to your characterization of him as 'mad as a hatter.'"

A muscle twitched along Langerton's jaw. "May I ask how any of this concerns either of you? We have only a passing acquaintance, Lord Fairfax," he drawled, then flicked a disparaging glance at Edward. "And with Mr. Cary, of course, I have none at all."

"You may rest assured, Langerton: I want none," Edward said.

But the duke was now studying Edward's features, as if seeing him for the first time. "Beckley," he murmured. "*Beckley*. The earl's estate is in the West Country, is it not?" Without waiting for an answer, he gave a low, humorless laugh. "Well, I'll be damned. *You're* the dark-haired stranger the papers have been talking about."

"Tell me where she's gone," Edward demanded.

Langerton lifted one shoulder. "I neither know nor care."

"Until very recently, you cared enough to offer a reward for information leading to her return," Fairfax observed. "What's changed?"

With a flourish, Langerton withdrew a folded paper from his breast pocket and tossed it onto the table. "See for yourselves."

Edward quickly snatched it up, then found himself reluctant to read it once it was in his grasp. Steeling himself, he dropped his eyes to the paper and saw it contained just a few hastily written lines.

> *With this letter, I hereby formally abjure all claim upon or interest in the estate of the late Duke of Langerton, my husband. It is my express wish that the inheritance granted to me by his last will and testament be declared the rightful property of his son and heir, Robert Blakemore, Duke of Langerton.*
>
> *Charlotte Blakemore*

The signatures of two others—witnesses—were scrawled across the bottom of the sheet.

Edward dropped the letter as if it were hot. "Why would she do this?"

Lifting the paper, Fairfax quickly scanned it, then let it flutter down to the tabletop. "She's under no obligation to take the money, of course."

"But in this case, I strongly suspect coercion."

With a slow blink, the duke registered his gaze on Edward's face. "I don't believe I have to answer to you, Mr. Cary."

"You're right," Edward acknowledged with a jerk of his chin. "You don't. I haven't the faintest interest in you or your father's fortune. I care only about Charlotte's well-being."

"*Charlotte*, is it?" Langerton's thin lips curled in a derisive smile. "Never say you've been taken in by that French whore, too?"

Conventional wisdom would have it that Edward's return to England marked a return to civilization. But it seemed civilization was not always civil.

Edward knew he possessed the strength to wipe that smile from Langerton's face. But he had no intention of using it. If twenty years in the bloody West Indies had not turned him into a violent man, Langerton's words would not be the breaking point. He would find a way to defend Charlotte's honor without sacrificing his own.

"That's quite a remark for a gentleman to make about a lady," Fairfax observed coolly, drawing Langerton's attention his way. "Fortunately for you, my friend is essentially a man of peace." Curling his long-fingered hand into a surprisingly formidable fist, Fairfax landed a solid punch in Langerton's face before the man could react to protect himself. Blood spurted from his nose, spraying the papers scattered across the table and pattering ominously onto Charlotte's letter. "Unfortunately for you, I suffer from no such compunction."

"You broke my dose," Langerton cried, clutching both hands belatedly to his face. "You athaulted a peer of the realm!"

"Call me out," Fairfax challenged, his voice as soft as his expression was hard. The silvery scar that curled along his cheek leapt into prominence—a relic of the exchange that had sent him into hiding, Edward had always suspected.

Langerton rummaged through the papers for a napkin and raised it to his battered face. "I wouldn't demean mythelf by giving you the thatithfaction."

"Suit yourself," said Fairfax, shaking out his fist. "What now, Beckley?"

Edward started at the unexpected address. "Let's go," he answered, moving toward the door. "There's nothing I want here."

Langerton lowered the blood-stained napkin and watched them leave. The swelling was already inching outward from his nose. By morning, his eyes would be ringed with bruises. Now, however, they were filled with loathing. When Edward was just about to cross the threshold, he muttered under his breath, "Even my father wasn't fool enough to fuck her."

Turning sharply, Edward took one step back into the breakfast room. Fairfax's hand caught his arm, but he shook it off and crossed to the duke, whose show of resolve faltered. When Edward reached out one hand, Langerton flinched.

But Edward had no intention—no desire—to strike the man. He did not fault Fairfax's action, could not regret that Langerton had been put in his place. What he wanted would not be gained by shedding more of the duke's blood, however.

Calmly, he picked up the document Charlotte had written and tucked it into his pocket. "If I am able to confirm that your stepmother gave up her inheritance willingly, I shall return this to you. I hope I shall not find she was coerced . . ."

Despite his injuries, Langerton shook his head vigorously in denial.

As they descended the stairs, they could hear the butler's exclamations of alarm and pity, the deeper rumblings of Langerton's voice as he brushed off the man's offers of assistance. A footman bowed them out the door, and they found themselves once more in the square, squinting against the glare of midday.

Out of the corner of his eye, Edward watched Fairfax flex his injured hand. "I hope Lady Fairfax won't have your head for those bruised knuckles."

"She might," he confessed with a wry laugh.

"Then why did you hit him?"

Fairfax's expression grew serious. "Because someone needed to, and I couldn't see letting you sacrifice your principles over someone like him."

In the lifetime he'd spent learning to control any propensity to temper, eschewing violence despite the viciousness of his surroundings, protecting those who were weaker than he, Edward had never really thought of any of it as a matter of principle. He had merely been determined not to become his father.

But perhaps Fairfax was right. In the end, one's actions were a matter of choice, not destiny.

"That was smart thinking to take her letter. I hate to imagine what Langerton did to get her to sign away what's rightfully hers." Something rather sly passed over Fairfax's expression. "How do you suppose she'll express her gratitude when you give her back that paper?"

"*If*, not when," Edward corrected, in no mood to be teased. "You forget, I haven't any notion of where she's gone."

The sound of hurrying footsteps behind them interrupted their conversation. Langerton's butler waved for them to stop, already huffing from his exertions. "My lords. Please, wait."

Edward regarded him warily. "What business have you with us?"

"You are searching for Her Grace, are you not?" He bent slightly and rested his hands on his knees, the better to draw breath. "I can help."

"How?"

"She came in a hackney coach, and when she left, I heard her give the direction to her driver. She asked to be taken to a place where she might board the Bristol-bound stage."

Edward felt his heart lift in his chest—not an entirely comfortable sensation.

"Why would you tell us this, Mr.—?" Fairfax asked.

"Aimes, my lord," the butler supplied. Some emotion flitted across his hound-like features. "I had not the honor of meeting Her Grace before today. And I have served His Grace only a short time. But from what I have seen, I feel certain she deserves better than she has received from him."

Edward gave a tight nod. "Yes, she does. Thank you."

Aimes bowed. "Of course, my lord. You are very welcome."

Fairfax watched the man return to Blakemore House before he said, "So, she's headed west."

"I'm well aware of the direction in which Bristol lies," Edward said. Far more aware than he'd like, or than Fairfax could guess. "But Bristol's a port town. She might be bound anywhere."

"If it was a ship she wanted, she could have found one here in London."

Such an unnecessary observation earned Fairfax a hard look. Could Edward dare to indulge the hope that had flickered to life in his breast?

"She can't have got far," Fairfax insisted as he began to walk in the direction of Sutliffe House at a faster pace. "With a little luck, you might even be able to catch her at Marlborough. Take my coach."

Edward hesitated. "I couldn't possibly accept the loan of your carriage. Didn't you tell me that Lady Fairfax is expecting you to return to Hampshire today?"

Fairfax smiled. "Sarah is a great believer in fairy-tale endings," he explained, and there was none of the customary cynicism in his voice. "*Love can blossom in the unlikeliest circumstance*, she's fond of saying. She would never forgive me if I did not do what I could to smooth the way for true love." He paused and gestured down the street with his injured hand—quite deliberately, Edward felt sure.

"True love?" he echoed.

"Good God, Car—er, Beckley. If you mean to deny that you're in love with this woman, I may just have to knock some sense into you as well." He laughed, but Edward had the distinct impression his friend was not joking. Fairfax slapped him on the shoulder. "When you find her, don't let her get away again."

Edward gripped Fairfax's forearm, met his cool blue gaze, and nodded once. "I won't."

Chapter 21

At Marlborough, Edward got the hostler of the posting inn to admit that there *might* have been a lady traveling alone on the west-bound stage. But as it had come and gone more than an hour ago, and the inn was busy, he simply could not be sure. Fairfax's coachman insisted his horses would be spry again after a brief rest. Edward did not hesitate to urge the man to drive on.

After the punishing pace they had set that day, however, they managed to go only a little farther before the sun began to dip toward the horizon. Which was how Edward found himself stepping into the shabby, all-too-familiar inn in a small village east of Chippenham. No cold rain stranded travelers this time; instead, many had settled in for the night. The place was crowded.

"No rooms, sir," the innkeeper proclaimed. "Just gave the last to a gouty old gentleman. On his way to Bath, I suppose." He scratched behind one ear, disordering a tuft of white hair and added, confidentially, "Fellow could hardly make it up the stairs. You seem fit enough, though. You're welcome to sit up in the pub."

Edward glanced through the wide doorway into the public room, taking in the scattered tables, the dingy windows, the long rustic settle beneath a series of cheap prints hanging on the wall. The day had been warm, and the hearth was empty now, but he had no difficulty conjuring an image of Charlotte shivering before it, refusing his offer of help.

"All right," he agreed reluctantly, bothered less by the room's uncomfortable accommodations than its uncomfortable memories. Ducking under the low beam that served as a lintel, he chose a table on quite the opposite side of the room from where he had once sat with Charlotte, and ordered a meal and a pint, though he had no appetite.

What if she was not returning to Gloucestershire as he firmly believed—or at least, fondly hoped? If he never found her, could he learn to accustom himself to the weight of his memories? He supposed he might someday forget the feeling of her beneath him—the eager exploration of her fingers, the brush of her lips. Mere physical sensations—both good and bad—faded over time, as he well knew.

But he did not think he could ever forget the host of other images his mind seemed eager to call up: Charlotte covered head to toe with mud, twigs and dead leaves caught in her hair, her curiosity warring with her pride. Charlotte coated in a layer of grime, surrounded by a cloud of dust, determined to bring Ravenswood back into the light. Charlotte with mud oozing between her bare toes, watching the minnows in undisguised delight. Just . . . *Charlotte*.

No wonder Langerton had disapproved of his father's marriage. When it came down to it, she had nothing more of a duchess's dignity than the stiff spine. Based on what Edward had gleaned from their conversations, he could guess that particular characteristic had been born of necessity, meager armor against the barbs and slings of her aunt, her stepson, and the world at large. Everyone around her had insisted she was unworthy—of comforts, of kindness, of love.

And though Charlotte had, in large measure, believed them, she had nonetheless found the strength to escape their cruelty, to run away. If she chose now to keep running, how could he begrudge her her freedom? Even if it meant he would never be free again.

Lost in his ruminations, he might not have noticed the innkeeper bustling past if the man had not jostled his elbow, causing him to slosh half the contents of his mug over the food he had been aimlessly pushing about his plate.

The expected apology did not come, so intent was the man upon his mission. "Fanny," he called to the barmaid, "have you fetched up that tray for Mrs. Cary yet?"

The bottom of Edward's pewter mug met the tabletop with a thump. *Mrs. Cary?* No. It must be a coincidence. Or perhaps he had misheard.

"Naw. I plum forgot. Jus' a mo'," Fanny called back, juggling an armful of tankards bound for another table. "Room three, in't?"

"Aye."

Against his better judgment, Edward snagged the arm of the innkeeper as he turned to go. "Mrs. Cary, did you say? Dark haired or fair? Young or old?"

"A widow lady," was the man's answer, as if that decided all other questions.

When Fanny stepped past a moment later carrying a laden tea tray, Edward pushed back his chair and rose. "Is that for Mrs. Cary?"

"Yes, sir."

"May I take it up?"

He had expected a denial, or at least an obligatory protest. Instead, Fanny blew a stray lock of reddish hair away from her sweat-dampened forehead, took one look around the busy public room, and handed off the tray with a grateful sigh. "Here you be, then. Top o' the stairs."

As he walked, the contents of the tray rattled in his hands, a circumstance he blamed on his general lack of experience with fetching and carrying, rather than his nerves. What if he was wrong? What would he say, or do, if a perfect stranger opened to his knock?

Ah, but what if Charlotte stood on the other side of that door?

At the head of the dark, narrow staircase, he hesitated. By the light of a single sconce, he could see six doors, three to either side, all unnumbered and none, properly speaking, at the top, as Fanny's instructions had indicated. Which one should he choose? To the left or the right?

He hadn't long to consider. A creak on the steps behind him signaled the ascent of another guest. Drawing a deep breath, he stepped left to allow the fellow to pass, balanced the tray on one palm, and knocked on the door in front of him.

Having long since accepted that her request for tea had been ignored or forgotten, Charlotte jumped when she heard a knock on the door to her room.

After all this time, the tea was bound to be cold. Poor service was to be expected at a run-down posting inn, she supposed; nevertheless, her breath had quickened as the coach had rolled to a stop before this particular inn. When had she become such a creature of sentiment? Perhaps at the same moment she had forced herself to acknowledge that this journey might end in humiliation and disappointment.

What if Edward refused to forgive her?

Better to extend her travels, to delay the inevitable. And if that delay also provided an excuse for indulging in a few memories that ought to be resigned to the past—memories of Edward's strong arms drawing her to safety, or the sweep of his blue eyes across her face—well . . .

Laying aside her book, now emptied of its banknotes, she rose and went to the door, opening it without looking at who was on its other side. "Just put the tray on the table by the bed," she said, rummaging in her reticule for a coin. But the person who had entered was not carrying a tray. Was not a maid, but a man—and not the innkeeper either. A man whose weathered face and hair touched with silver were neither familiar nor strange. The man who had followed her once to this inn and apparently had been awaiting her return.

Why, oh why, had she been so foolish as to come back to this place?

Did she scream? No, the harsh sound jangling in her ears was the crash of china and silver. Oh, but her aunt would have her head when she found out Charlotte had been so clumsy as to drop the tea tray. Then she was slipping, scrambling, falling, while her cousins' faces taunted her from the rim of the narrow trap door that led to the root cellar. How long would her uncle leave her in the darkness this time? A hand, a strong hand extended to help her rise from the mud and the muck at the rear of the Rookery. Edward looking down at her with laughing eyes. No, he was not here—none of them was here. Just her imagination, playing tricks . . .

But then he *was* there, stepping between her and the stranger. "Are you harmed, Charlotte?"

Once more, Edward had come to her rescue at this ramshackle inn. But what was he doing here? Had he been searching for her? Her head told her it was the cruelest of coincidences. Her heart, however . . .

"I'm fine." Pushing up from the rough carpet, she came unsteadily to her feet. How had she ended up on the floor? Had she really fainted? How humiliating.

She turned to the stranger. "I suppose you were sent by my stepson? Even though I begged him to call off his dogs."

"You *are* the Duchess of Langerton, then?" he asked.

She nodded before recalling that she had meant never to answer to that title again.

"Oh, thank God," the man murmured, his lower lip beginning to tremble. "I've found you at last. No, I was not sent by the duke." The suggestion seemed almost to offend him. "I tried more than once to enlist his help in finding you, but he could—or would—offer me no assistance."

"Who are you?" she asked.

"James Winstead," he said, with an old-fashioned bow. "Earl of Belmont."

Charlotte swept one hand behind her, feeling for the bedpost, gripping it with all her might. "My . . . father?"

"Have you proof?" Edward demanded of the man as he jerked around to face him.

"Oh . . . well, yes. I have papers, and other things that will attest to the fact that I am who I claim to be. And my sister, Lady Penhurst, knows me."

Finding the bedpost insufficient support, Charlotte allowed herself to sag against the bed itself. "This cannot be."

Edward took a step closer, warmth and understanding in his eyes. "You've sustained quite a shock, I know. It is not every day one recovers a parent believed to be lost forever."

With those words she could guess that her parting instructions to Garrick had been followed. "Was I right about Tessie?"

He took one of her icy hands in his warmer one and squeezed, as if words could not convey what he felt. "Yes. But all that can wait. For now, talk to your father, Charlotte." Her fingers slipped from his grasp as he turned toward the door. "Pardon my interruption," he said with a nod to each of them.

"Please," she whispered, "don't go."

"I won't be far away. If you need me, you have only to call."

When the door latched behind him, she returned her attention to her father, who was studying her with his head tilted to one side. "From the moment I laid eyes on you in Bath, I knew," he said. "There's something of your dear mother in your face and in your bearing."

Those words brought forth an unexpected surge of strength, fueled in large measure by anger, forcing her to her feet again. "My *dear* mother? The poor woman you got with child and then abandoned?"

"I did not abandon her," he insisted. Then, more softly, "Or at least, I did not mean to. We were living just outside Paris. I was called half a day's journey away on business. Her time was not yet so near that I felt a risk in going. But I should've known better than to have trusted her brother. He'd been against us from the start. When I returned, delayed some days by bad weather, the nuns at the hospital showed me your mother's cold form, told me the babe she carried had never even drawn breath . . ." He shook his head, as if trying to dispel a particularly tenacious memory. "They must have given you into her brother's care, but how was I to have known? I had no will left—even to doubt. Grief struck me like a fever. Once I recovered my senses, I left France, headed east. Across Europe, through the Levant. All the way to China. Twenty years of wandering. An adventure, to be sure, though it never succeeded in making me forget what I had lost."

"You ran away." She made no effort to keep the accusatory tone from her voice.

The notion seemed to catch him by surprise. "I . . . I suppose you could say that. I think that deep down"—he sounded exhausted—"deep down, I hoped I would die, too. A bandito's knife between the ribs, some exotic illness. But I enjoyed no such luck. The worst I ever suffered was a fall from my horse," he said, nodding down at his left leg, which stuck out stiffly at an awkward angle. "Broken crossing through the Khyber Pass. Took months to heal. But left me with nothing worse than a limp."

Occasionally—when she was not grumbling about the thoughtlessness of people who ran off, expecting others to clean up the messes they left behind, without so much as a word of thanks—Aunt Penhurst had wondered aloud if her brother might not be dead. Then a letter would arrive from some faraway place where a reply was unlikely to reach him. Although those rare pieces of correspondence never inquired after his daughter, they did confirm his continued existence.

Charlotte had never considered that he might know nothing of hers.

Feeling the first stirrings of pity, she waved him toward the only chair in the room, into which he settled with a sigh of gratitude. The faint light coming through the window made it easier for her to take in his weather-beaten appearance, his hair flecked with silver. The places to which he had traveled over these last twenty-five years had not treated him kindly. Though she knew he could not be much older than fifty, no one who saw him now would believe it. His adventures, as he called them, combined with the shock of his recent discoveries, had left him rather the worse for wear.

Absently, she reached for her mother's book, her last connection to the woman who had brought her into the world before leaving it herself. "Yes, I was raised by my mother's brother in Rouen. He was . . . never kind," she whispered, tracing one finger across the book's battered cover. "He never let me forget what had become of my mother. What becomes of the sort of woman who acts with her heart and not her head."

The sort of woman she had become, despite her best efforts to the contrary.

"We *were* impulsive," her father acknowledged, sounding chagrined. "Marrying though we had known each other such a little time. But—"

The book nearly slipped from her hands to the floor. "Y-you were m-married?"

"Oh, yes. I persuaded her to elope with me to Guernsey. By marrying in the Church of England, I hoped to ensure that our union would be recognized here. When we returned to Paris, we planned to wed again, according to the rites of her church. I wanted there to be no objection, on any score. But we could find no priest sympathetic to our plight."

"My uncle always claimed there was no marriage of any sort."

Her father's face settled into harder lines. "From the first, her brother tried to convince her I had played her a wretched trick. She showed him her copy of our marriage lines, but he insisted they were forged. Afterward, I urged her to put them in a safe place, so that he would not try to destroy them. So that if anything happened to me, she would be able to prove she was my wife. I watched her—" His eyes fell on the book resting against Charlotte's thigh. "Is that—? Did that book once belong to your mother?"

With an uncertain nod, she held it out to him, and he took it reverently with both hands. "Ah, my darling," he breathed, whispering to a ghost. Lifting the cover with his thumb, he traced over the flyleaf with the fingers of the other hand, as Charlotte herself had often done, though the intricate, inked design had been smudged beyond legibility long before she had been able to decipher it. "You see," he said, displaying the page to her. "*S.C.W.*—Simone le Clerq Winstead. My wife."

"By itself, that proves very little."

"Yes, but..." He opened the book wider; she winced at the cracking sound. Into the narrow channel between the bound edge of the pages and the brittle leather spine, he slipped one finger, withdrew a carefully folded sheet of paper, and handed it to Charlotte. "This, I think, will attest to the truth of my story—the truth of yours, as well."

Carefully, she unfolded the yellowed parchment and saw, in formal script, the record of her parents' marriage.

Once more, she leaned heavily against the quilt-covered mattress, overwhelmed at the discovery. By joy, yes, because one scourge had been lifted. But also by sorrow. Sorrow at the loss of her mother. At the indignities Charlotte had suffered all her life because she was believed—wrongly, as it turned out—to be illegitimate.

"I will not ask for your forgiveness, daughter," he said, holding out the book. "I have done nothing to earn it—as yet. But I mean to try."

With a shaking hand she took the book from him, uncertain what else she might be willing to accept. Her father's return might mean another chance to build a family, another chance to be loved. Or it might mean more heartache.

Despite the difficulty posed by her trembling fingers, she managed to fold the parchment and slip it between the pages of the book. "May I ask why you returned?"

"At some point, a man grows tired of adventure. I decided it was time to come home."

It was, she sensed, a partial explanation. But she did not blame him. Nor did she press him for more than he was able to give. What would Edward's reply have been if she had asked him the same question?

"When I arrived in England a fortnight ago," her father continued, "I went first to my sister. It was she who informed me of the misunderstanding under which I had been laboring all these years. You were alive, she said, and recently married to the Duke of Langerton. By the time I arrived in Bath and tracked down his place of residence, however, he had died. I came to find you, to offer what comfort I could, but the servants told me you'd left, gone back to London. I followed you to this very inn, glimpsed you from a distance, and then... why, it was as if you simply vanished."

"I thought you were a spy, sent by my stepson. I fled into the country. To Gloucestershire."

"Alone?"

She hesitated. "Not exactly."

"Ah." He nodded his understanding. "The young man who barged in here to rescue you?"

"Edward—that is, the Earl of Beckley. Yes. Also recently returned after many years abroad. When he saw me in distress that day, he offered his assistance. It is his way."

Wrinkles formed at the corners of his eyes as he narrowed his gaze, trying to read her expression by the fading light. "I . . . see. Well, I went on to London, hoping to discover where you might have gone. I heard nothing but the vilest gossip. Then this morning, as I was attempting to speak once more with the duke, I saw that young man and another on the doorstep of Blakemore House, also looking for you. The butler told him you were traveling west. You planned to meet here, I suppose?"

Edward had gone to London? To Robert? "No."

The faintest frown notched his brow, then disappeared. But she knew disbelief when she saw it. "Aunt Penhurst has told you, I suppose, that I am . . . prone to invention. A liar."

"She would not dare to say as much to me, daughter." Charlotte could not entirely contain her incredulous huff. "But if she had," he continued, "I would have told her that your mother was also a teller of tales. Lovely tales, in verse that sang like the stars in the night sky. Those are her poems," he explained, gesturing toward the book. "Did you know? I had them printed and bound—for her, I claimed, though really, I had more selfish reasons. I wanted to be able to hold her precious gift in my hands."

Turning the aged volume, she felt as if she were seeing it for the first time. And to think, just a moment ago, she had imagined the book of little real value to her, now that the banknotes had been removed. Slowly, she rose, took three small steps toward him, and laid the book in his lap. Before she could let go, he caught her hand along with it, and held her there, looking not at the book, but at her. "I am so sorry, my daughter. And also glad. So very glad. That does not make much sense, I suppose, but—"

"I understand." Without extracting her hand from his grasp, she knelt beside the chair. His free hand reached up, as if he would touch her cheek, though he did not. So she tipped her head toward his palm, closing the distance between them. "Tell me about her."

Over the next hour or more, he did just that, and through his words, she met her mother—no, not *met*. She had known her through her poems, first, without realizing it. Poems that had spoken of love and joy and beauty and all the other things Charlotte had discovered in them, and only in them, when she was a child.

"I had traveled to Paris with friends, serious about nothing but wine and vingt-et-un," he told her. "Then early one drizzly morning, I was staggering home and I stumbled right into your mama, who was just leaving mass, as it happened. She gave a nervous giggle, then tried to hide it." While her father spoke, she let her head drift until it was resting on the edge of the chair. His hand passed over her hair. "Do you believe in love at first sight, Charlotte?"

Her first impulse was denial. But at the question, her mind had conjured an image of Edward as she had first seen him, damp curls plastered to his forehead, gazing down at her with those blue eyes that drove away the rain and the cold. "I think, perhaps, that I do."

"Then you understand. When I saw her, I knew. I couldn't just let her go. I tried to apologize, but she hurried after her family. So I went back to that church every morning until I saw her again. Father Biet must have thought he had made a convert. Once I found her, I was determined to win her."

She had to swallow twice before she could get a sound past the lump in her throat. "But you lost her instead."

"No, my child. No. I won her. For a time, I had her love. And so much more. I would only have truly lost if I had given up." She felt him shift as if he would rise. "I should leave you to your rest. I hope this will not be our only opportunity to talk. I should like the chance to know my daughter."

Though she longed for him to stay and talk now, another part of her heart tugged her in the opposite direction, to the place where Edward waited. She pictured him at Ravenswood with his mother, shocked by the joy of their unexpected reunion. Yet somehow, he had torn himself from her side to follow Charlotte. Until this moment, she could not have understood the strength it had required. Until now, she had not fully understood what it meant that he had attempted to do it at all.

"And I should like to know you better . . . Papa." But she got to her feet as she spoke.

He caught her hand. "Tell me, where were you bound?"

Instinctively, she scrambled for a story to cover the scandalous truth. "I hadn't quite decided—"

"Charlotte," he chided. "Do not prove your aunt right."

"Gloucestershire," she whispered. "Ravenswood Manor."

"The name of the place is not familiar to me," he said, lifting one shoulder. "Would I be safe in assuming it has some tie to the Earl of Beckley?"

When an answer would not come, she merely nodded.

He nodded, too, then rose and limped to the door. "The inn is full tonight. We are lucky to have beds. Some who arrived later were not so lucky. I believe at least one young man was obliged to make do with that hard bench in the public room."

There could be no doubt as to the guest to which her father referred.

"Bound to be uncomfortable," he added. "And lonely. Well, good night."

"Good night, Papa."

Before the door had fully latched, she was gathering the quilt and pillow from her bed. Before the door to her father's room had closed, she was halfway down the stairs. When she glanced over her shoulder, his door opened a fraction wider as he looked out into the corridor.

Surely it was a trick of the light, the single candle flickering in the sconce, but she could have sworn she saw him wink.

Chapter 22

As darkness fell, the public room emptied of its few remaining patrons: two local gentlemen who had been playing chess, a scattering of coachmen who reluctantly made their way to the stables for the night, and the guests whose limited coin had not secured them a private dining room. Before she retired, Fanny snuffed all the candles but one.

"Be there ought else I can do for ye, sir?"

Wary that if he said yes, he might be presented with another slice of the worst beef-and-onion pie in the history of beef-and-onion pies, accompanied by another mug of ale unequal to the task of washing it down, Edward shook his head. "I'll be fine, thank you."

At least the massive settle—around which he suspected the inn must have been built a hundred or so years ago—was wide enough to accommodate his shoulders. Time was, the exhaustion he felt would have been sufficient to ensure a good night's sleep almost anywhere. But if he spent this night tossing and turning, he did not think the hard wooden bench would be even a little bit to blame.

He lay with his head closest to the empty hearth, his feet pointed toward the wide entrance to the room, debating whether to use his greatcoat for pillow or blanket. When the stairwell just beyond the doorway beckoned to him, he closed his eyes. But when closed eyes invited his mind to wander to Charlotte, he opened them again.

The image that seemed to be seared into his memory did not disappear, however.

She stood in the doorway, her face a pale oval shining out of the gloom, her expression hidden in shadow. She looked as polished and proper as he had ever seen her, nary a speck of mud nor wayward lock of hair in sight. Easier, now, to imagine her a duchess.

But she was not more beautiful, for all that. He had grown accustomed to the other Charlotte.

His Charlotte.

As before, his good sense tried to resist the claiming. But his heart had other ideas.

For what seemed an eternity, neither of them moved. Perhaps she thought he was asleep. When at last she stepped closer, he could see she held a bundle in her arms. A flicker of fear passed through him. Was she fleeing in the night?

With creeping steps, she came to the far end of the settle and laid down what he now realized was a pillow and blanket, then turned to go.

"Charlotte, wait."

Relief swept over him when she heeded his command. He scrambled to sit upright, held out one hand to her, and ventured another. "Come."

She did. Slowly, rather warily. When she stopped a foot or so away from him, she did not take his hand, so he patted the bench beside him and invited her to sit instead. With care, she arranged her skirts as she took a place farther down the settle.

"Thank you for encouraging me to talk to my father," she said after a moment. "He is . . . eccentric. But he was able to tell me things no one else ever would or could. About my mother." A pause. "They were married."

He could hear the relief in her voice, and it irritated him beyond measure. She should never have been shamed or mistreated, even if her parents had not been wed. He swept the palm of his hand across the expanse of wood between them, feeling the ridges and ripples of the grain, worn smooth by a century or more of patrons' abuse. "For your sake," he managed to say, "I am glad."

"He has been searching for me for some time. I saw him here, that day—though of course, I did not know him. I thought him one of Robert's spies."

"So you ran."

Her gaze dropped to her hands, folded neatly in her lap. "After my husband died, I promised myself that I would never again let my happiness, or my misery, depend on another person. My stepson intended to make me the center of a terrible scandal. I wanted nothing more than to be left alone." As she spoke, her fingers twisted themselves into knots. "So when the chance to disappear presented itself,

I took it. At first, Ravenswood seemed an ideal hiding place. Remote. Secluded. Then Jack showed up."

"And threatened to expose you."

"I realized I could not go on living that way. When I saw that Mr. Sykes was leaving, it seemed the perfect chance to return to London and confront Robert once and for all, so I took it. I worried that if I delayed, even a moment, Jack would catch me. Or I would lose my nerve. Or you would try to stop me from doing what I meant to do." Although he could see the effort it cost her, she forced herself to lift her eyes to his face. "I spoke to my stepson. I gave up my inheritance in exchange—I hope—for my peace."

"I know." He reached into his coat pocket, pulled out the folded parchment, and handed it to her. "That is the letter you wrote. I feared Langerton might have forced your hand. You may return it to him, if you wish. Or you may destroy it."

With restless fingers, she traced the edges of the document. "You believe I ought to fight him?"

"His case is weak. With your father's revelation, I believe the tide of public opinion will turn in your favor. But only you can decide what to do, and I will respect your decision."

After a long pause, she rose and stepped toward the hearth, clutching the folded note in one trembling hand. Holding it out toward the candle, she hesitated, then touched the paper to the feeble flame. The sudden flare of light showed him her expression—half fear, half determination—before she tossed the burning note into the empty fireplace, where soon nothing more remained of it than a few cinders.

"I made a terrible mistake once where you were concerned, Charlotte," he said as she returned to her seat. Her strength and her bravery awed him. "When I met you here, I assumed you needed to be saved. I swooped in, as if you were a damsel in distress and I fancied myself your knight in shining armor."

Once more, only a faint, flickering light limned her profile. "Mari says it has always been your way."

"It has. And do you know why?" A quick shake of her head made her dark hair gleam. "Because when I saw others as vulnerable, it made it easier to deny my own vulnerabilities. You saw through that. When we met in this musty little inn, I believed I was rescuing you. Instead, you rescued me."

Her chin dipped downward, and after a tremulous breath, she said, "I *lied* to you."

"Were we not both guilty of keeping secrets, Mrs. Cary?"

Those words returned her gaze to his face. "I—I suppose."

"You did not tell me your full name. Nor your title. But you were honest about what mattered. You showed me who you *are*."

"Yes," she whispered, sounding resigned. "Aunt Penhurst always said my ill nature was stamped on my face for anyone to read."

"That is not what I meant." Good God, but Lady Penhurst ought to thank her lucky stars that he was not prone to violence. "I will not pretend I was not shocked to discover your identity. Shocked, and disappointed to think that you did not think me worthy of your trust. But even if you'd introduced yourself from the first as Duchess of Langerton," he insisted, "it would not have revealed anything more important to me than what you showed in so many other ways. The respect with which you spoke to Mari. How hard you worked to restore Ravenswood Manor, merely because you sensed my pain and hoped to ease it. And my mother . . ." The lump that rose in his throat made his words sound thick. "For all those years, she had been hiding in plain sight, scarred beyond recognition. You saw past the scars. And even when you were desperate to flee, you made sure she knew that I—that I had come home." He wished it were not too dim to see the expression in her dark eyes. "I told myself that if you did not care for me, at least a little, you would never have done it."

As always, she held herself immobile. He could not decide whether his words had surprised her. "You followed me."

Sliding closer to her, he tilted his head and held her gaze a long moment. "I love you, Charlotte." When her lips parted, he touched them with one finger to silence any protest, any reply. "No. Don't speak. Just listen. You have heard those words too rarely in your life. Hear them now. I love you for seeing beyond the surface of things to what is beneath . . . to what is beautiful. I love you for marching straight toward whatever frightens you. I love the way you laugh." Sensing that one of those little giggles was about to bubble from her lips, he drew his finger away to let it escape. "I love *you*. And I was not about to let you get away."

With an awkward motion, she slid across the smooth seat of the wooden bench, far enough that they were no longer touching. "If you hope to resume your place in English society, you must distance yourself from me. It is bad enough that people will say I duped you into . . ." If the light were better, he would have sworn that she blushed. "That I hoped to make it more difficult for my stepson to prove my marriage was a sham."

"And *is* that why you gave yourself to me?"

"No. *Non.*" More emphatic the second time, as if the English word had been insufficient to express her feelings. "I did not even know until I got to London that I was believed to be in search of—of a gentleman willing to do a most ungentlemanly thing."

He could not deny feeling somewhat relieved. "Then why?"

A pause. "*Je t'aime aussi.*"

Although he was certain of what she said, she had spoken so low that he was tempted to ask her to say it again. Thinking better of it, he moved closer and kissed her instead, his lips caressing hers, then skating across her cheek to nuzzle her ear. Her fingers crept up his arms, over his collar, to curl in his hair, coaxing him with gentle pressure to return his mouth to hers.

When their lips parted, she looked at him with wide eyes. "How strange that chance should have brought us together here."

"I have never been a great believer in coincidence."

She smiled. "The first time I came to this inn, I wanted a place to be *by* myself. But now, I realize that what I truly craved was a place where I could *be* myself. A home."

"And have you found one, Charlotte?"

"Yes. With you." She leaned closer and whispered across his lips, "I love you, too."

He stopped just short of returning her kiss. "The other night, I longed to ask you an important question, but a foolish fear kept me from speaking the words. You see, I swore never to marry. That way, no woman would risk becoming to me what my mother was to my father."

Her eyes widened and she shook her head in disbelief. "You are nothing like him," she insisted.

"No. I'm not. When I was a boy, I thought he was powerful. Now, I realize he was weak. But I'm strong. Strong enough to confess how frightened I felt when you left without a word." He tangled his fingers with hers where they lay in her lap. "Strong enough to admit how much I need you. I know your life as a duchess has not always been what you hoped. And I cannot promise that life as my countess will always be easy. But—"

"Oh no, you mustn't," she said, though she made no effort to pull her hand away. "I am nothing more than scandal now. Look at what happened to poor, dear George. People will say you are mad to—to—"

"To marry a clever beauty of noble blood? Madness, indeed," he murmured, dipping his head to press a string of kisses along the turn of her throat.

He felt a giggle ripple through her. "Perhaps you forget that I am in mourning, my lord," she said, as she smoothed her inky skirts with her free hand.

"Mm." His lips moved higher. "In six months the scandalmongers will have moved on to something new."

"Six months? We must wait a year, at least."

He thought—hoped—he had caught a teasing note in her voice. "A year?" He nipped at her earlobe. "However shall we pass the time?"

"I suppose I might take up residence in Little Norbury," she suggested, studiously ignoring his kisses. "Perhaps the hermitage, now that Tessie—*excusez-moi*, Lady Beckley—has been restored to her rightful place. I promise I would not trouble you."

"I beg to differ," he whispered against her hair. "If you were living in Little Norbury or the Ravenswood hermitage, it would trouble me a great deal."

"Then I might . . ." She drummed her fingers on the bench as she contemplated her options. "I might go back to Bath. I could take your mother, act as her companion. The waters would no doubt do her good."

"Bath?" He drew back. "Worse and worse."

"Why, whatever do you mean? It's only a half-day's ride from Ravenswood. You might visit us whenever you choose. And though it would not be proper for us to correspond, when your mother writes to you, as I'm sure she will, I might sneak in a postscript, now and then."

Remembering the story of their supposed cross-Atlantic courtship, he said, "About the weather, I suppose?"

"No. I cannot think the differences between the weather in Bath and the weather in Gloucestershire would be anything to speak of. I was thinking of the usual subjects." Her eyes glittered rather impishly in the near darkness. "Pump Room gossip. The latest fashions. You can tell us about the work on the manor, and whether the Toomeys' baby is teething, and . . ."

"Sheep?" he suggested wryly. "Oh, no, my dear. I can promise that any note I write to you won't be fit for my mother's eyes."

She tilted her head in a way that suggested a scold, though the room was too dark to allow him to see her expression. The effect was further spoiled when she laughed again. "In all seriousness, *mon cher*, I need a little time. Things have changed so fast. I am . . . overwhelmed. My father. My stepson's suit, and"—she twisted her wedding band with her thumb—"I would not wish to become the person the gossips believe me to be. My husband was a dear man, worthy of honor, and I—"

"I will wait," he assured her, stopping her words with a fingertip, brushing away her worries. "As long as you need. As long as I have your promise. Will you marry me, Charlotte? Just one word. Yes or no." The gentle reminder of their night together was only half in jest. Then, as now, the choice must be hers. "In French or in English. It does not matter."

Curling into his embrace, she laid her head against his shoulder. "Yes," she breathed. "*Oui*. Always."

Later, when the candle had guttered and the only light came from a rising moon, he swept the hair from her cheek and lifted her face to his. "You should go back to your bed."

"I would much rather stay here with you."

"Aren't you at all worried we'll be caught in this compromising position?" he teased. It was not a cozy spot for lovemaking. It was not even comfortable. But he made no move to let her go, either. "I might be forced to make an honest woman of you."

With a sly smile, she reached for the blanket she had brought down, and wrapped it clumsily around them both. "You can try."

Epilogue

Ravenswood Manor
Some years later

Soft morning light filled the earl's bedchamber, bringing with it birdsong and the first stirrings of wakefulness. Clinging to sleep, Charlotte burrowed deeper under the covers, closer to Edward. He pulled her into his arms with a drowsy murmur, and she rested one cheek against his chest. When his hand began inscribing lazy circles on her back, a sigh escaped her lips. As the hand slid lower, its touch grew more focused, and the lingering desire for sleep gave way to the desire for something else entirely.

"*Bonjour, madame*. Fancy finding you in my bed." With a low laugh, he hitched her higher against his hard body. She lifted her lips to his face, and—

"Mama! Jamie won't let me play with Nana's soldiers."

Reluctantly, Charlotte shifted back into a sitting position, half propped against Edward, and faced their younger son. "Kit," she admonished. "I've told you a dozen times that you boys must work it out between yourselves." The basketful of toy soldiers, found and preserved so many years ago by Edward's mother—who had been happy to give up her renewed claim to the title of Countess of Beckley in favor of Charlotte's assumption of it, and now much preferred her new title of Nana—had long been a source of conflict between the boys. But she hadn't the heart to punish them for it.

"And did he give a reason?" asked Edward, scrubbing the dark stubble on his jaw and mustering a yawn Charlotte knew must be false. Positioned as she was, she could tell very well he was wide-awake.

"He says I'm too old," Kit sobbed.

Edward cast off all pretense of drowsiness. "He said what?"

"Now, now," she began, recognizing the reason for her husband's sharp reaction and trying to soothe both of them at once.

But Edward spoke first, and his voice was gentle. "Too old, eh? Well, you might remind him about that battle I saw him waging with Grandpapa just yesterday."

The boy pushed his unruly mop of dark curls out of his damp eyes. "Really?"

"Really," his father confirmed. "Now, back to the nursery with you."

"Aww . . . Can't I climb in bed with you?"

Tilting her head in what she hoped was a show of sternness, Charlotte pointed toward the door. "You heard your papa." With a huff and a scowl that made her want to gather the boy into her arms, Kit turned to go. "Oh, and Kit?" she added. "You'll never be too old for those soldiers. But Letty is still too young. Make sure to keep them out of your sister's hands, or they'll find their way into her mouth."

"Yes, Mama."

When the door closed behind him, Edward wrapped his arms around her. "Now, my dear. Where were we?" His kisses down her neck and along the top of her shoulder worked their magic, as they always had, but as if unsatisfied with mere magic, he shifted away from the head of the bed, allowing her body to slide down into the mountain of pillows as he transferred his kisses to her lips, her jaw, the turn of her throat. Lower . . . lower. Her breast, the curve of her waist, her—

"Ow!"

Tail fluffed and eyes bright, Noir prepared to pounce on her feet once more. Beyond the end of the bed, she could see that the heavy oak door had been pushed open just enough to allow the cat to slip into the room. Kit must not have closed it tightly behind him.

"Ignore him," Edward advised, sliding lower still, until he was entirely lost beneath the blankets and quilts which he insisted were necessary in all but the warmest months—for he was still inclined to find England a bit chilly, even after all these years.

"Really, though . . . Noir and Kit have the right of it. I should get up. I've a million things to do. The Corrvans will be here this afternoon, and . . . oh, I *do* hope Thomasina has outgrown that terrible phase she was in at Christmas. I don't think Noir ever forgave her for that tug on his tail."

Studiously ignoring her, Edward traced one fingertip along the curve of her belly, then followed its movements with his lips.

"And Lord and Lady Fairfax, and their children . . . Oh, why did I ever think an Easter house party was a good idea? I haven't had a moment to look at those illustrations Jack sent for my latest book of stories . . ."

"Charlotte."

She glanced down at him. *"Oui?"*

"That's more like it." When he began idly stroking the soft skin of her inner thigh she forgot to mind the cat nipping at her curling toes. And when his kisses followed his fingers, she forgot everything else. Until—

"Milady?"

Peg Eakins's head poked around the edge of the door that Noir had opened. Startled, Charlotte shuffled more upright, propping herself against the bolster. But Edward did not follow suit. He stayed nestled between her spread legs. The shadows cast by the bed hangings and the mountain of coverings on the enormous bed perfectly hid him from Peg's view.

"Sorry, ma'am. But the door was open. Nurse sent me to look for the boys," she explained. Though she had never quite got the knack of knocking, she had turned out to be a fine housemaid in all other respects.

"Ah. Well, they're not here, I'm afraid. Kit popped in a moment ago, but he's gone again."

"All right, then." Just as Peg turned to go, Edward's fingers struck a ticklish spot, and Charlotte could not contain a giggle. Peg's head twisted around. "Was there something else you wanted, milady?"

Charlotte managed a quick shake of her head.

"Oh," said Peg. Struck by some recollection, she paused on the threshold. "Would you happen to know where Lord Beckley is, ma'am?"

"I—ah—"

"Because Mr. Markham's below. Said he hoped t' meet with his lordship before his comp'ny arrived. Somethin' about the wheat field on the Westons' farm."

Naming Matthew Markham as steward of Ravenswood had been one of Edward's first official acts as Earl of Beckley. She had never doubted it was the right decision. But right now, the state of crops was the last thing on her mind. "I will—ah—let him know, when I see him. First thing."

Peg tilted her head to one side. "You feelin' yourself, ma'am? You look a bit flushed."

"Oh. I'm fine. Just . . . oh. A bit tired, yet, I suppose. Perhaps I'll close my eyes for a moment more."

"As you wish, ma'am." She hesitated. "But you should know Mrs. Markham came along wit' her husband. Went right into the kitchen and made herself t' home." The Rookery had long since been repaired to accommodate the Markhams' little family, which more than occupied Mari's time—whatever was not taken up by her duties as midwife to the rapidly growing village, that is. But none of those changes had altered her sense of possessiveness where Ravenswood's kitchen was concerned. "You know how Cook feels about—"

"I'll take care of it, Peg. Momentarily." She could not keep the note of impatience from her voice—or perhaps it was just the familiar tension Edward's caresses were building in every part of her body.

"Very good, milady." With a curtsy, she slipped out the door, and this time, Charlotte waited until she heard the click of the latch.

"Edward Cary," she gasped, twitching the covers away, "just what do you think you're doing?"

He looked up at her with those summery blue eyes and a wicked grin. "If you don't know, we haven't done it often enough."

"After four children, I think I have some idea of how it works."

Her words seemed to take a moment to penetrate. Suddenly scrambling free of the coverings, he rose up until they were face-to-face. "Charlotte?"

"Hmm?"

"Did you say . . . *four* children?"

"I did." At his wide-eyed expression, she laughed. "Come, come, my lord. I have heard Mr. Markham claim that he's never known a man so skilled at tallying figures in his head."

When she held up four fingers and waggled them, he leaned in and pressed a kiss to each one in turn. "Four. Well. If we're going to have another mouth to feed, perhaps I'd best go meet with Markham about that wheat field right away," he teased. "No time to waste."

Wrapping her arms around his neck, she wriggled her hips until their bodies were perfectly aligned and pulled him closer.

"Maybe a little time," he murmured, lowering his mouth to hers. "But first, I'm going to lock that door."

Historical Note

In *Slave Populations of the British Caribbean*, historian B. W. Higman says that "the ultimate aim of the British sugar planter [was] to return home once he had amassed his fortune." Despite their wealth, that homecoming was not necessarily an easy one. In this book, I consider how time spent in the violent world of the West Indies might have shaped the return to life in Great Britain.

Of course, British planters were not the only ones whose lives were transformed by a journey across the Atlantic. The Africans who came to England—some free, some enslaved and traveling with their owners—faced their own challenges. Mari's romance in this book was inspired by the interracial marriage between an English farm girl and a former slave from Jamaica in Maria Edgeworth's 1801 novel, *Belinda*. The plot point was deemed so shocking by Edgeworth's father that he insisted she take it out. It does not appear in the 1810 edition of the work.

The frequent mention of the West Indies in the work of an Anglo-Irish author is one sign of the pervasiveness of discussions of slavery and abolition in Britain at the close of the eighteenth century and the start of the nineteenth. Edgeworth's personal stance is somewhat ambiguous; like many of her contemporaries, she seems to have opposed the slave trade, but remained skeptical of efforts to abolish slavery. An antislavery boycott of West Indian sugar, and the proposed substitution of honey as a sweetener, inspired her to ask (in a 1792 letter to her friend Sophy Ruxton), "Will it not be rather hard upon the poor bees in the end?"—a remark I give to Charlotte's heartless aunt in this story.

Finally, the character of Charlotte, a refugee from the French Revolution, draws on the work of another late-eighteenth-century novelist, Frances Burney. *Evelina* (1778), a novel in letters, traces the coming of age of a young woman of uncertain birth (and French extraction) who has the temerity to fall in love with an earl. Some details of Charlotte's story were suggested by the case studies in historian Lawrence Stone's *Broken Lives: Separation and Divorce in England, 1660-1857*.

ABOUT THE AUTHOR

A love affair with historical romances led **SUSANNA CRAIG** to a degree (okay, three degrees) in literature and a career as an English professor. When she's not teaching or writing academic essays about Jane Austen and her contemporaries, she enjoys putting her fascination with words and knowledge of the period to better use: writing Regency-era romances she hopes readers will find both smart and sexy. She makes her home among the rolling hills of Kentucky horse country, along with her historian husband, their unstoppable little girl, and a genuinely grumpy cat. Find her online at www.susannacraig.com.

TO KISS A THIEF

In this captivating new series set in Georgian England, a disgraced woman hides from her marriage—for better or worse . . .

Sarah Pevensey had hoped her arranged marriage to St. John Sutliffe, Viscount Fairfax, could become something more. But almost before it began, it ended in a scandal that shocked London society. Accused of being a jewel thief, Sarah fled to a small fishing village to rebuild her life.

The last time St. John saw his new wife, she was nestled in the lap of a soldier, disheveled, and no longer in possession of his family's heirloom sapphire necklace. Now, three years later, he has located Sarah and is determined she pay for her crimes. But the woman he finds is far from what he expected. Humble and hardworking, Sarah has nothing to hide from her husband—or so it appears. Yet as he attempts to woo her to uncover her secrets, St. John soon realizes that if he's not careful, she'll steal his heart . . .

SUSANNA
CRAIG

"A stunning, sensual storyteller,
Susanna Craig is an author to watch!"
*—*New York Times *bestselling*
author Jennifer McQuiston

LYRICAL

TO KISS A THIEF

RUNAWAY DESIRES

TO TEMPT AN HEIRESS

Susanna Craig's dazzling series set in Georgian England sails to the Caribbean—where a willful young woman and a worldly man do their best to run every which way but towards each other . . .

After her beloved father dies, Tempest Holderin wants nothing more than to fulfill his wish to free the slaves on their Antiguan sugar plantation. But the now wealthy woman finds herself pursued by a pack of unsavory suitors with other plans for her inheritance. To keep her from danger, her dearest friend arranges a most unconventional solution: have Tempest kidnapped and taken to safety.

Captain Andrew Corrvan has an unseemly reputation as a ruthless, money-hungry blackguard—but those on his ship know differently. He is driven by only one thing: the quest to avenge his father's death on the high seas. Until he agrees to abduct a headstrong heiress . . .

If traveling for weeks—without a chaperone—isn't enough to ruin Tempest, the desire she feels for her dark and dangerously attractive captor will do the rest. The storm brewing between them will only gather strength when they reach England, where past and present perils threaten to tear them apart—even more so than their own stubborn hearts . . .

SUSANNA
CRAIG

TO TEMPT AN HEIRESS

RUNAWAY DESIRES

CPSIA information can be obtained
at www.ICGtesting.com
Printed in the USA
BVOW08s0309200617
487318BV00001B/17/P